"Hello, my darling."

She brushed the tangles from Lavinia's cheek. "My, you had a long nap. Are you hungry?"

"Uh-huh." Her gaze was aimed over Viola's shoulder, and her brown eyes grew round.

"Good. Now, I want you to say hello to your father. He's eager to meet you." She glared at Robert, silently forbidding him to disappoint this vulnerable child. Oddly, at the moment, Robert also appeared a bit vulnerable.

He joined them on the couch. "Hello, Lavinia." His voice sounded thick with emotion.

"What do we say?"

"'Lo." A half smile graced her lips.

Robert's eyes reddened. "Will you let me hold you?"

She buried her face in Viola's shoulder.

"Give her time."

Robbie sauntered over to join them. "Hi, Lavinia. Remember me?"

She lifted her head and nodded.

"Want to see some kittens?" He offered his hand.

With a happy squeal, she jumped from Viola's lap and scampered from the room with her brother.

Swallowing so hard Viola could hear him, Robert pressed a hand to his chest, stood and strode from the room.

Viola's heart twisted. So the man had feelings after all. At least for his daughter.

Florida author **Louise M. Gouge** writes historical fiction for Harlequin's Love Inspired Historical line. She received the prestigious Inspirational Readers' Choice Award in 2005 and placed in 2011 and 2015; she also placed in the Laurel Wreath contest in 2012. In addition to writing, she enjoys copyediting for her fellow authors of Christian historical romance novels. Please visit her at louisemgougeauthor.blogspot.com, www.Facebook.com/louisemgougeauthor and www.bookbub.com/profile/louise-m-gouge.

Books by Louise M. Gouge

Love Inspired Historical

Finding Her Frontier Family

Four Stones Ranch

Cowboy to the Rescue
Cowboy Seeks a Bride
Cowgirl for Keeps
Cowgirl Under the Mistletoe
Cowboy Homecoming
Cowboy Lawman's Christmas Reunion

Visit the Author Profile page
at LoveInspired.com for more titles.

Finding Her Frontier Family

LOUISE M. GOUGE

LOVE INSPIRED
INSPIRATIONAL ROMANCE

LOVE INSPIRED®
INSPIRATIONAL ROMANCE

ISBN-13: 978-1-335-41895-1

Finding Her Frontier Family

Love Inspired
22 Adelaide St. West, 41st Floor
Toronto, Ontario M5H 4E3, Canada
www.LoveInspired.com

Printed in U.S.A.

Recycling programs for this product may not exist in your area.

And be ye kind one to another, tenderhearted, forgiving one another, even as God for Christ's sake hath forgiven you.
—*Ephesians* 4:32

This book is dedicated to my beloved husband, David, my one and only love, who encouraged me to write the stories of my heart and continued to encourage me throughout my writing career. David, I will always love you and miss you.

My special thanks go to my wonderful agent, Tamela Hancock Murray, and my fabulous editors, Shana Asaro and Rachel Beck. Thank you for all you do.

Thank you, Rudy Ramos, for making sure my Mexican Spanish was correct.

Chapter One

Riverton, New Mexico
Spring 1887

No. No. Not that man, please, Lord.

Standing on the train platform, Viola Brinson clutched the hand of her tiny charge and searched the crowd for the rancher who was to meet her. Of the dozen or so men who milled about collecting baggage and greeting other newly arrived passengers, only one stared at her with any sense of purpose. Dusty from the crown of his battered, wide-brimmed hat to the poorly mended shirt and trousers to the toes of his badly scuffed boots, he had the look of an outlaw, not a successful rancher. Beside him stood a young boy, just as unkempt, another indication that this was the person to whom she had brought Lavinia.

Thumb stuck in her mouth, eyes round with fear, the dear little four-year-old even now tried to lose herself in Viola's skirts, knocking her bonnet askew in the process. Viola forbade herself to tremble so as not to further alarm the child.

"Shh. It is all right." The words tried to stick in her throat, but she forced them out. "That is your papa." After righting the bonnet, Viola lifted her own chin and stared back at the man who held Lavinia's future in his hands.

Beside her, Lavinia shivered.

Removing his hat, the man strode toward her. His young companion copied the gesture and followed. The gentlemanly gesture inspired a slightly improved opinion of him.

"Viola Brinson?" He spoke her name almost like an accusation. Her good opinion vanished.

Closer now, she could see his startling blue eyes set in a deeply tanned—and dirty—face. His strong jaw appeared clenched. In fact, anger seemed to radiate from every inch of his person. Worse, the smell of sweat and cattle permeated his clothing, even the air around him, and nearly knocked her over. Could he not have bathed before meeting his daughter?

She stiffened her spine, determined not to let him see her waver. "I am she. Are you Mr. Robert Mattson?"

He nodded toward the carpetbag she held. "Where's the rest of your luggage?"

She narrowed her eyes. "I said, are you Mr. Robert Mattson?"

"Lady, I wouldn't be here if I wasn't." He slapped his hat back on his head, took a step closer and loomed over her. "Now where's your luggage?"

Despite his superior height, Viola refused to cringe. With three bossy older brothers, she wouldn't let this

ill-mannered brute frighten her. Of course, her brothers were all gentlemen, reared in polite society where
ladies were treated with respect, not terrorized. She
and her sisters had always been treated well, even cosseted. If this man truly was Lavinia's father, such gentle
treatment probably would not be in the child's future.

"I believe our trunks are in the baggage car. Perhaps
the porters have unloaded them by now."

The words had not left her lips before he strode away
toward the back of the train she and Lavinia had traveled in these past few days. Like a faithful puppy, the
boy trotted after him. Viola noted he didn't seem afraid
of the man. But then, what did she know of children who
grew up on ranches? As the youngest of seven, she'd
seen each of her elder siblings marry and bear offspring,
but the children had all been gently reared to take their
places beside their parents in society.

A soft whimper came from Lavinia, and she clung to
Viola's hand. Did the dear child know Viola was supposed to leave her here? That even now, she had a return train ticket in her reticule? Had she overheard the
plans made on her behalf by people who had seemed
eager to be rid of the little girl whose mother had died
nearly penniless?

How well Viola knew what that meant and how it felt.
At twenty-five and lacking sufficient funds to secure
a suitable match, she'd become her family's redundant
woman. Unmarried, unnecessary, unwanted.

Stop it. Such self-pitying thoughts could only drag
her down. Besides, she had an important responsibility, making sure Lavinia had a safe and secure home

before she traveled back East, where no responsibilities awaited her at all.

A sudden determination struck her. If Robert Mattson would not provide safety and security for his daughter, Viola would find a way to do it herself, even if it meant taking the child back to Charleston and scrubbing floors to provide for the both of them.

Mr. Mattson strode back their way, her trunk on his back as if it were as light as her carpetbag. Viola's heart skittered about inside her. Goodness, the man was as strong as the biblical Samson. Behind him, his son helped a porter carry Lavinia's baggage. They delivered it to the back of a nearby surrey. Then father and son climbed into the front seat of the conveyance. As if she and Lavinia were an afterthought, Mr. Mattson looked their way.

"You comin'?"

The nerve of the man! He hadn't even offered to help them into the carriage. Without a word, she guided Lavinia to the surrey and lifted her onto the second bench. If she were one of her sisters, she would fuss and simper until Mr. Mattson got down and helped her. But a redundant woman quickly learned to fend for herself or get left behind. She gathered her skirt and petticoats and climbed aboard to sit beside her charge, barely settling before the man slapped the reins on the horses' haunches and shouted, "Hyah!" The horses set off at a brisk pace, almost a canter.

With one hand, Viola grabbed the upright post that supported the fringed canopy. With the other, she held Lavinia to keep her from bouncing out onto the dusty roadway. Before she could voice a complaint or ask

Mr. Mattson to slow down, the boy turned around and stared at Lavinia.

"Hello." His bright blue eyes sparkled in the daylight like his father's, and his sweet grin seemed to offer friendship.

Lavinia buried her face in Viola's skirt, once again knocking her bonnet askew.

"It is all right, my darling." Her heart twisting, Viola removed the bonnet and caressed Lavinia's dark brown hair. They had warned her not to become attached to the child, but she couldn't help herself. "This is your brother." To the boy, she asked, "What is your name?"

"Robbie."

Of course. Named for his father.

Determined not to let the surrey's fast pace interfere with these all-important introductions, she smiled. "I am pleased to meet you, Robbie. I am Miss Brinson, and this is your sister, Lavinia." She lifted Lavinia's chin. "My darling, this is your brother. Remember? We talked about him." Not that she'd known what to say about him, only that Lavinia had an older brother and, from her own experience, that *some* brothers could be very nice.

Fear ebbed from Lavinia's eyes, and she offered a quivering smile before sticking her thumb into her mouth.

The surrey hit a bump, and everyone bounced in their seats. Lavinia looked frightened until Robbie giggled. "Whee!"

"Whee!" Lavinia giggled, too, a sound that brought tears to Viola's eyes. She hadn't heard the child laugh since before they had taken her kitten away, saying the

creature couldn't go with her to New Mexico Territory. Now, with every bump in the road that bounced
them around in their seats, she and Robbie giggled and
shouted "Whee!" The seat being only lightly padded,
Viola couldn't quite share their glee.

The road ran beside a winding river some thirty
yards wide. She supposed this was the Rio Grande,
but for the life of her, she would not ask Mr. Mattson
if that was true.

The drive took perhaps a half hour, during which
Viola studied the back of the man who had fathered
such a sweet, delicate child. She hadn't known Lavinia's
mother, Maybelle Mattson, although they were distant
cousins. All she knew was that Maybelle had fled her
marriage when Lavinia was an infant, leaving behind
a young son and a heartless husband. Mr. Mattson's
hunched shoulders seemed to verify that description.
He hadn't even spoken to his daughter…or his son, for
that matter.

They reached a turnoff and drove under an archway,
then up a long hilly driveway that led to a two-story
white clapboard house set on a rocky bluff above the
river. Numerous outbuildings dotted the property, some
clapboard and others pink adobe. With none of the ar-
chitecture matching and no symmetry in the layout, it
seemed somewhat of a hodgepodge to Viola. But then,
no one had asked her opinion.

Behind the main house stood a large red barn with a
network of corrals attached. Dust and the stink of burning leather filled the air, along with the shouts of men
and the bawling of countless cattle.

For some odd reason, Mr. Mattson didn't drive up to

the attractive columned front porch. Instead, he drove around to the back of the house and jumped down from the driver's bench. There he unloaded the trunks. "Robbie, take care of the horses, then go help your grandpa." He strode away toward the barn.

"Yessir." The boy hurried to take the lead rope.

"Mr. Mattson!" Viola burst out before she could stop herself.

He spun around and faced her, fists at his waist. "What?"

Viola clambered down from the surrey and lifted Lavinia to the ground. Taking the child by the hand, she stalked toward him, stopping short of meeting him nose to nose. "Mr. Mattson, may I introduce your daughter, Lavinia Maybelle Mattson?" She narrowed her eyes, silently daring him not to respond.

He blinked. Then looked at the child as if she were some strange creature.

Lavinia once again sucked her thumb and tried to hide in Viola's skirt.

"A simple hello would suffice."

The slightest softening crossed his face. "Hello." He turned away.

"Mr. Mattson." She should let him go but simply could not.

He spun back around. "There are six men around here who go by that name. My father is Mr. Mattson. I am Robert. And I have cattle to brand." He strode away.

This time, she did not call him back.

Striding toward the corral where his brothers and ranch hands had continued to work after he left, Rob pressed his fingers to his chest, knowing he couldn't massage away the pain. It was far too deep. He'd thought he'd forgotten Maybelle or at least stopped loving her. But when this morning's mail brought the shocking news that she'd died six months ago, leaving behind their four-year-old daughter, his world seemed to crash around him. He *had* loved Maybelle. *Had* tried to make a life that pleased her, made her comfortable, gave her a place in society. She'd just never understood he couldn't do that back in Charleston. As the oldest of five brothers, he'd needed to come with his family to New Mexico Territory to work the land Pop had bought. It hadn't helped that Mother had abandoned them all after the first few years and fled back East. It gave Maybelle an excuse to do the same.

Of course, he'd been sending her money every month for the past three and a half years. If only he'd known she'd died, he would have arranged for Lavinia's care back in Charleston, would have arranged for her to live at a boarding school.

But then this morning's letter, followed by a telegram—both from one Miss Viola Brinson—announced the imminent arrival of his daughter, so he never had a chance to do that. Instead, right when he needed to be overseeing the cattle branding, he had to leave the work and go fetch her. Not that Will and Drew couldn't manage the job themselves, but his two brothers who still lived here weren't privy to Pop's suspicions about a couple of their hands.

Someone was changing their brand to one that looked very similar, one that a rustler could easily change with a running brand, and when the work got hectic, a man had no time to look close to see the difference. Rob thought Pop should just tell his brothers, but Pop had only ever trusted him with secrets. Maybe it was because he was the oldest. Maybe it had to do with both of them being abandoned by their wives. Rob couldn't figure it out, and with so much work to do, he didn't have time to ponder it. He'd accept the weight of responsibility as long as necessary, especially since Pop seemed to be slowing down these past few months.

Taking his place back at work, he wrestled a calf to the ground and tied its legs, then held it while ranch hand Patrick Ahern applied the red-hot brand...the right brand. Eyes wide, the calf bawled its protest until Rob untied its legs and sent it to join its mama.

As he grabbed for the next calf, the fear in its wide brown eyes struck him in the chest. Lavinia had stared at him like that with her big brown eyes. Man, she was a pretty little thing. Just like Maybelle.

No wonder she'd been scared. He was big, he was ill-tempered, and he was a stinking mess. But branding took strength, and it wasn't a dainty job. Maybe when they were through for the day, he could clean up and make amends to her.

As for that Miss Brinson, she couldn't have stuck her nose any higher in the air. Just like with Maybelle, disapproval shone from those narrowed eyes. He wasn't about to try to please this woman. He'd get matters sorted out and send her packing, along with Lavinia, as soon as possible. The arrival of her letter and wire this morning had shattered his safe world, knocking him plumb off balance right in the middle of branding. Why hadn't she written sooner? If Maybelle had been gone six months, shouldn't someone have notified him by telegram? He'd have to ask Miss—

"Okay, boss, this one's ready to go." Ahern plunged the iron back in the fire where four others were reheating and set the calf loose before Rob could check the brand.

The critter scampered away and got lost among the rest of the herd. Rob shook his head in disgust. This was why females had no business on a cattle ranch. Living or dead, they caused a man enough worry to keep him from concentrating on his work.

Once the branding was done for the day, Rob headed to the house with his brothers. An odd desire to see Miss Brinson again flared up inside him. What was that all about? He seemed to recall blond hair piled on top of her head and a little furry hat cocked to one side. Green eyes narrowed with haughtiness and indignation and…

"So, what's she like?" Will took off his hat and wiped away sweat with his sleeve.

"Yeah, Rob." Drew stepped up beside him. "Tell us all about her."

"Well, she's not bad to look at—"

Each of their faces, similar to all the Mattson men, registered shock.

"That's what you have to say about your daughter?" Drew frowned. "She's not bad to look at?"

"Don't you get it?" Chortling, Will slapped his hat against his thigh. "He's not talking about the little one. He's talking about the lady who brought her."

"Ooooeee!" Drew hooted so loud Rob came near to belting him. "I can't wait to meet this lady."

Only one way to get control of this situation. "My

daughter is a pretty little thing like her mama." He swung around in front of his brothers. "The next one to suggest anything about Miss Brinson and me will be picking himself up off the ground minus a couple of teeth."

Despite their answering laughter, he stomped away and onto the back porch where washbasins and buckets of water awaited them, courtesy of their cook, Old Fuzzy. Rob observed both Will and Drew taking so much special care with their ablutions that they didn't notice he was doing the same. What ailed the two of them? Since their two youngest brothers had married sisters and moved to the sheep ranch five miles away, these two had gotten downright ridiculous when it came to women. Well, they could do as they wished. As for him, he was cleaning up for his daughter.

They finished about the same time. Also at the same time, the aroma of cooked chicken wafted out through the screen door, and their eyes widened.

"Man, that can't be Old Fuzzy's cooking." Will glanced down at his clothes. "I think I'll go put on a clean shirt."

"Me, too." Drew followed Will into the house.

"Hey." Rob spoke to thin air. He snorted. What nincompoops. On second thought, a clean shirt might go a long way to winning Lavinia's trust.

He stepped into the mudroom and climbed the back stairs to change his shirt. All the while, his mouth watered from the aroma of stewed chicken that filled the house.

Drew and Will beat him back down to the kitchen. They sat at the table drinking coffee with Miss Brinson while Old Fuzzy regaled them all with stories of his many years of cooking for cattle drives.

"Yessiree-bob." The old man chortled, then wheezed. "Nobody ever knew how often I served 'em rattlesnake or armadillo. One time I even served up a couple of prairie dogs in a stew. The drovers were always too tired at the end of the day to pay attention."

"Either that," Will said, "or all of your cooking tastes the same. I never notice any difference, do you, Drew?"

"Nope. Not a bit. Always tastes just like boot leather."

Miss Brinson's unquestionably pretty face wore a look of concern as she glanced at Old Fuzzy. When she saw him laughing loudest of all, she smiled…and became beautiful.

Uh-oh. What was he thinking? He didn't have the time or inclination for women. Maybelle had been gone for almost four years, had been dead for six months. But for Rob, it wasn't until today he'd actually become a widower. His heart ached at the thought, and he rubbed his chest, unable to make the pain stop.

He shook off his thoughts and cleared his throat.

Everyone turned to look at him.

He stared at Miss Brinson. "Where's my daughter?"

Heat flooded Viola's face, but not from the hot stove nearby where two chickens stewed in a pot. The nerve of this man. She should make plans right now to pack up Lavinia and leave tomorrow.

"Well?" Mr. Mattson—*Robert*—put his fists on his waist, probably to intimidate her.

She would have none of that. "Lavinia is sleeping on the divan in the parlor."

He looked toward the inside kitchen door as if he would go there.

"Please let her rest." It was an order, not a request. Viola didn't want the child to have another fright from this man. No matter what he said, she would manage their first real meeting.

To her relief, he nodded. "Fine." He ran a hand down his cheek—his *clean* cheek that sported dark stubble—and took a seat at the large round kitchen table.

My, these handsome brothers cleaned up nicely. Well, she'd not seen Andrew and William before but imagined they had looked as dirty as Robert had earlier.

"Tell you what, Miss Brinson." Andrew gave her a dimpled smile. "If that chicken tastes as good as it smells, I'll be hard-pressed to let you go back East. We're in dire need of some good cooking around here."

"That's right," Old Fuzzy said. "Women are scarce in these parts. I reckon one of us oughter marry you so you'll stick around." The twinkle in his eye showed he was teasing and that he was not offended by the insults to his cooking.

Andrew and William laughed.

Robert's scowl deepened. Before Viola could respond in kind to the old man's teasing, he snorted. "Where's Pop?" He directed the question to Old Fuzzy.

Viola started. She'd forgotten Lavinia had a grandfather. Would he be ill-tempered like Robert or friendly like his other sons?

"Last I saw him, he and Robbie was goin' out to check on that applewood branch to see if it's ready to carve." Old Fuzzy scratched his fuzzy chin. "They was gonna whittle me some new cooking spoons and such, but maybe Miss Viola would like one of them fancy metal ones from the dry goods store." He winked at her. "That is, if you felt like cookin' fer us again."

"Wellll…" She drew out the word to return his teasing. "I'll have to think about that."

"Don't bother. You won't be here that long." Robert stood and stepped toward the back hallway. "And Old Fuzzy's cooking is good enough for us." He walked out, and soon the screen door slammed shut.

Her face burning again, Viola stood and busied herself at the stove. The man was insufferable. At least these three men were kinder, more welcoming. Andrew and William had displayed manners nearly as fine as her own brothers. And Old Fuzzy had already endeared himself to Lavinia by giving her a sweet.

When she and the child had arrived at the *back* door, of all things, she hadn't known what to expect. But the old cook had greeted them warmly and showed them upstairs to the small bedchamber they would share. Lavinia refused to nap by herself, so Viola took her down to the parlor, where she fell asleep under a soft patchwork quilt Old Fuzzy found for her. He then invited Viola to have a much-needed cup of coffee.

It was awful, but she managed to drink it…in a kitchen that looked as if a tornado had swept through. In fact, the entire house looked as if spring cleaning was a foreign concept. Tired of sitting idly on a train or in train stations for over a week, she secured Old Fuzzy's permission to occupy herself. It had taken several hours for the two of them to clean and organize the kitchen and formal dining room, but afterward, they agreed it was a job well done. The kindly old man had been near to tears with gratitude, further endearing himself to her.

"Miss Brinson." William refilled his cup from the pot on the stove. "This is the best coffee I've ever tasted. Is it something you brought with you?"

She glanced at Old Fuzzy, who chortled.

"No, sonny. She just washed the pot."

They all shared another laugh.

What kind gentlemen they were. If not for Robert's harsh pronouncement, she might consider staying here. But did he have the final say? Maybe the others could overrule him. After all, she didn't feel right leaving Lavinia in the care of these busy ranchers with not a woman in sight. What would happen to the child? At the very least, she would be neglected and would grow up like a weed, all femininity stamped out. At the worst, she would never learn proper manners or obtain a suitable education.

No, Viola could not, would not permit that to happen. She would find a way to charm the patriarch, Mr. Mattson, into letting her stay, perhaps through her cooking. That cake she'd whipped up earlier should help. She would win them all over through their stomachs. And she would take care of Lavinia as if she were her own.

Rob found Pop and Robbie seated on a log outside the woodshed. "What're you making there, son?" The boy was learning to whittle from the expert, as Rob and his brothers had done.

"A spoon." He held up the applewood stick, which was already taking the shape of a usable utensil.

"Good job." Rob ruffled his son's hair. "How you doin', Pop? You meet your granddaughter yet?"

"Huh!" Pop eyed him crossly. "Not with that female hovering around. I saw 'em inside and ran for cover. How soon before she leaves?" From the jerky way he moved his hands, Rob could see he was seriously out of sorts.

"Soon." Rob sat beside them, pulled out his pocketknife and picked up a stick. "You feeling all right?"

"Fine." His tone said he was anything but fine.

So the old man was having as much trouble as Rob over today's shattering news. They needed to talk about it.

"Son." He placed a hand on Robbie's shoulder. "I want you to go inside and see how supper's coming along." Another thought struck. "Peek in the parlor and see if your sister's waked up yet. From the way you made her laugh on the way home, I have a feeling you and she are going to be best friends." Rob never had a sister, so maybe that wasn't quite true. Besides, the girl would be gone soon. He'd have to be careful what he promised his son.

Robbie's eyes brightened. "Yessir." He folded his knife and stuck it in his pocket. "Thanks for the lesson, Pop."

"Glad to. We'll finish it tomorrow, then maybe work on those cradles for your cousins."

After he left, Rob looked at his dad, and they both heaved out a weary sigh.

"So, what are we going to do with the girl?"

Rob winced at the way he referenced Lavinia. But

then, he'd been thinking of her that way, too. "You got any ideas?"

"We could send her over to Jared and Cal. Their wives'll know how to raise a girl."

A sudden feeling of possessiveness overcame Rob. No! Nobody was going to take his baby girl away from him. But where did that thought come from?

"That wouldn't be fair. Emma and Julia are both expecting." He grunted. "And may I remind you how pleased you were to learn about that? Isn't that why you told everybody you'd be the one making the cradles?" Against all of his and Pop's efforts to keep women out of the family so they could build their ranch without the drama women brought, Jared and Cal had married two sweet sisters. Not one of the other Mattson men had objected. Probably because they'd be living on a different ranch, and the women wouldn't be here to cause drama and disruptions.

"Yeah, well." Pop snorted. "So, what are we going to do?"

Rob scratched his chin. "On the way back from the train, Robbie got Lavinia to giggle. Maybe he's the key to helping her feel at home." The idea of keeping his daughter here was growing on him all too fast.

"That's all well and good, but girls need different training from boys. They need a woman to bring them up. I still say Julia and Emma or maybe even their ma could help out."

Before Rob could object again, the dinner bell clanged noisily, so they made their way to the kitchen.

Instead of supper being laid out on the kitchen table as usual, the dining room table was now covered with the damask cloth Mother had left behind all those years ago. Her china and silver were set out to designate seven place settings, folded linen napkins beside each one. Filled with delicious-smelling chicken and dumplings, the large china tureen from above the china cabinet sat in the center of the table. A cloth-covered basket of biscuits and a steaming serving bowl of baby carrots added to the fare. Cut glass bowls held butter and jam. Crystal salt cellars sat before each place setting, and water had been served in crystal goblets.

Pop took one look at the feast, one look at Miss Brinson, and blinked. "You did all this?"

"Yes, I did, Mr. Mattson, with Old Fuzzy's help." She reached out to him. "I am Viola Brinson, and I am pleased to meet you."

Pop chuckled as he shook her hand. "And I'm more than pleased to meet you, Miss Brinson. Would you like a job?"

Chapter Two

Standing by the table, Viola started to grab the back of the nearest chair. As her grandmother used to say, somebody could have knocked her over with a feather. Here she'd been ready to fight to stay with Lavinia, but Mr. Mattson had offered her a job. Regaining her balance and finding her voice with some difficulty, she managed to speak without stuttering.

"How very kind of you. May I presume you require a cook and housekeeper?"

"You may presume." The older man waved a hand around the table at his sons. "Take a seat, boys."

William stepped over and pulled out a chair for her. "Ma'am?"

"Why, thank you." Viola gave him a smile that would rival one from her most coquettish sister…at the same moment she noticed the scowl on Robert's face.

Mr. Matson offered grace, thanking the Lord for each dish, even wondering aloud about the carrots being ready to pull so early in the spring. When he finished, they passed the bowls in a rather haphazard way, but

Viola masked her chagrin with a benign smile. Their table manners would set a terrible example for Lavinia, so she would begin their lessons tomorrow. As they all began eating, no one spoke, and for a moment, Viola wondered if she should introduce some generic topic.

"Where is my granddaughter?" His tone not unkind, Mr. Mattson indicated the vacant chair beside Viola.

"Still asleep, I am afraid."

Robert's gaze darted toward the inner door. "Is she sick?"

"No, no. Not at all." Viola kept her voice light. "She barely slept during our travels, so once her exhaustion finally took over, I didn't think it wise to waken her."

"So you know about children?" Mr. Mattson's blue eyes showed interest, perhaps eagerness.

"Yes, I do, sir. I have a dozen nieces and nephews back home. They are all my delight." It was true. She did adore children and wished for some of her own, a useless wish for a redundant woman.

"Then you'll want to get back to them." Robert didn't look her way.

"Now, hold on, son." Mr. Mattson paused with his dumpling-laden fork halfway to his mouth. "I have offered the young lady a job as my housekeeper, and that would include taking care of Lavinia. Don't you think that would solve the problem we discussed?"

While his brothers and even little Robbie laughed, Robert appeared just short of frowning at his father. Clearly, he did not intend to show such disrespect, for which Viola had to admire him. Although he had no such compunctions over frowning at *her*.

"As I recall, sir, we discussed a different solution."

"No. We decided that wouldn't work." Mr. Mattson turned his weathered but still handsome face—so much like his eldest son's—in Viola's direction. "Miss Brinson, will you accept my offer? You may take some time to think it over, if you like."

"Do say yes, Miss Brinson," William said.

"We'd all love for you to stay," Andrew offered.

"You're real pretty," Robbie piped up, a sweet grin on his sweet face. Robert scowled at him, so he added, "I mean, pretty please stay."

To avoid joining the others as they laughed at the adorable boy's winsomeness, Viola focused on Mr. Mattson. "Thank you. I would be delighted to stay as your housekeeper and Lavinia's governess." And perhaps help with Robbie's education, too, she thought but didn't say.

A soft sob emanating from the direction of the parlor caught everyone's attention. Viola rose quickly, as did Robert. Closer to the door, he took a step toward it.

"Permit me." Viola feared he would do irreparable damage to the child if he barged into the room first.

His shoulders slumped, and he impatiently waved a hand toward the door.

In the parlor, Viola knelt beside the dark pink brocade divan, another relic of the woman who had borne five sons, come to this wilderness with her husband and then fled back to the safety of civilized society. While Viola and Old Fuzzy had cleaned the kitchen and dining room, he'd given her a history of the family.

"Hello, my darling." She brushed the tangles from Lavinia's cheek. "My, you had a long nap. Are you hungry?"

"Uh-huh." Her gaze was aimed over Viola's shoulder, and her brown eyes grew round.

Viola moved up to sit on the divan and pulled the child onto her lap. "What would you think if I stayed here with you for a while?"

Her thumb went into her mouth, but she nodded.

"Good. Now I want you to say hello to your father. He's eager to meet you." She glared at Robert, silently forbidding him to disappoint this vulnerable child. Oddly, at the moment, Robert also appeared a bit vulnerable.

He joined them on the couch. "Hello, Lavinia." His voice sounded thick with emotion.

"What do we say?" Viola gently removed the wrinkled thumb from Lavinia's mouth.

"'Lo." A half smile graced her lips.

Robert's eyes reddened. "Will you let me hold you?"

She reclaimed her thumb and buried her face in Viola's shoulder.

"Give her time."

Robbie sauntered over to join them. "Hi, Lavinia. Remember me?"

She lifted her head and nodded.

"Want to see some kittens?" He offered his hand.

With a happy squeal, she jumped from Viola's lap and scampered from the room with her brother, not bothering to look back.

Swallowing so hard Viola could hear him, Robert pressed a hand to his chest, stood and strode from the room.

Viola's heart twisted. So the man had feelings, after all. At least for his daughter.

"Miss Brinson." William entered the parlor, closely followed by Andrew. "It's my turn to help you with supper cleanup. Would you like me to wash or dry?"

"I think you're mistaken, brother." Andrew practically fell on his face trying to move in front of William. "It's my turn."

Viola pursed her lips to keep from laughing. These men were more like her young nephews than grownups. "I believe there is plenty of work for everyone."

With evening chores still to be done, Rob couldn't take refuge in his room to sort out this miserable situation. Once Pop made up his mind, there was no way he could overrule it, not even when it came to Rob's daughter.

He followed the children to the barn, staying far enough behind to avoid frightening Lavinia. After his brusqueness this morning, he knew it would take time to win her trust. Maybe she'd like to watch him milk the cows. He'd guess that prissy Miss Brinson hadn't ever seen it done. She probably expected milk to suddenly appear in the kitchen.

Maybelle had hated the barn, hated the smell of a hardworking man. Had refused to strain the milk or skim off the cream to make the butter. She'd often neglected to prepare supper, preferring to sit in the parlor and sew useless samplers. If not for Old Fuzzy, the family would have starved.

Rob rubbed his chest. After supper it hadn't hurt as bad as usual. The chicken and dumplings went down easy and actually seemed to soothe what ailed him.

Oh, no. He wasn't going there. No matter how well

she cooked, Miss Viola Brinson would soon be on a train headed east. Except Pop had hired her. Rob's pain moved from his chest to his head.

"Hey, boss." Old Fuzzy met him by the barn door. "I'll be happy to do the milkin' fer ya."

Was that worry in his eyes? He hadn't eaten supper with them, probably preferring to eat in the bunkhouse with the other ranch hands. But maybe by now he'd heard that Pop had hired that woman. Despite his cheerfulness earlier, did he think they'd find him useless?

"Now that you mention it, that would be real fine. Would you take over that chore? In fact, if you'd still strain the milk and make the butter, that would be a big help." He paused. "And keep up the good work on the kitchen garden. Those new carrots were mighty fine at supper."

Old Fuzzy's face lit up. "I'd be proud to, sir." He headed into the barn and grabbed a milk bucket from a nail. No doubt hearing the metallic clatter, both milk cows mooed their eagerness to be relieved of their fullness.

From a back stall, the sounds of giggling children wafted on the cool evening air. Rob hesitated. If he joined them, would he frighten Lavinia? His feet made up his mind for him by walking in that direction. Or maybe his heart led him toward his daughter, despite his concerns that the ranch was no place for her.

Robbie was all boy and would make a fine rancher. He already knew how to train horses and do many other grown-up jobs. But Lavinia was dainty like her mother. She'd be lost in this all-male family. On the other hand, maybe having her around would help him remember the better parts of his failed marriage.

He braced his arms on the wall and peered into the half-darkened stall. Six or eight kittens were climbing all over both children, inciting their giggles. Rob decided he could get used to that sound. At nine years old, Robbie hadn't had much of a childhood. He had friends his age at church, but they all came from hard-working families and generally saw each other only on Sundays. Having another child on the ranch might be good for him.

The mother cat sat to the side giving herself a bath. One of the numerous barn cats that kept down the mouse population, she was obviously unconcerned about her offspring, which looked about old enough for weaning.

Robbie looked up at him. "Hey, Dad."

Alarm covered Lavinia's sweet face, and Rob's chest began to hurt again. As softly as if he were taming a wary mustang, he responded. "Hey, there. Looks like you two have made some friends."

"Yessir." Robbie glanced at his sister. "Can we, I mean, may we take Puff to the house?"

Hope brightened Lavinia's brown eyes.

They'd already named the critter? "Now, son, you know the rule about cats not being in the house."

Her thumb went into her mouth. Her dirty thumb. Uh-oh. Not good. Thankfully, stuffy Miss Brinson wasn't here to see that.

"But Dad, Lavinia had to leave her kitten behind. Can't she please have this one?"

His son never argued with him, yet here he was, already fighting for his sister.

Rob leaned back and stared down at his boots. And prayed for the first time in he didn't know how long. How was he going to be a father to this child? A Bible verse came to mind about the Lord being so gentle that he wouldn't break a bruised reed. Losing her mother and being forced to leave all she knew to go across this wide land with a stranger, tiny Lavinia was as emotionally bruised as anybody he'd ever seen. Rob decided he'd do his best to follow the Lord's example.

He gave his daughter a smile for the first time. "You promise to take care of it?" As in teaching it to go outside when necessary and keeping it from shredding the curtains.

She took her thumb out, gazed up at him with those big brown eyes—only this time without fear in them—and gave him a solemn nod.

"All right, then. Puff may come inside the house." He wouldn't consider whether Pop would agree. Somehow the old man would just have to.

The smile Lavinia gave him as she nuzzled the wiggling kitten warmed his chest enough to make the last of his pain disappear, at least for now.

"Lavinia!" Studying the various outbuildings, Viola tried to keep the alarm from her voice, but it was no use. It had grown dark, and the child had not eaten supper. Where had Robbie taken her? In the distance, near the barn, several grown cats wandered around. But Robbie had said *kittens*. Where could the children be? "Lavinia! Robbie!"

Old Fuzzy ambled toward her, a large bucket of milk in each hand. "No need to worry, missy. They're safe in there." He tilted his head toward the barn. "Rob's watching over 'em."

Oh, no. Lavinia was so frightened of her ruffian father. Viola dashed toward the barn, sending Old Fuzzy a quick thank-you over her shoulder and a quick prayer upward for Lavinia.

A single hanging lantern illuminated the aisle of the large building, causing shadows to dance on the walls. The smells of hay, manure and livestock mingled in the air. In two of the nearest stalls, two cows, presumably the producers of the milk Old Fuzzy carried, munched on the hay in their mangers.

Children's giggles and the deep rumble of male chuckling came from the back stall. Viola slowed her pace and caught her breath, then ambled toward the sounds as though unconcerned. She peered around the corner and came near to gasping. There sat Mr. Robert Mattson on a bale of hay, the children at his feet, all of them playing with kittens too numerous to count.

Lavinia noticed her first and popped up, lifting a calico kitten for display. "This is Puff."

"Oh, how sweet." Viola bent down and brushed a finger over the kitten's tiny head. "Hello, Puff. How adorable you are." And a nearly identical replacement for the larger calico she'd had to leave behind.

"Huh." A grunt of disgust emanated from Robert. Despite the dark, Viola could see him rolling his eyes. "Cats, adorable?" He stood and brushed at the straw clinging to his clothing. "Necessary, but not adorable."

Even as Viola's feelings stung at his contradiction of her simple comment, her heart hiccoughed at the reminder of his height. *My oh my, he has an imposing presence.*

But he was also rude, even boorish, so she refused to give thought to her nearly breathless response.

"Lavinia, my darling, you have not eaten supper. Come along now." Viola reached for her hand and led her from the barn. Halfway across the barnyard, she realized the child still cradled the kitten in her other arm. "Oh, dear, I'm sure Puff wants to stay with her mother."

"I said she could have it." Robert's gruff voice sounded behind her.

Viola stopped to stare at him. "How very kind." She didn't intend to sound snippy, but from the way he scowled, she must have. It was his fault. If he hadn't spoken so gruffly...

No, there was never an excuse for rudeness, even when another person had been rude first. But words spoken couldn't be taken back, so nothing could be done about it now. She must settle it in her mind that they would never get along, never agree on anything. But at least the elder Mr. Mattson had said she could stay. And with Robert and his brothers busy working the ranch, she would be able to take care of Lavinia and rear her to be a lady.

As for Viola, she would finally be useful. No longer the redundant woman who had to sleep on one of her sisters' divans or in her nieces' trundle beds. No longer an object of her brothers' pity and annoyance because their late father's money had run out, and no society gentleman wanted to marry a woman who could bring no wealth or influence to the marriage.

She'd prayed for a purpose in life, and she adored the

children. But why did the Lord have to plop her down in the middle of such a wretched wilderness? Still, she would trust Him, whatever His plan for her. And although she could sympathize with Mrs. Mattson and Maybelle for leaving this place, for Lavinia's sake she would refuse to let fear or revulsion chase her away.

Later, with Lavinia fed and put to bed, her kitty keeping her company in the small bedroom assigned to them, Viola returned to examine the kitchen. She and Old Fuzzy had agreed he would help her prepare breakfast tomorrow, but she wanted to inventory the pantry. With the right items available, she would make a breakfast fit for a king…or a hardworking family of men. She made her way down the front stairway and past the partially open parlor door.

"Maybe it's a scheme to snare herself a husband."

She recognized Robert's voice, which was a little deeper than his brothers'.

"No surprise about that, son. Don't you know a woman's foremost job in life is to trap a husband?"

"Huh! I do know it. Maybelle couldn't get me to the altar fast enough."

Viola's face burned. The nerve of that man! But here she was eavesdropping when she should barge right in and tell him off.

"Psst." Andrew appeared beside her, a teasing grin lighting his face, a leftover biscuit in his hand.

She gasped and jumped. "Shh!"

"Go on in," he whispered. He didn't give her a chance to respond but guided her though the door.

The startled looks on Robert's and Mr. Mattson's

faces would have been comical if Viola didn't feel guilty for listening to their conversation. But then, maybe they felt guilty for talking about her. She noticed that William had his nose stuck in a book, so maybe he didn't agree with their unkind assessment of women.

"So, as I was saying—" Andrew spoke as if they had been conversing all along "—your biscuits even beat my sister-in-law Julia's. You haven't met her or Emma yet, but don't worry. I know you'll get along just fine."

Viola pursed her lips to keep from giggling like a schoolgirl. Andrew was saving her from embarrassment. "I'm sure I will. And your other brothers, too, if they're as gentlemanly as you."

He gave her an exaggerated bow. "Thank you, ma'am."

Over Andrew's bent form, she noticed Robert's dark eyebrows formed a frown deeper than any he'd worn yet today. *My, my. Such a disagreeable man.* She was glad she would be staying so she could prevent his bad temper from rubbing off on Lavinia and maybe even Robbie.

In apparent deference to her being there, the other men stood.

"Miss Brinson, please come in." Mr. Mattson waved a hand toward a delicate chair with dark pink flowered upholstery. So many things in this room, this house, seemed to be relics of the senior Mrs. Mattson's former presence, perhaps even Maybelle's. "Have a seat. Most evenings we have a family meeting after supper, mostly to sort out the day and make plans for the next one. We also share any news or concerns."

"Why, thank you, sir. I am honored to be included."

She gazed around at each of these four men who held her future in their hands. "If you will permit me, before you get down to family business, I am sure you would like to know more about the circumstances that brought Lavinia and me here." And give her a chance to forestall any accusations that she sought to "snare" a husband from among them.

All but Robert voiced their agreement.

"As you know, Maybelle was my distant cousin." She didn't have to feign the catch in her voice. If she'd actually known Maybelle, perhaps she could have helped her during her illness. "When we learned she'd died, I gladly offered to care for Lavinia until she could be adopted."

Grumbles and protests resounded in the room. Viola didn't look to see who said what.

"I assumed I would be taking care of her in Charleston, but Maybelle's will stated that she was to be taken to her father." She focused on Mr. Mattson, but in the corner of her eye saw Robert's startled look. "You can imagine my shock at learning she had a living father. We all thought Maybelle was a widow.

"Of course, I immediately wrote to you—" she snuck Robert a full glance "—and said we would be arriving this month. When we reached Santa Fe yesterday, I sent the wire you received this morning."

"You wrote immediately?" Was it an accusation? "When did you say Maybelle died?"

Viola stiffened her spine. "You no doubt noted my letter was dated last October fifteenth. We couldn't come right away because matters needed to be settled, and I was advised it was not wise to travel west with a child in winter."

"If you ask me, it makes sense," Andrew said.

"Nobody asked you." Robert crossed his arms. "Why did it take so long for your letter to reach me?"

Viola's jaw dropped in the most unladylike way. Heat once again infusing her cheeks, she snapped it shut.

"How would she know that?" Mr. Mattson glared at his eldest son like he was lacking good sense. Then to Viola, he said, "We're much obliged to you for taking care of our little girl. I'm sure there are more details we'll learn as you think of them."

"For instance, what happened to all the money I've been sending every month for the past four years?" Robert leaned forward. "More to the point, the last six months?"

At that moment, the day caught up with Viola. Chin raised, she stood and walked toward the door. "Good night, gentlemen." She almost added "and Robert" but thought better of it.

Upstairs in the small bedroom she would be sharing with Lavinia, she made sure the child was fast asleep, with Puff curled up beside her on the pillow. Then Viola took her own pillow and muffled the torrent of sobs she could no longer hold inside her.

"What was that all about?" Will stood over Rob, hands posted at his waist.

"Yeah." Drew stood beside Will in a similar posture. "Why'd you accuse Miss Brinson that way? You got no cause."

Rob stood and took a defensive position. Not that

he'd actually fight his younger brothers in the house, but he might just throw them outside and see what they were made of.

"Now, boys." Pop's voice rumbled throughout the room as it hadn't done since they'd all been in their teens. "If you're going to fight over this woman, I may just have to send her packing."

"Right." Rob emitted a bitter laugh. "Why don't you do that?" He ran a hand through his hair, dislodging some of the dirt his earlier washing had missed. "Women. Nothing but trouble."

"Will. Drew. Off to bed." Pop waved his hand toward the door. After they complied, he pointed to a chair. "Sit."

"Yessir." Close to thirty years old, Rob still sat when Pop said *sit*, especially in that tone of voice.

"Now, son, you know that of all people I understand about Maybelle. I'll never forgive your mother for abandoning us all those years ago. But Maybelle is dead, and Lavinia is here. Let's make the best of it." He opened the humidor on the table beside him and pulled out the pipe he no longer smoked. "That little girl needs you, and she needs Miss Viola." He clamped the pipe between his teeth, then took it out and stared at it like it tasted bad. He'd quit smoking before Mother left because of her complaints, but that hadn't kept her here. Nor had love for her sons.

"What about the money?" Rob fumed when he thought about his faithful monthly payments to his wife while he wore poorly mended clothes and his son wore hand-me-downs. "Maybelle never once acknowledged it or thanked me. What am I supposed to feel?

Folks back there thought she was a widow." His chest started aching again.

"I know. I know. I send your mother money every month, and she never writes either. We just have to do the right thing by providing for our wives. They'll have to answer to the Lord for their part."

Rob gave his father a sidelong look. He'd always taken them to church and offered grace before supper, but he rarely mentioned God. Since Jared and Cal had married into a family of more *dedicated* Christians, maybe Pop had begun to think about the Lord more.

Or maybe he really was slowing down and realizing his days were numbered. The thought caused Rob's chest to ache even worse.

Chapter Three

Viola and Old Fuzzy bustled about the kitchen as they prepared Sunday morning breakfast. Over the past three days, they had developed a routine that kept them from colliding, at least most of the time. They fried bacon, ham and eggs, whipped up biscuits, fried potatoes and pancakes, and brewed several pots of coffee.

Old Fuzzy had taught her to fetch the eggs from the chicken coop some twenty yards from the house. Once she learned how to make sure no snakes had crept into the coop, she actually enjoyed the chore because it got her out into the crisp morning air just as the sun came up. Each day, she gazed northeast toward the majestic snow-crowned Sangre de Cristo Mountains and lifted a prayer of thanks for her new home, her new purpose in life. Yet, no matter how early she rose, one or more of the men were out at the barn tending to chores, even on Sunday.

For her part, she still had much work to do to whip this household into a shape fit for a little girl to grow up in. Following the examples of her older sisters, she brooked no contradiction when it came to order and cleanliness. Spring cleaning still needed to be done, something she might have to do bit by bit. To keep the house from getting even dirtier, she required that the men clean their barn-soiled boots in the mudroom before coming inside. That simple act cut down the number of times a day she had to sweep the rest of the house. She also required that they brush more dirt from their clothes and hair before sitting down to eat. To her surprise, the men complied without complaint, although Robert continued to scowl at her.

"Looks like another fine breakfast, Miss Viola." Mr. Mattson entered the kitchen dressed in a black suit, white shirt and dark blue tie. His constant praise always cheered her.

Fresh from their Saturday night baths and dressed in their Sunday best, the other men came in and found their places at the table. Robbie's trousers seemed a bit short, so Viola made a mental note to check to see if they could be lengthened or if new ones needed to be bought or made. She'd noticed a Singer treadle machine covered with a sheet in the corner of the parlor but had not had time to inspect it. If it worked well, she could easily manage the children's mending.

After breakfast, Viola wakened Lavinia and dressed her in her finest frock, a blue taffeta and lace creation Viola had made from some fabric Maybelle had purchased before she died. Viola removed the rag ties from the child's hair and arranged the resulting curls.

"There. You're a picture of perfection and ready for church." She kissed the child's cheek.

"Can Puff go?" Lavinia's thumb hovered near her mouth.

"Oh, I do not think Puff would like to ride into town. She'll be much happier at home with a nice saucer of milk." Before Lavinia could object, Viola took her hand. "Shall we take her downstairs so she can go outside for a few minutes and then both of you can have your breakfast?"

Robert was the only one left in the kitchen. Dressed in a handsome black frock coat, white shirt and black tie, he sat nursing a cup of coffee that was probably cold. When Viola and Lavinia entered, his eyes lit briefly, then clouded. Still, he held his hand out to his daughter. She skipped over to him.

Happy to see progress in their relationship, Viola busied herself preparing a plate for the child. She also checked the firebox to be sure the roast in the oven would continue to cook while they were gone.

"My, that's a pretty dress." Robert gently turned Lavinia around in a circle, then eyed Viola. "Pretty expensive."

She gave him a ladylike shrug. "From the clothes she left behind, I would say Maybelle had excellent taste." She wouldn't tell him she'd made Lavinia's dress lest it sound like boasting.

Snorting in obvious disgust, he lifted Lavinia into her chair. "That she did."

"Bacon?" Lavinia offered her father a slice from her plate.

"No, thanks, sweetheart. I've eaten." His gentle smile caused a small hiccough in Viola's heart. "And now you need to eat so we won't be late for church."

While Lavinia complied, Robert leveled a stare on Viola. "Tell me more about Maybelle's *clothes*." His tone suggested he was not interested in fashion but, rather, the money he'd been sending his wife. They still had not discussed the matter.

"What we couldn't sell, we gave to charity. Lavinia chose a few small mementos to remind her of her mother."

"Who's this *we* you're talking about?" As it often did, his tone sounded accusatory.

"Her lawyer, her pastor and his wife, and I." Viola couldn't fault him for his concern. After all, he *had* been providing for the wife he'd driven away. "Perhaps if you wrote to Mr. Purcell, the lawyer, he could ease your mind. I have his address."

"I'll do that." He rose and kissed the top of Lavinia's head. "Hurry up, sweetheart."

Seated on the back bench of the surrey with Lavinia and Robbie, Viola gazed at the scenery they passed on the way to town. Yes, it was dry and mostly barren, but it also had a wild beauty about it. Were the people as wild as the landscape? She'd heard that the notorious Billy the Kid had been killed not far from here some seven years ago. Even now, all the Mattson men had strapped on gun belts, and two rifles hung in a rack behind the front bench of the surrey. Did they expect trouble? A shudder traveled down her spine.

They passed many adobe houses, their pink walls bright in the morning sun. Well-dressed people emerged from several abodes and appeared to be on their way to church. Surely if they were churchgoers, they had some semblance of civility about them.

William and Mr. Mattson occupied the surrey's front seat, with William driving. The other men rode horses—very fine ones, from Viola's viewpoint. Back when Father had money, she'd owned a pony and learned to ride like a lady. Those had been days of hope and promise. Why should she not have expected to make an excellent match and live in a mansion in the best part of town? Father and her brothers never discussed money with Mother or her sisters, so Viola never learned what happened to the family fortune. She only knew that her brothers now owned grand houses and worked at successful careers, and her sisters had married well. Yet somehow, nothing had been left for her. In fact, with their own families to care for, they had all become rather parsimonious in regard to her.

Stop it! This was not the way to prepare for worship. She would be grateful that the Lord had given her a position in a comfortable house and children, though not her own, to care for. But why did it have to be in the middle of this dusty, barren wilderness?

Rob usually drove Pop to town, but today he wanted to watch him from a distance. Despite the bumps in the road, he seemed to be all right. Almost jovial. Was he proud to have a chance to show off his beautiful granddaughter to the other church members? Rob felt a little bit of that same pride, though he'd had nothing to do with her upbringing so far.

As for that expensive taffeta dress, he certainly didn't resent her having it. He'd done his best to properly clothe Robbie, as any responsible father would. But those monthly wire transfers to Maybelle's bank had made it hard to spread his share of the ranch income to cover two households.

Thoughts of the bank grated on his nerves. Why hadn't they wired him when Maybelle died? There were too many questions that had no answers, and he didn't have time to travel to Charleston to investigate. He'd have to rely on that lawyer, Mr. Purcell, and pray the man was honest.

He had to admit that Miss Viola, as they'd all decided to call her, was doing well with his daughter. She was firm but gentle regarding behavior and had even begun to teach Lavinia to read. In regard to his brothers and especially him, he'd noticed she sometimes shuddered when they broke some rule they hadn't minded since Mother left. In fact, she'd begun to correct their table manners in a passive way by telling Lavinia or Robbie what not to do and whom *not* to emulate—mainly Rob—when they breached some point of etiquette.

While his brothers and Pop didn't seem to mind, it grated on Rob's nerves to be educated in society's rules, not one of which made him a better rancher. Now, all gussied up in a stylish dress, bustle and all, how would Miss Viola react to the plainer clothes worn by the ladies at church?

They arrived in Riverton with time to spare. After vying with other carriages from their own church and the Mission de Santa María across the street, Will found a place to park. Then he and Drew vied with each other over who would help Miss Viola down from the surrey. She offered a hand to each of them along with that fetching smile. She hadn't once smiled at Rob that way. Not that he wanted her to.

Robbie had already lifted Lavinia down, so Rob helped Pop. From the way his father leaned on him, it was a good thing he'd done so. He wouldn't embarrass Pop by mentioning his failing condition to church folks, but he'd be sure to take Pastor Daniel aside and ask for prayer.

Folks milling around the churchyard began to notice their arrival. As happened most Sunday mornings, a passel of young ladies scurried over to greet Rob's brothers. But both Will and Drew had already offered an elbow to Miss Viola, drawing downright indignant looks from the other females. As if sensing a potential crisis, she politely declined both offers and accepted Pop's. She then clasped Lavinia's hand, and the three of them headed toward the white clapboard building. Rob's brothers blithely followed, as if unaware of the stir they'd caused, leaving all the fair young ladies to sigh after them.

He should laugh at the foolishness of it all—would have if it didn't reinforce what he and Pop had discussed the other evening. Single women were always out to snare an eligible man. A sudden chill went down his spine. Now that he was a widower, many would regard *him* as eligible. Fat chance they'd have any success. God rest Maybelle's soul, but she'd showed him he wasn't cut out for wedded *bliss*. One disastrous marriage was enough for him.

"Dad?" Robbie stood beside him, his head cocked and a puzzled expression on his face. "Are you going in?"

Rob chuckled. "Yes, indeed." He put a hand on his

son's shoulder and urged him forward. How he loved this boy! And now that Lavinia was here, he loved her, too. He wouldn't trade them for anything. If for nothing else, he was grateful to Maybelle for giving him these dear children.

The hair on Viola's neck seemed to stand on end, a sure sign someone was watching her. It couldn't be Robert. He'd seated himself on the far end of the same pew she sat in, along with the rest of the Mattson family.

"Did you see the way she sashayed in here on poor old Mr. Mattson's arm?" The female voice, though hushed, still carried up from several rows back amid the hubbub of people entering the church for worship. "Taking advantage of an old man that way."

"Humph." Another woman spoke. "You think her nose could get any higher in the air?"

"And look at that dress. Must have cost a fortune. I wonder if—"

"Hello, ladies." Another voice, one similar to Robert's, interrupted the gossipers.

The women giggled. "Good morning, Cal," one said.

The man appeared at the end of the pew. "Good morning, Pop."

The young man, looking so much like his brothers Viola couldn't mistake his identity, gave her a warm smile. "I'm Cal Mattson. You must be Miss Viola. Will came over and told us about you. Welcome to Riverton." He reached his hand out to her.

"Thank you." She shook his offered hand. Now was not the time to correct him by explaining that a lady must offer her hand first.

As music from the pump organ began to fill the air, Cal and the small crowd with him filed into the opposite pew. "We'll introduce you to the rest of the family after church."

The two pretty, *enceinte* young ladies with him smiled and gave her little waves. She waved back. Their friendliness eased her hurt feelings over the other ladies' whispered insinuations.

But why should her feelings be hurt? Maybe the other girls had never learned proper manners, never learned what damage and division gossip could cause. While enjoying the pastor's sermon on seeking to serve the Lord, she felt the strong urge to do just that. And what could better serve Him than teaching these young ladies that women were to be the civilizing influence in any community, the ones who united instead of divided people?

During the final prayer, she made up her mind to ask Mr. Mattson for permission to invite a few of these girls into the ranch house parlor to discuss the establishment of her school.

When church let out, Rob was surprised to see the folks from the mission across the road also pouring out of their adobe building. Their services usually lasted longer. He waved to a few friends as he helped Pop into the surrey, then climbed into the driver's seat and took hold of the reins.

"Aren't you forgetting something?" Pop set a hand on Rob's and tilted his head to the back of the carriage.

Miss Viola had already lifted Lavinia up and was now struggling to climb in herself. And no surprise.

With that ridiculous bustle on the back of her dress, it was a wonder she didn't fall over backward.

To placate Pop, he jumped down and held out both hands. "May I assist you, ma'am?" Did he sound sarcastic? Yes, he did. She'd managed to climb into the surrey on her own the other day at the train station.

"No, thank you. I can man—"

He didn't give her time to finish but gripped her waist and lifted. She gasped and grabbed his shoulders, and her feet flailed for a moment before she landed safely on the surrey's floorboards. Before turning away, he saw fire in her eyes and flame on her cheeks. He would have laughed if Robbie and Lavinia weren't watching, their eyes round and their mouths hanging open.

Or if Pop wasn't glaring at him like he wanted to take him to the woodshed…and not to carve a spoon.

Once he was back on the driver's bench, they rode in blissful silence for several miles until Miss Viola decided to make some noise.

"Shall we sing that song from church? Do you remember it?"

He didn't turn around to see if she included him in that suggestion.

"Amazing grace, how sweet the sound that saved a wretch like me…"

The children joined in, their sweet voices mostly in tune with her pleasant soprano. Even Pop added his gravelly bass toward the end of the stanza.

"…but now I'm found, was blind but now I see."

The thunder of hooves coming up fast behind them put Rob on the alert. He glanced back and saw an unwelcome sight.

"Martinez," he murmured to Pop as he reached back to remove a rifle from the rack between the seats and lay it across his lap. He paid no attention to Miss Viola's gasp. She'd have to get used to this sort of thing. Of course the outlaw would come upon them when Will and Drew weren't there to help. They'd gone over to the Sharps' ranch to help their brothers move furniture.

Pop slid his Colt .45 from his holster and hid it in his lap under his coat.

The Mexican and his caballeros surrounded the surrey, and real panic struck Rob's chest. Would this bandido harm his children? He must not let Martinez see his fear. Must not let the children see it either. He kept driving, kept praying, praying…

"*Buenos dias, Patron* Mattson, Señor Mattson." As he rode beside them, Martinez addressed Pop and then Rob, touching the brim of his silver- and turquoise-decorated sombrero. The hat was a bit fancy to wear to a holdup. But then, the man was nothing if not vain. "I see you have a lovely guest with you today. Perhaps you would be so kind as to present me to her."

Rob kept driving. They would reach their turnoff soon, and his men who'd stayed home to guard the herd would recognize the problem. *Please, Lord, let somebody be out in the front field to see us.*

"Señor Mattson, you wound me with *su silencio.*" Martinez put his hand over his heart. "When I come out of church just now, I look across the road and see the most beautiful woman to grace our town since my sister married the *alcalde*, the governor's son, and moved to Santa Fe. Surely it will do no harm to present me to her." The man's eyes turned toward the back of the surrey. Was Miss Viola returning his gaze?

"You were in church?" Rob couldn't keep the sarcasm from his voice. "That's new."

"Ah, again you wound me. Did you not know that since last *Navidad* when our two churches joined together for *Las Posadas*, that I have been faithful in my church attendance?" Martinez's laugh sounded jovial, not threatening. "That was when my little cousin María gave birth to a healthy baby boy in *Patron* Sharp's barn on, what you call it? Christmas Eve, just like *Niño Jesús* was born in a stable so long ago. María lost her first *bebé* before its time, so *mi familia* and I prayed for a healthy birth. When our prayer was granted, I knew this was a *muy especial* gift from God, and He was speaking to Julio Alejandro Martinez. Me, the fearsome *bandido* you *Americano*s despise. I now know *Jesucristo* as *mi Salvador*. You did not know this?"

"I did not know this." Or believe it. Rob kept driving. They rode in silence for several minutes.

"A man can change, Señor Mattson." An odd intensity filled Martinez's voice. "Or, should I say, God can change a man." He again touched the brim of his sombrero. "Señorita, perhaps another day." He clicked his tongue at his horse. *"Vamos, muchachos."* The band of five men rode away in a flurry of dust.

After several moments, Miss Viola broke the silence. "Lavinia, Robbie, I think we will add learning Spanish to our lessons. What would you think of that?" Her cheerful tone showed not a hint of fear.

A snort burst from Pop, followed by a deep chuckle.

As relief flowed through him like a soothing stream,

Rob had a hard time stifling his own laughter. If nothing else, he'd have to admit that Miss Viola had spunk.

Viola washed the last pan and handed it to Robbie to dry. Sunday dinner had been another success, with the roast and potatoes cooked to perfection. Her favorite apple tarts, which she and Lavinia had made on Saturday, had been a bit too sweet, but no one complained. She'd had a hard time saving two for William and Andrew from Robert and his father.

No one had spoken about the men who had accosted them on the road. Maybe *accosted* was the wrong word. After all, they had done no harm, and their leader seemed sincere when he proclaimed he was no longer an outlaw. As propriety demanded, she'd only glanced at him before turning to face Robert's back.

If nothing else, the gentleman certainly was handsome, with his piercing dark eyes and well-trimmed mustache. She wouldn't have minded an introduction but would depend on Robert and Mr. Mattson for wisdom in that regard. It felt good to be protected, a feeling she'd not experienced since Father died and her last brother married. She admitted to herself that it also felt good to be complimented so profusely by the well-dressed Mexican gentleman who was obviously a man of prominence.

"Miss Viola." Leaning on a cane, Mr. Mattson entered the kitchen. "What would you think of entertaining the rest of my family one of these Sundays?" He eased himself into a chair at the table.

"That would be lovely." When introduced to them after church, she'd taken to Jared, Cal and their wives right away, along with the girls' parents, Mr. and Mrs. Sharp. Even though the other ladies had been everything from standoffish to rude, Julia, Emma and their mother had freely offered their friendship.

"Pop?" Robert stuck his head in the door, and Mr. Mattson quickly slid his cane under the table. "You feel like playing horseshoes?"

Mr. Mattson perked up. "Sure do. Robbie, go get your sister. It's never too soon to start learning."

Robbie dashed from the room and soon brought Lavinia, Puff in her arms, to the kitchen.

"Let's go." Mr. Mattson didn't retrieve his cane but walked with a limp toward the door.

Although concerned, Viola wouldn't offend his dignity by asking if he needed help.

The game was set up just outside the kitchen garden fence. Right away Robert and his father traded boasts and made it a competition.

Viola had never tossed a horseshoe. Had never even held one. "It's heavy, dear." She helped Lavinia lift and try to toss the iron. It didn't go far.

"Don't worry, sis." Robbie patted her shoulder. "It just takes practice."

"I don't like it." Lavinia settled on a grassy spot nearby and teased Puff with a long blade of grass.

"You try, Miss Viola." Robbie offered her a horseshoe.

"Very well. It cannot be too hard."

The men chuckled.

"Let's see what you've got," Mr. Mattson said.

"All right." She practiced swinging her arm as she'd seen them do, then let the iron go. Instead of sailing across the yard toward the spike, it flew straight up in the air and landed near Lavinia.

Viola gasped. "No more for me." She took Lavinia's hand. "Let's watch from a safer spot."

Robbie and the men offered no objections, so she and Lavinia wandered around the property. Always alert for snakes, Viola carried a stick she'd found by the fence.

They passed several outbuildings, coming at last to a tidy little one-story clapboard house. Viola peeked in the front window. It was empty and had much more room than the main house parlor.

"Thank You, Lord," she said aloud. Just what she needed for her school.

That evening over supper, she waited until William and Andrew had given their reports on the other branch of the family. When the subject seemed exhausted, she cleared her throat in a ladylike manner.

Every eye turned toward her.

"Mr. Mattson, I was inspired by Pastor Daniel's sermon this morning. I would like to do some of the Lord's work, and I can think of nothing this community needs more than a young ladies' school of etiquette. What would you think of my using that adorable little house on the other side of the property to hold classes for some of the girls I met at church today?"

While the older man's face lit up with interest, Robert put on his usual scowl and slammed his hand down on the table.

"Absolutely not!"

Chapter Four

Before the china resettled on the table, before Lavinia's shriek had ended, Rob knew he'd made a mistake...a bad one. Eyes wide with terror, his daughter jumped from her chair and flung herself into Miss Viola's arms. Chin lifted, lips in a tight line, the lady herself viewed him with narrowed eyes, an expression that shouted her disapproval of his display of temper. That, or her anger was at his dismissal of her request. Either way, at least she hadn't cowered. He had to admire that.

Will and Drew appeared dumbfounded. Didn't they agree that women had no place on a ranch? Pop and Robbie just stared at him.

"Shh. It's all right." Miss Viola urged Lavinia back to her chair. "Let's finish those string beans so you can have dessert."

Slowly returning to her chair, Lavinia eyed Rob as though he were an enraged grizzly bear, which in these last few seconds he'd begun to feel like. He offered her the best smile he could muster.

"Mmm. Dessert. Better eat those string beans."

Though not fond of this particular vegetable, he shoved a forkful into his mouth to set an example for her.

Silence filled the room as everyone resumed eating. Finally Pop set down his knife and fork and wiped his lips with one of the linen napkins Miss Viola had started setting out. "When the good Lord puts a calling on a man's *or* a lady's heart, it's always wise to follow it. If you think you can interest those gals in such classes, I'd be hard-pressed to find a reason to say no."

Rob choked on a bean that hadn't been fully destrung but managed to wash it down with a gulp of coffee. When had his father become so interested in God's will? "Pop, I don't think—"

"I can see I've failed." Pop went on as though Rob hadn't said a word. "I haven't taught you boys to appreciate finer manners." He harrumphed. "The way I've let things go, you'd never know I grew up a Southern gentleman."

"Pop—" Will began, protest clear in his tone.

"Sir—" Drew said.

Rob opened his mouth to add his own protest.

"Why, Mr. Mattson." When Miss Viola began to speak, everyone else went quiet. "I think your manners are charming. As I know you know, manners are simply a way of showing respect for others, of making others feel at ease in our company. You have made Lavinia and me feel at ease in your company from the moment we arrived." She shot a glance toward Rob, one eyebrow raised, making clear that he had *not* behaved in such a welcoming manner.

Pop's eyes twinkled. "That's the foundation of it all,

isn't it?" He scanned the table, settling his gaze at last on Rob. "Making folks feel at ease."

Heat rising up his neck from this second censure, Rob stood and tossed his napkin on the table. "If you all will excuse me, it's time for milking."

He strode from the room and grabbed his hat on the way out the back door. Halfway to the barn, he saw lantern light beaming from the doorway and remembered he'd given Old Fuzzy the milking chore so he wouldn't feel set out to pasture in his old age. Under the circumstances, he couldn't exactly go back inside the house, so he continued his trek. Branding had been completed on Saturday, so he would examine the irons to find the one that left a gap. How had he forgotten to do that important task?

After greeting Old Fuzzy, he moved on to the storage room and lit a lantern. He pulled four irons from their storage box. Four. But he'd counted five in the fire last week. A thorough search of the room failed to turn up that fifth one, and the head of each of these four bore a perfect Double Bar M brand, a tilted *M* with a bar over the top and bottom. The single false brand he'd seen on one of their calves lacked the lower bar, making it possible for rustlers to change it with a running brand and claim the calf as theirs.

Which of their cowhands had knowingly snuck that missing iron into the fire? How many of their calves had been branded with it? And after the cattle were driven up to mountain pasture next week, who would cut them from the herd and rebrand them?

A more worrisome question was why hadn't he just checked the irons last week? Easy answer. He'd been distracted from his work by two females who should have stayed back in Charleston instead of coming out here to intrude on his peaceful existence. And now, with Pop agreeing to more females coming to the ranch for that ridiculous school Miss Viola intended to establish, the Double Bar M ranch would be nothing short of chaotic.

Out of habit, Rob rubbed his chest above the spot that usually ached. These past few days, he hadn't felt that old familiar pain, at least not as bad. Was it Miss Viola's cooking? Or the trusting way Lavinia had begun to look at him? And had he destroyed that trust with his angry outburst? How could he make it right, at least to his sweet daughter, so she wouldn't be afraid of him again?

Too many questions with no answers. His chest began to ache again.

Early Monday morning, as Viola prepared breakfast, she heard unfamiliar female voices and the sound of clattering outside the kitchen door. Setting the ham-filled cast iron skillet to the back of the stove, she went to investigate.

Two middle-aged women bustled about the yard, one starting a fire in a pit, the other filling tubs with water from the hand pump.

"Good morning, ladies." Viola stepped outside. "I am Viola Brinson, Mr. Mattson's new housekeeper. I see you're preparing to do the laundry." And what a relief that was. Her employer had not mentioned this particular chore, and she'd feared she would be responsible for it. Washing and ironing clothes for four men and a boy, not to mention her and Lavinia, would be an overwhelming task and reduce her time for educating Lavinia and Robbie.

"Si, señora." The dark-haired woman kept pumping water but cast a wary glance her way.

"Yes, missus." The redhead didn't spare her a look as she stacked more kindling on the fire.

"It's Viola, ladies. And señorita." At least that was what Señor Martinez had called her. She hoped it was correct. "May I offer you some coffee or toast before you begin?"

Now they gave her their full attention.

"The washin' gen'rally takes all day, ma'am, so I don't have time to eat afore I come." Offering a shy smile, the redhead spoke with a slight Irish accent. "I'm Agnes Ahern."

"I am pleased to meet you, Agnes." Viola looked expectantly at the other woman.

"Rosa Garcia, señorita."

"How do you do, Rosa and Agnes. Excuse me. I'll be right back." Viola hurried into the kitchen the same moment Robert entered from the hallway, Mr. Mattson right behind him. "Oh. Oh, dear. I'll have breakfast in five minutes. Everything is ready but the eggs."

She found a tray and loaded it with filled coffee mugs and toast. She speared two ham slices from the skillet and set them on the bread. "I'll be right back."

"Where—?"

Viola didn't give Robert a chance to finish his question lest he criticize her. Her sisters would be appalled to see her serving the servants. But she was in essence a servant herself now. Making friends with these women would do no harm and possibly do some good.

The gratitude beaming from their eyes as she set the tray on a nearby stump confirmed she'd done the right thing.

"I hope you do not mind." Back in the kitchen, she addressed Mr. Mattson, who now sat at the table with his sons and grandson. "They have a big job to do today, and it will be easier if they have eaten."

"Speaking of eating—" Robert began.

"The eggs will be ready by the time you have passed everything else around the table." She wouldn't give him a chance to criticize her work. If he objected to the small expense of sharing food with the help, she would pay for it out of her wages.

"That was mighty thoughtful of you, Miss Viola." After saying grace, Mr. Mattson heaped pancakes onto his plate. "I just figured the washerwomen ate before they came. I reckon it takes another woman to see—" He interrupted himself by taking a syrup-laden bite.

"I sure do work better with a full belly." William copied his father by digging into his breakfast.

His mouth full, Andrew hummed his agreement.

"Miss Viola, is that more good manners?" Robbie blinked his bright blue eyes at her. "I mean, feeding those ladics so they're 'at ease,' like you talked about last night?"

Robert paused, fork halfway to his mouth. His gaze, wary but curious, moved from his son to Viola.

To her chagrin, Viola's eyes burned. She turned back to the stove and scooped two dozen fried eggs from the skillet to a platter. "Why, I suppose so, Robbie." She managed to speak without betraying her emotions to this room full of men. Just think—she was already having a good influence on at least one of them.

"Boys," Mr. Mattson said, "the first thing I want you to do today is clear the land around Miss Viola's schoolhouse."

Viola's heart skipped. Not only had he accepted her idea for the school, but he was also fully engaged in the project. And he called it *her* schoolhouse!

"But Pop—" Robert began.

"And Rob, I want you to ride into town and invite all the young ladies you can think of to attend classes, starting… Miss Viola, when would you like to start?"

Viola took her place at the table. "If you will give me a few days to prepare lessons, I think next Monday would be fine."

"Pop." Despite addressing his father, Robert frowned at her. "You wanted me to inventory the supplies for the cattle drive. Can't you send Will or Drew?"

"I'll go."

"I can do it." The two younger brothers spoke at once.

"Nope, nope. You two'll just start flirtin' with every pretty gal you see, and they'll start settin' their caps for you. Rob's married, so that won't be a problem."

The table went quiet.

Mr. Mattson blinked, clearly realizing his mistake. "Sorry, son. Guess I need to revise my thinking on that."

Viola had not missed the way Robert cringed at his father's mistake. She tried to think of some way to smooth over the situation, but no words would come.

"Hey, look who finally woke up." Robert's cheery tone seemed forced as he drew everyone's attention to Lavinia, who stood in the doorway, her eyes wide and her thumb firmly stuck in her mouth. He rose and walked to her, then knelt down to her eye level. "Good morning, Miss Mattson. May I escort you to your seat?" He held out his arm.

She smiled around her thumb and nodded.

Viola breathed out a quiet sigh of relief. After Robert's burst of temper last evening, it had taken her some time to convince the child not to be frightened of her father. Now as he seated Lavinia at the table and tied her bib around her neck, his gentleness brought more tears to Viola's eyes. Thankfully for her, everyone's attention, even Robbie's, was on the little girl who was quickly becoming the darling of the ranch.

Rob couldn't fault Pop for thinking of him as still married. It had been less than a week since they'd learned of Maybelle's death. Although he'd grieved the loss of his marriage years ago, he'd just begun to discover true grief over the finality of it all. But a hardworking rancher had little time to park on his feelings, especially when the whole ranch needed to prepare for the cattle drive. Nor did they have time to clear the land around the little house.

Schoolhouse? Once Pop used that term, Rob knew his hopes for quashing the whole plan would be dwindling. In fact, since last week, Pop had been reclaiming the big decisions around the ranch, decisions he'd delegated to Rob months ago. In a way, Rob was glad to see him get back some of his old energy. But after running the place himself for so long, he felt a kick in his pride over having to surrender those responsibilities.

The ride into town gave him time to decide which of the town gals he would approach first and how he would sound convincing when he told her about the school of etiquette he most definitely did not want on the ranch. The first problem was easily solved. Suzette Pursers, daughter of mercantile owner Abner Pursers, was the unofficial social leader of the younger set. Now that he thought of it, Pop was right to send him. Suzette was sweet on Will, so she might misunderstand an invitation coming from him. Rob wouldn't wish that on either brother.

As for Rob sounding like he really wanted the school to open, Suzette might solve that problem, too. Anytime anybody spoke to her, the eighteen-year-old generally took over the conversation before they got two words out.

True to her nature, she saw Rob enter the store and pasted on her brightest smile before he even removed his hat.

"Good morning, Rob. I hope everyone at the Double Bar M is doing well. What can I do for you today?" She fussed with several items displayed on the counter. "Everybody sure was surprised to see that pretty lady with you at church yesterday. And that darling little girl. Miz Whitman says she's your daughter and that—" Suzette gasped, and her eyes reddened. "Oh, Rob, I'm so sorry about your wife…"

He should have known the whole town would be gossiping about his family. They gossiped about everything and everybody, so he didn't take it personally.

"Thank you kindly, Suzette. We all have our share of troubles, don't we?" He cleared his throat and tried to remember the speech he'd prepared. "Of course, my daughter is a pure joy. As for the lady, she's eager to meet you and the rest of the young women in town. Seems she didn't have much chance to speak to you all yesterday after church, what with talking to my younger brothers' wives and in-laws and all."

Suzette blinked her light brown eyes in surprise. "So she'll be staying around? We just thought she brought your daughter and planned to head back East."

Rob swallowed a laugh at everything that remark revealed. "No, no. We decided she needed to stay on as Lavinia's governess." For some reason, he couldn't bring himself to say *housekeeper*. That might diminish Miss Viola in the town's opinion. But why did he feel the need to protect her? Or to include himself among those who'd decided?

"Not only that, but Miss Brinson is a highly trained teacher of etiquette, having graduated from a fine finishing school back in Norfolk. In fact, she has generously offered to establish a school of etiquette for our town, seeing as how most folks around here can't afford to send their daughters back East for such training." He gave Suzette a paternal smile. "Present company excluded, of course."

She blinked again, not the least bit flirtatiously. "School of etiquette? Oh, that sounds wonderful. Do you suppose she'd let me come?"

"She sure would. So spread the word and bring all your friends. School starts next Monday. I'm sure you can find out all the particulars from her on Sunday." And unlike yesterday, maybe offer her some sort of welcome to the community. He pulled Miss Viola's shopping list from his pocket. "Speaking of particulars, here's what we need for this week."

Headed back home a short time later with saddlebags full of supplies, Rob pondered his feelings of protectiveness for Miss Viola. After all, he did want her to leave, didn't he? But then who would take care of Lavinia? He didn't want her to establish a school on the ranch, did he? But someone should teach the local gals about finer manners.

As much as he hated to admit it, women did provide a civilizing effect. Although Billy the Kid and his gang had been sent to their reward seven years ago, too many other outlaws and bandidos still lived in this area. To edge out the lawless, the community needed to be strengthened with decent, God-fearing families. Yet the new arrivals generally turned out to be single men hoping to strike it rich. If ladies back East knew they would find civilized towns where manners were appreciated, more of them might be persuaded to come.

Even Mama and Maybelle might have stayed if they'd found other refined ladies to socialize with. Instead, where the Mattson men had found a rough but promising land to conquer, the Mattson women found a bleak desert that had conquered them. Would Miss Viola be conquered, too? Somehow, from the way those intense green eyes of hers stared down every challenge she'd met here so far, he doubted it. Oddly, and against all his former hopes that she'd leave, he admired her for it.

By the time Rob turned down the lane to the ranch, he'd decided Miss Viola's school of etiquette would be the best thing to come to this community since the railroad. Now if he could figure out a way to move the operation into town…

Viola accepted Robert's help down from the surrey, adjusted her skirts and surveyed the busy churchyard for young ladies whom she could meet after the service. Was it her imagination, or were there more young men than women in the milling crowd?

"Huh." Mr. Mattson leaned on William to get down, but his eyes were bright. "Appears to me that all the young bucks have suddenly decided to come to church." He winked at Viola, a social error she would ignore coming from him but not younger men. "Guess they've all turned out to meet the pretty new lady in the neighborhood."

As if his quiet words were a loudly spoken invitation, a half dozen men removed their hats and headed her way.

"Howdy, miss," the first one said. "I'm—"

"Ma'am, I'm Josh—" A second man shoved him aside.

"May I escort you—" A third man offered his arm.

"Hold on, boys." Mr. Mattson spoke with such authority that they all froze in place. "We've come to church to worship the Lord. There's plenty of time to socialize afterward." He offered his arm. "Shall we, Miss Viola?"

"Yes, sir." Her face on fire, Viola placed a gloved hand on his arm with one hand and grasped Lavinia's hand with the other.

When they entered the pretty little clapboard church,

she heard a female voice behind her. "Who does she think she is, enticing all them fellas to her that way?"

As if she had invited *those* "fellas" over to meet her! If all the young ladies agreed with that girl, it didn't bode well for Viola's school.

True to the lessons she'd planned to teach them, she set aside a problem she couldn't solve so she could concentrate on the immediate situation. She enjoyed the hymn singing and paid attention to Pastor Daniel's sermon. Once again, he spoke about following the path the Lord set before a person, so she searched her heart. Had she misunderstood God's direction last week? Had her desire to have a school been presumptuous? Surely not.

After Robert's initial outburst, even he had seemed willing, if not eager, to help her prepare the little house. He'd brought some chairs and a table out of storage and made sure the Ben Franklin stove would provide both heat and a cooking surface. Andrew remarked that the schoolhouse in town wasn't nearly so well furnished.

Yet what good would the little cottage do if none of the young ladies attended?

Oh, dear. She'd let her mind wander, and now the organist had begun the final hymn. She stood with the rest of the congregation and sang "What a Friend We Have in Jesus."

What a perfect message to receive from the Lord on this day. If no one else befriended her, the Lord Jesus Christ was her constant friend. She could carry everything to Him in prayer.

Church was dismissed, and she once again walked between Mr. Mattson and Lavinia as they proceeded toward the surrey. Although she'd thought to pause in the churchyard to meet some of the young ladies, Mr. Mattson kept walking, the other Mattson men following behind them. The older man's jaw was set, and his eyebrows were bent in a frown. She couldn't imagine why. In her ten or so days here, he had not shown a temper.

Robert helped the three of them into the surrey, then whistled for Robbie. The boy said goodbye to his friends and ran over to obey.

Right behind him, one of the young ladies charged across the yard and grasped William's arm. "Aren't you going to introduce me to your houseguest?" She batted her dark brown eyelashes and gave him a coy grin. William tugged at his collar and gulped.

Viola sucked in her cheeks to keep from laughing.

"Sure thing." William led the girl to the buggy. "Miss Viola, may I present Miss Suzette Pursers?"

"Miss Pursers, I am delighted to meet you." Noting William's proper introduction, Viola gave him an approving smile before reaching out to the girl.

Shaking Viola's hand a little too enthusiastically, Suzette grinned broadly. "Howdy, ma'am, eh, miss."

"Robert tells me you're interested in my school of etiquette. Will you come tomorrow morning at nine o'clock…and bring your friends?"

Excitement filled the girl's face. "Yes, ma'am. We'll be there."

"I am so pleased. I'll see you then."

The menfolk didn't speak during this exchange, but on the way home, Viola could see Mr. Mattson's jaw had relaxed. Seated on the front bench, he chatted easily with Robert about their plans for the coming week. William, Old Fuzzy and most of the cowhands would be driving the herd of cattle up into the mountains, and they had to carry four months' worth of supplies with them. Those left behind would busy themselves with ranch maintenance.

Although the church across the road had again been dismissed at the same time, none of the mounted caballeros attempted to stop the Mattsons, perhaps because William and Andrew rode behind the surrey. She'd hoped to discover more about the Martinez ranch, but Robert and Mr. Mattson seemed unwilling to discuss those particular neighbors.

She spied Rosa Garcia walking beside the road with several children. Her heart going out to the widow, she smiled and waved at her. Rosa stopped and blinked, as though she was surprised. Then she returned a smile and a wave. Viola knew her sisters and sisters-in-law would be appalled at her acknowledging a servant in public. But a new sense of freedom was growing inside her. Mama had always said being kind was more important than following rules. In Viola's school, she hoped to instill both kindness and manners in her students.

The next morning, the ranch hummed with activity. The cattle drive began at first light and continued for several hours until the last steer had been driven beyond the ranch's eastern fence line. The dust had not settled before Robert and Andrew started their repairs on the north side of the barn.

Having washed breakfast dishes and set a pot of stew simmering on the stove, Viola gathered her books and Lavinia and made her way to the cottage. Her pin watch read eight forty-nine, so she had plenty of time to settle her thoughts before her students arrived.

At ten minutes after nine, she made a note in her lesson plan to teach the importance of punctuality.

At nine-thirty, she pondered the possible reasons no one had come, not even Suzette. Perhaps she should have personally invited each of the young ladies, despite their failure to welcome her. She must not find herself in a situation like the one she'd endured back home, where she had nothing to offer the women of her community. She must, *must* find her place here among them and earn their respect. It would simply require more work on her part.

Before she fell too far into self-pity, Robert knocked on the door. "How's everything…" His words trailed off as he entered and glanced around the room, focusing at last on Lavinia, who sat at a low table practicing her letters on a slate.

Dismissing her disappointment, Viola waved a hand to indicate the otherwise empty room. "As you can see, nobody came." She knew very well his dislike for her school plans. Had he come to gloat?

Instead, he walked over to Lavinia and knelt beside her. "Say, you're doing a mighty fine job of writing those letters." His voice was soft, his expression even softer.

Lavinia gave him a winsome smile.

Viola joined them. "What do we say when someone compliments us?"

"Thank you?" Lavinia blinked those big brown eyes.

"You're welcome. Keep up the good work." He raised a hand as though he would ruffle her hair.

Viola cleared her throat more sharply than she intended.

Robert shot her a look of annoyance. "I know. I know." He patted Lavinia's shoulder, then stood and walked toward the door. "Sorry about your class."

She gave him her cheeriest smile. "Thank you, Robert."

She followed him outside, intending to ask whether he wanted Robbie to come for his lessons. But the sound of a horse galloping down the lane caught their attention. Suzette Pursers headed toward the main house but seemed to notice her mistake and whipped her little mare around and rode up to the cottage.

"Sorry I'm late." She hopped off the horse and tied her to the hitching rail. "Pa needed me to make a delivery before I came here. Is everybody else already here?"

"No. You're the first." Viola's heart lifted. *Oh, ye of little faith.* "Please come in." She gave Robert what she hoped was a dismissing nod.

He posted his fists at his waist. "Did you ride all the way out here by yourself?"

"Sure did." Suzette pulled out a brightly colored handkerchief and mopped her brow.

Robert shook his head. "Suzette, don't you know it's downright dangerous for a girl to ride around alone? There's all sorts of outlaws roaming around out here. What if you'd run into some of them?"

"Oh, pshaw." She laughed in a rather boisterous way. "I ride all over delivering for Pa. Nobody's gonna bother me, or they'll lose their credit at the store."

Robert huffed out a sigh of disgust. "Then I guess

I'll have to talk to him." He strode away muttering to himself.

Suzette gazed beyond him toward the barn and waved. "Hey, Will!" she yelled. "Oh, that's Drew. They look almost like twins."

"Shall we go inside?" Viola waved a hand toward the house. "Lavinia is working on her letters, so you and I can discuss your course of study."

"Oooh." Suzette playfully minced toward the door. "My *course of study*. That sounds so grand."

"And it is." Inside, Viola poured boiling water from the kettle into the porcelain teapot and added two spoons of tea leaves. "Shall we sit and get acquainted?"

"Have you seen Will this morning?" Suzette glanced toward the door as though expecting him to enter.

"Yes, at breakfast. But he left on the trail drive to the mountains and…"

"Oh!" Suzette stamped her foot and came close to pouting. "And here I thought…"

Viola's heart dropped. Suzette had not come to receive lessons in etiquette but to be close to William. "What did you think, dear?" She poured a cup of tea and offered it to the girl.

"Well…" She took it and added two lumps of sugar. "Oh, horsefeathers. I do want to learn etiquette." She giggled, and her creamy cheeks turned pink. "I was just hoping maybe to see Will at recess."

Recess? At her age? Viola laughed. "Think of it this way. When William returns, he will be impressed with all you have learned."

Suzette giggled. "You think so? He sure is like a skittish colt around me. Maybe I'll just show him what he's missing out on." She blew on her tea, then sipped it. "So where do we start?"

Viola thought for a moment. She couldn't conduct a lesson for one in the same way she would for a full classroom. Suzette didn't seem dismayed by not having any classmates though. Had she actually invited her friends, as promised? Viola would not ask her. After all, she'd seemed surprised about being the first to arrive.

She smiled at Suzette. "I believe the best place to begin is with an overview." At the girl's puzzled expression, she explained further. "An outline that will explain all the areas we will discuss in our lessons."

Understanding dawned on her pretty face. "Sounds good to me."

"Good. Now, tell me what you think etiquette is."

Suzette stared off for a moment. "Manners? Knowing the right thing to say?" She straightened in her chair. "Good posture?"

"Very good." Viola copied her favorite teacher from years ago by praising her student before correcting her. "All of those are part of etiquette. Can you tell me the foundation for those behaviors?"

Suzette blinked. "The Bible?"

Now Viola blinked. "Why, yes. That is our foundation for all good behaviors." Well, maybe not posture, but she would figure that out later. "In fact, if we love our neighbor as ourselves, we fulfill the law of Christ, as the scriptures say." She would have to employ that principle with Robert, difficult though it might be. "In addition, etiquette is founded in comportment, which goes beyond outward behavior that we can put on like a garment. It comes from within when we have an assurance of who we are, when we possess a sense of spiritual well-being." She still struggled with both concepts. "When we are self-assured in our innermost being, not based upon how society sees us, but upon how God sees us, we are free to treat others with respect and kindness."

Suzette nodded, her eager expression conveying at least partial understanding. As for Viola, she'd not expected this turn of conversation, but she knew in her deepest being it was true. Although a redundant woman might live on the edges of society and be invisible to most, God still saw her, still loved her, still assigned worth to her. In recent years, when it became clear she wouldn't find a husband back home, she still struggled to believe in that worth. Perhaps through teaching this young woman about etiquette and comportment, Viola had become her own student.

Two hours later, their overview completed, Suzette prepared to leave. "I sure do like this, Miss Viola." She hesitated, as though considering her next words. "Y'know, I'm gonna tell my friends you aren't snooty at all. Then maybe they'll want to come next week."

Viola did her best to hide a gasp. Was that how she appeared to the other girls—snobbish and unapproachable instead of refined, as she had intended? Was that why they disliked her without even knowing her? And, having made such a poor first impression, could she somehow find a way to win them over?

Chapter Five

After a long day of replacing boards and beams on the north side of the barn, where winter storms had weakened the structure, Rob surveyed the steaming bowls of food Miss Viola had laid out for supper. What with teaching Suzette and Lavinia all morning and then Robbie after lunch, then dealing with the laundry women, when had she had time to fix stew, biscuits, gravy and pie and set the table with freshly ironed linens and Mother's best china?

"Is something missing?" She brought in a glass dish filled with preserves and set it beside the biscuits.

"No. Not at all." Rob lifted a hand to rub his chest, a gesture now more habitual than necessary. He could see everything on the table would go down easy, so he let his hand fall back to his side. "'Scuse me. I need to go change." He hadn't been able to shake off all the dirt from his workday. He sure didn't want to be the one to soil the white tablecloth just by sitting down to eat. Before Miss Viola came, nobody in the household ever noticed such things. They always ate in the kitchen and hadn't even used tablecloths.

Since only one student showed up, he'd planned to offer a few words of consolation over the failure of her school, as he would try to encourage a new cowhand who fell short on his first day. But Miss Viola surprised him again. She carried herself with even more confidence than usual. Yep, she sure had spunk. And from the way Suzette had given him a cheerful wave as she left, she wasn't discouraged either. Too bad she hadn't been able to bring any friends.

Rob still worried about the girl riding out alone, and he still planned to speak to Abner about it. When he'd invited her to Miss Viola's school, he'd expected a wagonful of gals from town and nearby ranches to arrive together. A few of them carried guns, and there would be safety in numbers.

He should have done a better job of inviting them. Should have visited the ones he knew in town. Having failed that, he should have talked to some of them after church yesterday. But Pop had been riled up about the way a couple of them had talked about Miss Viola behind her back, not even trying to soften their snippy remarks to a whisper. If Suzette hadn't come over to the surrey and introduced herself after church, there was no telling what Pop would have done. If Will ever decided to get hitched, Suzette Pursers would be a good catch. Well, she'd be catching *him*, but the end result would be the same.

Where had these thoughts come from? After seeing Rob's and Pop's marriages fail, his four brothers had decided long ago not to get lassoed by females. Then

Cal and Jared had changed their minds and married the Sharp sisters. Now Will and Drew would probably follow suit. The ranch would go downhill from there, and Rob had no way of stopping it. Since Miss Viola arrived, nobody listened to him anymore.

Energized by the modest successes of the day, Viola decided to present her next important idea to Mr. Mattson. With supper dishes washed and put away and the children settled in bed, she joined the men in the parlor. Robert kept glancing her way as they discussed ranch business. Perhaps he thought she wouldn't be interested in how they would manage the various chores now that William and five of the cowhands were away for the summer. But she was. Three men still lived in the bunkhouse, and she would be certain to send desserts out to them from time to time to reward their hard work. Further, they might have sweethearts who would be interested in her school if their beaux suggested it.

"Well, now, Miss Viola." Mr. Mattson gave her a paternal smile. "I can see you have something on your mind."

"Yes, I do." She summoned to mind the speech she'd rehearsed, hoping to avoid sounding *snooty*, to use Suzette's word. "It takes my breath away to see all the work you men do to keep this ranch running. It's no wonder you have not been able to keep the house in order as well."

While Mr. Mattson appeared interested, she heard a slight growl coming from Robert's direction and a snicker from Andrew. She ignored the younger men and focused on their father.

"You may have noticed our dear little Lavinia frequently sneezes, and I fear she will develop a lung ailment. The climate here is so much drier than back in Charleston."

"Huh. I did notice that sneezing. Didn't you, Rob?" Mr. Mattson scratched his chin. "Never even thought about it, though. Wouldn't want our little girl to get sick, would we?"

"No sir." A worried frown on his brow, Robert focused on Viola. "You got any ideas?"

Viola smiled. "In fact, I do. Mr. Mattson, with your permission, I would like to do some spring cleaning."

He chortled. "*Spring* cleaning? How about eight years' worth of cleaning? My wife gave up on that two years in, even after I built this house just like she wanted. And bought her all the furniture and curtains and such that she asked for from back East." He scowled and seemed to shrink back into his chair.

"We can remedy that, sir." Viola spoke in a cheerful tone, reinforcing her words with another smile. She'd grown fond of the old gentleman, and she didn't like to see him depressed. Besides, every conflict had two sides, and she could only imagine what Mrs. Mattson endured before the railroad came and the town began to grow. "If you'll permit me, I'll ask Rosa and Agnes to give us some extra days so we can accomplish the task."

Was that approval she saw in Robert's eyes and maybe a half smile on his lips?

"Sounds good to me." Andrew laughed. "Maybe you'll find some of the stuff we've lost over the years."

Mr. Mattson scratched his chin again. After a minute, his face lit up. "Miss Viola, you're a blessing. If you're willing to soil your hands with some deep house-cleaning, I'll be willing to pay as many helpers as you need."

"Just stay out of my room." Robert's approving expression disappeared, replaced by suspicion.

"As you wish." Viola turned to Andrew. "Do you have any special requests?"

"No, ma'am." His eyes twinkled with mischief. "Well, you might just keep an eye out for my pet lizard. She went missing about five years ago."

The other two men chuckled.

Viola hid a shudder. "I'll do that. What is her name so I can properly address her?"

Andrew hooted. "You're a good sport, Miss Viola." He gave her a wily grin. "Just call her Liz."

"I'll do that, and I am certain she and I will become good friends." Perhaps the lizard, if she was still alive, had kept down the insect population in the house. "And I'll protect her from Puff, should she decide Liz looks appetizing."

More laughter from the men, even a mild chuckle from Robert.

"Now, would one of you be so kind as to drive me to Rosa's and Agnes's homes tomorrow morning so I can arrange the details? I also need to purchase cleaning supplies at the dry goods store. Oh, and new shoes for Lavinia."

"I'd be pleased to take you, ma'am," Andrew said.

Just as she began to feel relief that he, not Robert, had offered, Robert spoke.

"I'll take you to town, and if my daughter needs

shoes, I'll buy them." The finality in his tone ended the discussion.

Andrew shrugged. "Next time." He winked at Viola, more a brotherly gesture than a flirtatious one, so she wouldn't scold him for it.

"I truly don't mind riding in back." When Robert indicated Viola should sit on the surrey's front bench, her heart seemed to skitter about in her chest. Sitting beside this ill-tempered man and bumping into his shoulder all the way to town did not appeal to her at all. "Robbie can ride beside you."

Robert snorted. "For a lady who's all about appearances, you sure don't understand what that would look like. My father gave you authority to hire those women, so you should be sitting in the front seat, not in back with the young'uns." He gripped her waist. "Up you go."

Viola gasped as he lifted her into the conveyance as though she weighed no more than Lavinia. He then helped his daughter into the back seat. "Keep an eye on her," he said to Robbie. "Don't let her fall out."

"Now, really, Robert." Still unsettled from his less than gentlemanly help into the carriage, Viola felt her alarm growing. How could he be so callous toward his little girl? "I should—"

"Don't worry, Miss Viola," Robbie said. "If she falls out, we can pick her up on the way back home."

Robert chuckled, and both children giggled. Lavinia clearly didn't share Viola's concerns. Or perhaps she didn't understand. She simply laughed because Robbie did. It was a good sign. She trusted her brother, and so did Viola, so far as watching out for his sister. But could a nine-year-old boy actually keep her from falling out of the fast-moving surrey, considering the way his father drove? Viola prayed for the child's safety.

As always, the bumpy ride tossed them all around, but when Viola glanced over her shoulder at the children, they seemed to take the jolts easily. However, just as she'd feared, she kept bumping into Robert's shoulder—his very muscular shoulder. It felt like a stone wall, every bit as unmovable as his behavior toward her. Despite his improved attitude toward her school, he still didn't seem to trust her. The very idea that he'd forbidden her to give his room a spring cleaning, as though she might steal something, still rankled. If one room remained dusty, that dust would spread to the whole house, and her efforts to maintain a clean house would be in vain. And did she not have sufficient opportunity to steal from him, if she were so inclined, while the men worked outside all day? This man simply did not make sense to her.

Not far from town, Robert slowed the horses and turned down a lane. A small cluster of pink adobe houses sat beside the river, with several dark-haired children playing in the center plaza. Seeing the surrey, they shouted greetings.

"My, how friendly." Viola smiled and waved back.

"What did you expect?" As usual, Robert's tone sounded accusatory.

She would not dignify his rude question with an answer.

"Hey, Pepe!" Robert called out to one of the older children. "Fetch your mama for me."

"Please," Viola prompted.

Robert snorted.

Before Viola could think of a way to correct his manners, several women emerged from the houses, suspicion on their faces. She spotted Rosa and waved to her.

"Rosa, may we speak with you?"

As Rosa walked toward them, worry now clouded her face. "*Sí*, Señorita Viola. Is something the matter?" She glanced around at the other women, who hung back and watched warily.

"No—" Robert began, his voice cross.

"Oh, no, not at all." Not giving him a chance to finish, Viola used her friendliest tone. "I know you're a busy mother, but I wonder if you could spare a few extra days to work for us. I need help with spring cleaning and…"

One of the other ladies called out to Rosa in Spanish. Rosa answered in kind before turning back to Viola. "Spring cleaning, señorita? *¿Qué es?* What is?"

Viola somehow managed not to show her surprise. "Cleaning out the soot and dirt after the house has been closed up all winter."

"Ah." Rosa spoke to the others, who appeared surprised. Then they talked among themselves and laughed.

"What are they saying?" Viola gave them a smile that felt a little tight. Beside her, Robert chuckled.

"They say why not keep *su casa* clean in winter?" Rosa's dark eyes twinkled.

Now Viola laughed. "Yes, well." She waved a hand toward Robert. "These men have been living without a woman's help all these years."

Rosa translated, and the women laughed again.

"*Sí*, we know about our men." Rosa rolled her eyes. "*Sí*, I will come. When?"

They arranged a day, dependent on Agnes's response, and soon the surrey was again traveling toward town. Robert seemed a bit taciturn, even surly, but that was nothing new. Viola wouldn't try to draw him out.

In Riverton, they drove to Agnes Ahern's small clapboard shack. Unlike in the little village, no one came out to meet them.

"I'll go." Viola moved to climb down from the surrey.

"No." Robert touched her arm. "I'll go." His voice conveyed caution, although Viola couldn't imagine why. She might not care for his rudeness, but she did trust his knowledge of the local customs.

"Very well."

He pounded on the door, and Agnes answered.

"Whaddaya want?" She looked over his shoulder. "Oh, it's you, Miss Viola."

Viola did her best not to recoil. This was not the tidy woman who came to do the Monday wash. Today Agnes's hair was uncombed, her clothes almost slovenly, and her gaze seemed blurred. Was she inebriated?

"Is it my boy?" Agnes dragged a hand through her graying red hair. "Is he all right?"

"Patrick's fine. He's riding fence today." Robert turned back to the surrey. "Let's go. She's probably been drinking—"

Viola shook her head. "Good morning, Agnes." No matter what her condition, this woman obviously needed more income. "Will you come this Thursday and Friday and do some extra work for us?"

Agnes blinked and straightened. "Yes, ma'am. I'll be

there first thing Thursday morning." She didn't sound the least bit intoxicated. Perhaps they had awakened her from a sound sleep.

"Good. I'll have breakfast for you and Rosa."

As they drove away, she could feel more than hear Robert's grumbling. Well, he could grumble all he wanted to. Mr. Mattson had given her the authority to hire these women, so she didn't have to answer to him. And if Robert had trusted them to wash his laundry and put it away in his room, maybe Viola could arrange for them to do a bit of cleaning in there as well. Clearly, she was the one he found untrustworthy, which hurt more than she could ever admit to anyone. Once considered above reproach by her family and community, in this place she had a mark against her that was in no way her fault, and she had no idea how to erase it.

As usual since Miss Viola Brinson's arrival, which had first put a dark shadow over his existence, Rob's thoughts took a downward turn. It was all well and good that the house would have its first thorough cleaning in years, but he wasn't so sure Agnes Ahern was the one to do it. For years, her son Patrick had worked off and on for the Mattsons and other ranchers, but he didn't have the best reputation for honesty or sobriety. Had he learned his shady ways from his widowed mother?

Rob felt certain the Irishman was the one who had tampered with the branding irons. That's why he hadn't sent him out to ride herd on summer grazing, where all the ranchers' cattle mingled in the same mountain meadows. At the end of summer, brands made it possible to sort out which ranch each steer belonged to. At least Rob had been able to persuade Pop to tell Will about their suspicions so he and the other cowhands could be on the lookout for any attempt at rebranding.

The surrey dipped into a hole in the road, and Miss Viola bumped against his shoulder. Each time she did that, each time Rob smelled that fancy perfume of hers, he was reminded of her womanliness, and it was starting to get to him. The last thing he needed was to get attached to a female—any female.

If he weren't holding the reins with both hands, he would rub that spot where worry often tried to bore a hole in his chest. It hadn't hurt so bad lately, but today he had an extra concern. Last night he and Pop had written a letter to a friend of Pop's back in Charleston to investigate that lawyer, Purcell, who had managed Maybelle's estate. If his letter took as long to get there as Miss Viola's had to arrive here, it might be years before they solved the problem of where his money had gone for the better part of these past four years, and especially these past six months. With trains running back and forth across the country every day, it made no sense that her letter had been delayed so long.

"Now, about Lavinia's shoes." Miss Viola spoke as if they'd been conversing all along.

He gave her a sidelong glance. She wore that bossy look on her face that both riled him up and tickled his funny bone. "Yeah, what about them?"

"I do have some funds left from the sale of Maybelle's belongings to purchase—"

"You mean to tell me you have some of *my* money, and this is the first time you decide to mention it?" Just as he'd suspected, she couldn't be trusted.

"*Mister* Mattson," she whispered, "the children are listening."

"So?" He glared at her.

She glared back but still whispered. "Perhaps we should discuss this later."

"No. I want to know now." Despite his annoyance at her, he softened his voice. "Why is this the first time you've mentioned that you have my money?"

She looked away and sighed—one of those "Lord, give me patience" sighs, as she often did. "Maybelle gave instructions that the money from selling her possessions should be kept by her guardian to see to Lavinia's needs. As her temporary guardian until we arrived here and the only woman currently in her life, I wanted to be certain she would be provided for."

"*You* wanted to be certain?" Rob felt as if his head might explode. "What gives you the right…?"

"Dad?" Robbie's plaintive voice from the back bench, along with an unmistakable sob from Lavinia, cut into his anger.

Miss Viola might be snooty, maybe even dishonest, but the children—*his* children—didn't need to be frightened by his anger.

"It's all right, son. Miss Viola and I are just discussing Lavinia's shoes. Say, aren't you about due for some new boots?" Rob hoped the distraction would soothe his son. He glanced over his shoulder to see Lavinia sucking her thumb, a habit Miss Viola forbade him to correct.

"I 'druther have a rifle." Robbie gave him a cheeky grin, clearly distracted from Rob's *discussion* with Miss Viola.

"You also need new trousers, Robbie." Miss Viola gave the boy a sweet, genuine smile, the one that made her beautiful and made Rob's collar feel too tight. "If the dry goods store does not carry them in your size, we can purchase material, and I'll make them."

Rob couldn't think of any response to her clever change of subject. Here she was willing to make new clothes for his son, who'd worn his uncles' hand-me-downs since he was a tyke, and Rob was treating her like a thief.

But he wouldn't rest easy until he found out about that money.

Impossible man!

With no little difficulty, Viola engaged every ounce of her upbringing to act as though nothing was the matter. The very idea that he would continue to suspect her of thievery had brought her to the brink of lashing out, which would have been a serious breach of etiquette and, more important, would distress the children as much as Robert's angry outbursts.

As discreetly as she could, she pulled the folded bank notes from her reticule and deposited them in the pocket of his black frock coat. Yes, it was too familiar a gesture, but she couldn't abide holding on to that money for another moment.

"I'll give you an accounting to the penny when we return to the ranch." She spoke in a quiet but cheerful tone, as if she were promising to bake him a cake.

His jaw dropped briefly, and he frowned. No surprise there. And no response. Instead, he turned away and concentrated on the road as if he were driving through

an unfamiliar labyrinth. He might have at least acknowledged what she'd done. But she would no doubt always
be disappointed when she expected gratitude or any
other courtesy from Mr. Robert Mattson.

She sighed softly, hoping he wouldn't hear her over
the rumble of the surrey wheels. How she'd looked forward to this shopping trip, her very first to the Riverton dry goods store. She had no needs for herself, but
buying clothes and shoes for Lavinia would have been
all her delight. Now she would have to ask him to make
the needed purchases. Once again she was the redundant woman begging for a pittance.

A giggle from Lavinia shook Viola from her self-
pity. As if they had forgotten the adults' disagreement,
the children once again chatted happily, with Robbie
pointing out various sights they drove past. Ah, the re-
silience of childhood. Viola could only smile.

Beside her, Robert grunted. "Pretty pleased with
yourself, eh?"

She refused to dignify his ridiculous comment with
a response.

Rob had expected Miss Viola to take charge of the
shopping in her usual bossy way. Instead, she led them
to the shoe display and waved a hand over the smaller
girls' sizes.

"You may find what Lavinia needs here." She stood
back with a smug smile.

As if he would know how to choose anything for his
daughter. Worse still, Lavinia took his hand and looked
up at him with trusting expectation in her eyes.

Rob scrubbed his other hand down his face, internally surrendering but still trying to hold on to his pride. "Miss Viola, would you be so kind as to choose the right shoes for Lavinia? I'll find some boots for Robbie." He delivered his daughter's hand to the lady and led his son to another display.

"Dad, I really want that rifle." Robbie's eyes shone with hope. "I can wear Uncle Drew's old boots for a while longer."

His son had no idea Rob had already bought the rifle for his upcoming birthday. "Now, son, you know those boots are still too big, even when you wear two pairs of socks. Let's find some that fit better."

"Yessir." Robbie shrugged off his disappointment, as he always did.

While they looked over the boots, chirping female voices came from across the store.

"Oh, Miss Brinson," Suzette Pursers said. "I've been practicing my lessons from yesterday and can't wait for next Monday."

"Very good, Suzette. I look forward to it as well. Now, give me your honest opinion about these shoes. Should Lavinia wear these high-tops or the lower cut tie shoes?"

The women then discussed the particulars of the choice as if deciding on a presidential election.

"Dad?" Robbie tugged on Rob's coat sleeve. "What about these?" He held up a fine brown pair with swirling tan designs.

"Hmm. Kinda fancy for ranch work, son." And pricey. Maybe Pop would buy them for Robbie's birthday. "Let's see what else they have."

As Robbie tried on a more serviceable boot, Lavinia danced over to him.

"Daddy, Miss Viola said to ask you if I can have these." She held up a pair of pink leather high-tops with pearly buttons down the side. A bit fancy, but also sturdy looking.

The lady in question stood several yards away, her expression bland. So this was her plan, putting the decision on him. Well, two could play her game.

"Why, I don't know, sweetheart. Do you like them?"

Her eyes bright, Lavinia nodded. "Yessir."

"Dad?" Robbie's voice held a hint of whining. "How come she gets fancy shoes?"

His son never whined. Never complained. If Rob bought his daughter the fancy shoes, Robbie might resent her. Rob knew from experience that sibling squabbles could lead to bitterness. He'd often felt his four younger brothers' resentment when he gave them orders. Besides, special purchases like new boots usually came in the fall after the cattle herd had been sold. How could he justify the expense of two pairs of boots in addition to Lavinia's shoes? The bank notes Miss Viola had slipped into his pocket seemed to shout the answer. He could afford both.

"Well, now you've ruined my surprise. I was going to save the fancy ones for your birthday. But you can have them today, along with the work boots." It wasn't quite a lie. "Besides, girls need more fancy stuff than us men."

Robbie's troubled expression dissolved into a wide grin. "Thanks, Dad."

Across the room, Miss Viola stood at a display fingering some material. What did she want now? He walked over to her, expecting to see more pink and probably some lace. Instead, she held up a bolt of dark blue denim.

"Would you please purchase four yards of this for Robbie's work trousers and four yards of the black flannel for his Sunday trousers?" Again, her bland expression gave no hint of her thoughts.

"Sure."

She lifted the two bolts, refusing his offer to carry them. *Stubborn woman.* He followed her to the counter, where Suzette measured and cut the material, then gathered the notions needed to make both pairs of trousers. A pinch of guilt struck Rob. Here she was taking care of his children, and he hadn't even appreciated it. What would he do if Maybelle were here? Ah, yes. Women liked to be spoiled as much as children, so maybe he just needed to buy her something. Within propriety, of course. "You want, uh, need anything, Miss Viola?"

"Why, yes, now that you ask." She pulled a folded paper from her reticule and handed it to him.

Expecting a list of gewgaws, he frowned. "Flour, sugar, coffee, jam, cleaning supplies…" Necessities for the kitchen but not one thing for herself. "You don't need anything?"

She lifted her chin, just as she had that first day, and speared him with a cold look. "I have all I need."

"Maybe you'd like some of this." Suzette held up a small wrapped package with elaborate lettering. "It's fancy perfumed soap directly from France. It's easy on the skin, so—"

"No, thank you."

"Yeah, we'll take it."

They spoke at the same time, and Rob chuckled.

Miss Viola glared up at him, her green eyes narrowed. *"No, thank you."*

Rob returned the look. "For Lavinia."

"Humph." Miss Viola turned away. "Very well."

Suzette looked back and forth between Rob and Miss Viola. "Why don't y'all take the young'uns over to the ice cream parlor while I get these supplies ready."

Miss Viola's eyes flickered briefly before she put her bland face back on. "You go on. I'm sure the children will enjoy it."

Rob took her elbow and guided her toward the door. "Come on, young'uns. Let's get some ice cream."

Giggles erupted from the two, while the lady beside Rob stiffened even more than usual, going so far as to mutter, "Will you kindly stop manhandling me?"

He let go of her like she was a branding iron straight out of the fire. No lady, not even Maybelle, had ever had cause to accuse him of manhandling. And here he was trying to do something nice for this one.

Stubborn, impossible woman.

Chapter Six

Even after Robert let go, Viola could still feel the grip of his hand on her elbow. It had not been physically painful, but her pride had suffered more than a little as he pushed her toward the door. She would have enjoyed wandering about the store perusing the wares, but she would never let him see her do that lest he regard her as covetous. As for her requiring any personal purchases, she would die before admitting it to Mr. Robert Mattson.

And yet, for those few minutes she and Lavinia had looked at the various displays, happy memories of Mama and Viola's older sisters taking her shopping stirred sweet nostalgia within her heart. The ice cream parlor would only do more of the same.

Now they were seated around a small square table, the children providing a buffer on either side. She had to admit her admiration—no, that was too strong—her *approval* of Robert's quick thinking to forestall Robbie's jealousy of his sister regarding the pink shoes and the fancy boots. Viola had observed many incidents of jealousy amongst her siblings over the years. As the youngest, she'd done her best to stay out of it, for she'd seen it never led to anything but discontent all around. And of course they all claimed she was spoiled.

"What can I get you folks?" The young man, dressed in a white shirt and trousers and wearing a little red-striped cap that matched the tablecloths, stood beside the table, pen and paper in hand.

At Robert's nod, the children gave their orders. Then he asked for three scoops of chocolate ice cream with raspberry syrup. Rude man, not asking her first. She should refuse to order just to show him she would not be bullied. But she hadn't eaten ice cream since her closest brother's wedding reception, so she would just be spiting herself.

"One scoop of vanilla, please."

"No syrup?" The young man grinned, showing a dimple.

"No syrup. Thank you."

"Just plain vanilla," Robert muttered. "That's a surprise."

She wouldn't ask him what he meant. *Would not.* She didn't find vanilla plain at all, but rich and thick and creamy and sweet…and a reminder of how good her life used to be.

The young man provided a bib for Lavinia, which ended up saving her dress from a significant amount of strawberry syrup. Refusing a bib, Robbie fared a little better, but the blueberry syrup came close to blending with his dark blue shirt. Viola would have to soak it tonight to keep the stain from becoming permanent.

"Well, who do we have here?" A well-dressed gentleman of perhaps fifty years approached the table, a young lady of perhaps twenty at his side. "Howdy, Robert. How're you doing? Sorry to hear about your w—"

"Shh!" Viola couldn't stop herself. Whoever this man was, he had no right to blurt out his condolences in the children's hearing. At his shocked expression, she tilted her head toward Lavinia.

"Ah. Yes." His frosted mustache twitched. "And you must be…?"

"Lavinia's governess." She smiled warmly to make up for shushing him. She looked at Robert and raised her eyebrows. Would he fail even at a simple introduction?

He stood and shook hands with the man. "Blake. Miss Blake. May I present Miss Viola Brinson. As she said, she's Lavinia's governess. Miss Viola, this is Mr. George Blake, our town banker, and his daughter, Iris."

Viola gave the girl a guarded smile. She was the one who had sat behind her and the Mattson family in church and gossiped about them. "How do you do, Miss Blake? I am so pleased to meet you at last. It seems we have never had time to stay and chat after church."

The girl gave her a curt nod before touching Robert's arm. "Hello, Robert. I must tell you how sad we all are for your loss." Her honeyed tone and the expression on her pretty face conveyed more flirtation than sorrow.

"Yes, well." Her father nudged her away. "Let's order our ice cream before your mother arrives. She never lets me order what I want." He chuckled and patted his slightly rounded belly.

Viola could see the struggle in Robert's face, a vulnerable yet hard expression that shut out anyone who mentioned his wife's death. As for Miss Blake, her behavior had been nothing less than predatory. The girl could use some lessons in etiquette, but from the way she ignored Viola's benign greeting, it was unlikely she would take instruction from an outsider, especially her.

Lavinia yawned as they returned to the dry goods store, where their purchases had been loaded onto the back of the surrey.

"I'll sit with her so she can nap." Viola didn't wait for Robert to answer but climbed onto the back bench with her charge.

He nodded and climbed in beside Robbie. He hadn't spoken much since encountering the Blakes, had only paid the young man who served them and answered the children's usual comments and questions. Despite their differences, Viola's heart went out to him. She too had suffered loss. Loss of her parents. Loss of her hopes and dreams. Loss of her brothers and sisters, who did not want her anymore because she was an embarrassment to them for not having secured a husband, an undesirable situation not of her making. How good it would feel to pour out her grief to an understanding friend. Perhaps she should write a letter to Virginia, her closest sister, and mention her loneliness. No, it wouldn't do for her family to think she was failing to cope with life. She couldn't bear their pity.

Did Robert have someone to talk to about his sorrow? Or was he like her brothers, who never spoke of their feelings? In any event, she wouldn't be the one to draw Robert out. After all, if he'd treated Maybelle as a husband should, she wouldn't have left him.

Halfway home, Rob remembered the letter in his pocket. He'd been so distracted with shopping for the children that he failed to give it to Abner Pursers. Suzette's father must have been working in the back room, because he hadn't appeared at the post office window at the back of the store. That would have been a helpful reminder.

Then there was that disastrous meeting with the Blakes. He always enjoyed meeting up with George, but Iris was another matter. Just as he'd feared, he would now be considered a single man and, coming from a successful ranching family, become a target for every unhitched gal in New Mexico Territory...*and* their mothers. Now he understood what Will and Drew endured every time they went to town. If he ever did decide to show interest in a woman, it wouldn't be one who snubbed Miss Viola after she'd spoken so nicely to her. But he doubted Lavinia's governess needed him to stick up for her. She might like plain vanilla ice cream, but she had plenty of backbone.

Should he go back now to mail the letter or wait for his next trip to Riverton? With Lavinia asleep on Miss Viola's lap, he probably should get her home as soon as possible. Funny how his perspective on so many things had changed since his daughter had come into his life. While Miss Viola might be an unwanted but necessary presence, Lavinia brought him pure joy. He would have bought her the whole store today if she'd asked him.

He had to hand it to Maybelle. She'd done a good job raising their daughter, who never threw tantrums like some of the younger children he'd seen at church. And Miss Viola kept her in line too, usually with just a word or a look. She doled out just the right amount of praise and correction to the children, as Rob tried to do with his cowhands and horses.

There he went again, thinking kindly of that troublesome woman. No matter how many pairs of trousers she made for Robbie, no matter how much Lavinia benefited from her presence, Rob would be glad to see the last of her, and the sooner, the better.

He managed to keep that thought in mind right up until he sat down to a supper of the best ham, beans and cornbread he'd ever eaten.

Having cleaned and oiled the Singer, Viola began work on Robbie's dress trousers, which she'd measured and cut using an old pair of Andrew's work pants as a pattern. She would make wide seams and hems to give him room to grow, especially in length. If he grew as tall as the other Mattson men, he'd be due for a growth spurt soon. She'd observed her nieces and nephews over the years and had learned a great deal about growing children. And if she pushed herself, she could finish these trousers before Sunday, even with spring cleaning to begin tomorrow.

"Lavinia, come watch me fill the bobbin." Viola put the spool of thread on the spool pin.

Lavinia set aside the scraps of material she was playing with and joined Viola.

Viola wound it through the guides to the bobbin winder by the balance wheel. "The thread goes through here and around here, then through this tiny hole in the bobbin." She hoped her own love of sewing would rub off on the child. "Now I turn the wheel and slowly begin to push the treadle." She glanced down at her foot, pleased to see the years of disuse had not rusted the treadle or impeded its movement.

Lavinia's eyes widened with interest as the thread on the bobbin seemed to grow before their eyes. She giggled, as she often did these past few days. It was a lovely, musical sound that gladdened Viola's heart.

"After we make these trousers, we can make a coat for your dolly. Would you like that?"

"Yes, ma'am." Lavinia fetched the rag doll Viola had made for her over the winter. She'd also made a doll dress of the blue taffeta remnants from Lavinia's Sunday dress. "Can we make a coat for Puff?" She pointed at her kitten, who was curled up on the material scrap bag Viola had brought from home.

"My darling, Puff already has the perfectly fine coat the Lord provided. And look, she's sharing it with us." She pointed to the gold and white fur that clung to the black fabric.

Lavinia giggled again. "Miss Viola, you're so silly."

Viola tweaked her nose. "And you are, too. But we are having fun, are we not?"

"Who's having fun?" Robert chose that moment to break into Viola's happy mood.

Lavinia ran to her father and held up her doll. "Miss Viola is going to help me make a coat for Dolly."

"She is?" He took the doll and turned it this way and that. "Is this the only doll you have?" He cast an accusing look at Viola.

She stiffened and turned back to the Singer to finish threading it. Whatever her supposed offense, she refused to justify herself to Robert. But she did glance back to see if her little charge required any defense against him.

"Yessir." Lavinia gave him a doubtful look. She retrieved the doll and hugged it close.

He seemed to understand his error. "Well, she's a mighty fine doll." He patted her head. "I don't know that your grandpa has ever seen her. Why don't you run out to the woodshed where he's working and show him?"

Lavinia looked at Viola. "May I?"

Robert scowled and seemed about to speak.

"If your father says you may, that is all the permission you require."

As the child skipped from the room, Viola turned once again to her work, hoping Robert would leave as well. Instead, as she'd feared, he sat on a nearby chair and cleared his throat.

"You have something to say?" She placed a material scrap on the throat plate so she could test the machine's thread tension.

"Didn't Lavinia have any dolls or toys? I sure sent plenty of money and told Maybelle to get whatever she needed. Not that she ever answered." He muttered that last under his breath.

Viola stopped working and turned to face him. To her chagrin, her eyes burned at the memory of her introduction to her precious charge. Sad, frightened and dressed in well-worn clothes, Lavinia had seemed like a lost little waif. "I learned from Mr. Purcell that the minister and his wife had given all of Lavinia's toys and much of her clothing to charity. I barely managed to save the material for her traveling suit and Sunday dress and a few other items before they could dispose of them."

True shock registered on his face. Then indignation. He seemed about to speak but merely huffed out a cross breath, stood and strode from the room.

Viola sighed. At least he hadn't accused her *again* of misusing his money.

Rosa and Agnes arrived early the next morning, bringing extra rags, brooms and other cleaning items. Rosa also brought her daughter, a fourteen-year-old wearing a sullen expression on her pretty face.

"Elena is good help." Rosa thumped the girl's shoulder.

Glaring at Viola, Elena spat out a string of Spanish words. Rosa returned a lengthy scolding in their native tongue. Not an auspicious beginning to a difficult but necessary work project.

Viola forced a smile. "Elena, I am pleased to meet you. Perhaps you would like to attend my school of etiquette next Monday." She looked at Rosa. "Would you please translate?"

"I speak English." Elena tossed her thick black hair over her shoulder. "I also read and write. We Mexicans are not all ignorant peasants."

"No, of course not." Viola continued to smile. "I wish I spoke Spanish. Would you and Rosa help me learn? In fact, I would be so pleased to add Spanish to my curriculum so Lavinia and Robbie can learn to speak it as well."

Clearly surprised, Elena batted her eyes. "You want me to teach you?"

"Yes, of course."

"You see." Rosa thumped her daughter's shoulder again. "I tell you she is a good lady."

The girl gave Viola a little smile. "I will do it."

"Well, gals." Agnes walked toward the house. "This day ain't gettin' any younger. Let's get started."

Her officious tone jolted Viola, yet also gave her some comfort. Agnes sounded like Viola's eldest sister, Augusta. Bossy and a know-it-all, but an accomplished household manager. While Viola had participated in spring cleaning for many years, she'd never organized the operation.

Once in the kitchen, Viola served them the simple breakfast she'd promised, then sat down with them to plan the day. "Ladies, where should we begin?"

"Take down them velvet drapes in the parlor and library." Agnes spoke around a mouthful of bread and jam. "We'll hang 'em over the clothesline and beat the dust out of 'em. If they got dirt or stains in 'em, we'll have to haul out the tubs and wash 'em. Otherwise, if the wind don't kick up, we leave 'em overnight to air. Next, we carry out the rugs 'cause they gotta be beaten, too. Rosa here can start by oiling the woodwork." She stared at the doorjamb. "Looks like it ain't been done in many a year, if ever."

To Viola's delight, Agnes laid out a plan for the next two days, giving each of them assignments according to their abilities. The woman was clear-eyed, articulate in her Irish accent and entirely sober. So much for Robert's concern that she was unfit for the task.

"I have only one stipulation," Viola said. "Mr. Robert said we are not to touch his room, so..."

The two older ladies laughed.

"Just like a man. *Don't touch me stuff.*" Agnes said those last words in a gruff bass voice. "Don't worry, love. He'll not even know we've been in there."

"Unless he misses the dust." Rosa chuckled.

A slight chill went down Viola's back. She tried to reason it away. These women had fetched and returned laundry for this household for several years and therefore had been trusted. Yet if anything went missing, it would fall on her shoulders. On the other hand, if she showed a lack of trust in them, they would be terribly offended, perhaps even leave and not come back. Therefore, she must not show any form of suspicion.

"Very well, then. Shall we get started?"

"Man, I'm not going anywhere near that, no matter how hungry I am." Drew waved a hand toward the big house, where dust swirled in the wind like a tornado. Walking next to Rob, he halted. "Patrick should have something for us to eat in the bunkhouse. You coming?"

"Naw, I need to check on Robbie and Lavinia to be sure they aren't being neglected." And Pop, but Rob wouldn't stir up his brother's worry about their dad.

"You really think Miss Viola would neglect them?" A smirk on his lips, Drew snorted. "That lady loves those kids as much as you do, and you know it. Seems like they could use a mama like her." He ducked away from Rob's attempt to swat him.

Rob wagged a threatening finger at his brother. "I've warned you about that. Don't you ever hint to anybody that something's going on between me and that..." He balled his hand into a fist.

"That sweet, beautiful lady." Drew danced out of reach. "You go ahead and check on those young'uns. I'm going to the bunkhouse." He walked away laughing.

Rob huffed out his frustration. Good thing Will was away, or he'd have two brothers torturing him about Miss Viola. Beautiful, yes. Sweet—again, yes. But only to the children and Pop and…just not to Rob. And that was the way he liked it. Encouraged it, in fact, to keep her from setting her sights on him.

He rubbed his chest where a slight burn had begun shortly after her revelation about that minister and his wife giving away Lavinia's toys. Right away, he'd re-written his letter to Pop's friend in Charleston. Then he'd ridden into town last evening to post it. He couldn't imagine a man of God being so cruel as to give away a child's toys and other belongings right after her mother died. If it was true, the man should be defrocked or something. And where did that lawyer, Purcell, fit into it all?

He couldn't solve the problem now, so he carefully made his way around the clotheslines, where Agnes was beating the carpets. Whew! That was a lot of dust. No wonder Lavinia sneezed so often. As much as he hated to admit it, Miss Viola's plan to clean the house was a good one.

He found the lady, his children and Pop seated at the table. Like the other females, Lavinia wore a scarf on her head, probably to keep her hair from getting dirty. She looked adorable…and far too much like Maybelle. If his stomach wasn't growling due to the aroma of the stew simmering on the stove, he'd scramble back to the bunkhouse and eat whatever pottage Patrick Ahern had prepared for himself and the few other cowhands.

"Have a seat, son." Pop waved a hand toward an empty chair. "Miss Viola is up to her usual fine standards of cooking." He took a bite. "Mmm-mm."

"To give due credit, Agnes prepared the biscuits." Miss Viola stood. "I'll bring you a bowl of the stew."

"I can serve myself." He didn't mean to sound so brusque, especially with the children sitting there, so he softened his tone and added, "Thank you anyway."

As he joined the others at the table, the children began to chatter about their morning.

"Miss Viola let me dust." Lavinia's eyes sparkled as if she'd said she got to ride a pony. Maybe it was time for him to buy one for her.

"I'm sure you did just fine."

"I got to help Mrs. Ahern carry out the carpets." Robbie lifted his arms as if to prove his strength. "It was easy."

Rob reached over and gripped one bicep. "My, just feel those muscles." The boy sure was growing fast, but more like a tree than a weed.

Mingled with the cooking aromas, the pungent scent of lemon oil invaded his senses. He studied the pine doorjamb. "Looks like somebody's shined up the woodwork."

"Yep. The ladies have been working hard." Pop's eyes took on a wistful look. "I spent a lot of money building this house just like your mama wanted. Two stories. Oak and mahogany in the parlor and bedrooms. Fancy velvet drapes in the colors she wanted. A Persian carpet in the parlor." His voice rose as he listed all he'd done for Mother. "Then she didn't even take care of them."

And Maybelle hadn't done much to help her either, but Rob wouldn't speak ill of the dead, especially in front of his children.

"It is a beautiful house, Mr. Mattson." Miss Viola spoke in that chirpy voice of hers, like she always did when trying to smooth things over. "It is a joy to see all that fine woodwork shine. Rosa and Elena have done a wonderful job. Of course, it will take more than one application, but we will do that tomorrow so the first one can soak in."

Her cheerfulness seemed to placate Pop. "That's right. You gotta treat wood with respect. Those cradles I'm making for my newest grandchildren are gonna shine."

"Lavinia, Robbie, won't it be wonderful to have two new cousins?" Again, Miss Viola kept the conversation light.

Rob had to admire her for it. She brought a little happiness to Pop, who hadn't deserved to be abandoned. A few times, Rob and his brothers had discussed going back East to fetch Mother, to bring her back here and show her how much easier life would be for her now. But with each having so many responsibilities on the ranch, they couldn't spare one of them to make the lengthy trip. Not that any of them would be able to convince Mother to come, what with her living a life of luxury in Charleston society.

Before his thoughts could turn bitter, he finished his dinner and excused himself. Exiting through the back door, he saw Agnes and Patrick talking on the far side of the clothesline, partially obscured by the airing drapes. Agnes handed her son a square item wrapped in a tea towel, and he took it carefully, as though it was something valuable. What were those two up to? Patrick glanced his way, gave him a quick nod, then turned and strode away toward the bunkhouse.

Seeing Rob, Agnes ducked away and joined Rosa, who stood over a large tub washing brown muslin curtains, the ones from his bedroom. So they'd gone into his room after all. So much for Miss Viola following his orders. She was in charge of this cleaning project. Hadn't she told the women what he'd said? And what would he find missing? He owned only a few valuables, and most of those were kept in the safe in Pop's study. The few mementos he'd saved for Robbie were tucked away in the bottom of his wardrobe, which he'd once shared with Maybelle. Nothing of hers, including her jewelry, remained anywhere on this property.

With fencing to mend and hay to haul, he couldn't worry about it now. But he would certainly call Miss Viola to task this evening after the women left.

Yet, as she sat in the parlor after supper, hemming his son's Sunday trousers after a long day of cleaning, he couldn't bring himself to scold or question her.

Eyes fixed on sewing the dark fabric in the dim light of the kerosene lantern beside her, Viola felt Robert's stare from across the room. But she wouldn't acknowledge it. If he had any questions about today's work, she would gladly answer him, even about Agnes's insistence on washing the curtains and quilt from his room.

Having once worked as a housemaid in a great house

in England, the Irishwoman truly was a gift from the Lord, as were Rosa and Elena. But Agnes's gift for organizing made the job run as smoothly as the well-oiled Singer. A little push of her foot on the treadle, a little turn by hand on the balance wheel, and everything was set in motion. She smiled at her silly little saying. Maybe she should write it down for Robbie's and Lavinia's language lessons.

"Something funny?"

Startled, she looked up to see Robert's dark eyebrows bent into an all-too-familiar frown, which made him resemble an angry bear. If only he would smile, he would be quite handsome. But then, Viola supposed men like Mr. Robert Mattson didn't care about such things.

"I asked you if something was funny." Now his bear-like growl completed the picture…and sent a nervous twinge through Viola. What had set him off?

"What's the matter with you, Robert?" Mr. Mattson lowered his *Riverton Journal* and stared at Robert, matching his son's glower. "Isn't it remarkable that this lady can smile at the end of such a hard day?"

For several moments, the only sound in the room was the ticking of the grandfather clock in the corner. Viola felt her sunny spirit flag and her eyes burn. Yes, it had been a hard day, and she was tired. But it was a good, satisfying kind of tired. Agnes said they would finish by tomorrow evening or Saturday morning at the latest. What part of their work had Robert found lacking?

"I do believe these trousers will be ready for Sunday." Viola's face warmed. What a silly thing to say, almost a boast.

"Well, I'd say that's something to smile about,

wouldn't you, Rob?" Mr. Mattson raised his newspaper then lowered it again. "I said, wouldn't you, Rob?"

Oddly, Viola felt a moment of sympathy for Robert. She couldn't imagine how an almost thirty-year-old man could endure such correction from his father. Yet he did. Papa had never corrected her brothers that way. Or perhaps she'd just never noticed.

Robert cleared his throat. "I'm much obliged to you for taking on such a task, Miss Viola. I'm sure Robbie will look mighty fine on Sunday."

His praise sent a foolish tickle through her. "Yes, I think so. I would also like to make him a dress shirt." She stopped herself before launching into further chatter about the children's needs.

At last, Robert's face softened. "We'll go to town next week and get what you need to do that."

"Thank you." She took the final stitch on the hem and snipped the thread, then held up the trousers to inspect the final product.

"No, ma'am. Thank *you*." Robert stood and took his leave of Mr. Mattson. As he passed Viola's chair, he nodded to her. If she was not mistaken, a hint of a smile lifted one corner of his lips.

She was most definitely not mistaken about the way that tiny smile made her heart hiccough.

Chapter Seven

~

"Miss Viola, where did you ever learn to sew such fine clothes?" Drew grinned at her as they came to Sunday morning breakfast. "Robbie's fine new trousers will put the rest of us to shame. We'll all have to get new duds."

Rob watched her reaction to this praise, sure she would beam with pride. Instead, her cheeks turned a bit pink. He sure did wish she weren't so pretty, especially when she smiled or blushed.

"I always enjoyed sewing for my nieces and nephews." She sat down and began to serve the breakfast she'd been up preparing for hours. "Practice makes perfect. Or if not perfect, at least it makes for improvement." She gave Drew her sweet smile that somehow made Rob wish it were aimed at him. *No*, he would not think that way.

"Now don't you be getting any ideas, son." Pop skewered Drew with a look. "Miss Viola has enough to do around here without sewing for all of us. Miss Viola, would you please pass those tasty-looking pancakes?"

As she handed him the platter, a hint of worry skittered across her smooth brow. "Of course I would be pleased to do any mending you might require. I can do it in the evenings…"

"Nope." The word was out before Rob could stop himself. "We've been mending our own clothes all our lives. As Pop says, you have enough to do around here."

She blinked those pretty green eyes in surprise. "Very well. If you say so." She offered Drew an apologetic smile, though what she needed to apologize for, Rob couldn't guess.

If he wasn't mistaken, his brother's silly grin in response held a mite too much admiration…the love-struck kind. Rob should put a stop to that. Drew was two years younger than Miss Viola. Surely she wouldn't fall for him. Or try to snare him. Would she? But maybe Drew's teasing about Rob liking her was a test to see if he would compete for her hand. That wasn't going to happen.

Trying to think of something to change the conversation, he took a deep breath and caught the now-familiar scent of lemon oil. The house sure did feel nice and fresh after its thorough top to bottom cleaning. But he'd already complimented the ladies yesterday as he paid Rosa, Agnes and Elena for their work. No need to thank Miss Viola again.

"Dad." Robbie saved him from his dilemma. "You don't think the boys will tease me about my new trousers, do you?"

"If they do, you laugh it off." Rob leaned toward him. "Just don't get into a fight in your new clothes, you hear me?"

Miss Viola's eyes widened briefly before she reclaimed her usual placid expression. If she knew anything about her nephews, as she claimed, surely she
knew little boys liked to fight.

When they arrived at church, the boys' behavior was
the least of Rob's worries. As usual, other than Suzette
Pursers and Rob's in-laws, the ladies offered no friendship to Miss Viola. Worse still, the other families had
brought food for dinner on the grounds, but no one had
informed them. Julia and Emma apologized, but Rob
couldn't fault them, as they were expecting and had a
lot on their minds. They probably figured the news had
gotten around to everybody.

Before the sermon began, an older woman sitting
behind the Mattsons said none too quietly that Miss
Brinson's school of etiquette was an insult to the ladies
of the town, as if they didn't know how to teach manners to their own daughters. Rob had a hard time not
turning around and telling her gossip and unfriendli-
ness were the worst sort of bad manners. But this was
church, and he wouldn't cause a disturbance. He always
liked to listen to Pastor Daniel's sermons, but today
he couldn't concentrate on a single word the man was
saying. Pop seemed just as riled, if his grim expression
was any indication.

After the final hymn, while the rest of the church
fixed up plank tables outside and set out food, the
Mattsons and Miss Viola prepared to go home. Suzette skipped over to the surrey, apology written all
over her face.

"Oh, Miss Brinson, I'm so sorry no one told you. Mr.

Mattson, won't you stay?" She took Pop's hand. "We have plenty to share."

"What do you think?" Pop looked over his shoulder at Miss Viola.

Her cheeks pinched and flushed, she shook her head. "Thank you, Suzette, but I have a roast in the oven. It will be dry and ruined if we leave it there."

"Will we still have class tomorrow?" Suzette must have heard the gossiping woman's rude remarks.

Miss Viola smiled. "Yes, of course. I look forward to seeing you at nine o'clock sharp."

No one, not even the children, said a word on the way home, and very few were spoken during dinner.

Foregoing his usual Sunday rest, after dinner Rob went out to the barn to be alone and to ponder why the church folks had deliberately left his branch of the family out of today's dinner on the grounds. He could tell Pop was angry. Hurt, in fact. Why, just last Christmas the whole community, including all the Mexican families, had come together to rebuild the Sharps' barn so they could celebrate *Las Posadas* together there on Christmas Eve. What was different now?

Miss Viola, that was what, with her fine clothes and snooty manners and...and...

He wasn't being fair. The banker's wife and daughter were just as snooty, yet every woman in town, in fact the whole community, wanted to keep company with them. Rob could only guess that their money drew more friends, though probably not true friends. And the worst part of the whole situation? He couldn't figure out how to fix it, just like he hadn't been able to fix his marriage.

Maybe he should just send Miss Viola away. But Lavinia depended on her, and her womanly influence on Robbie was already improving his manners. In truth, Rob found it surprising she didn't just leave after the way she'd been treated. For all she'd done for his family, Rob should try to make her life easier. Despite his lingering concerns over the money he'd sent to Maybelle and Miss Viola's possible part in its disappearance, he'd give it a try and see what happened.

Viola rarely took a Sunday nap, but today she felt the need for a long rest. Tired though she'd been the previous night, she'd lain awake on the trundle bed beside Lavinia's higher bed, trying to create some defense against her foolish reactions to Robert's smallest kindness toward her. Had she become like one of her unmarried aunts, a silly old maid who swooned at any small attention from a gentleman?

And today had brought more unpleasantness with the ladies at church. Once Lavinia was asleep, she lay down and surrendered to her unhappy thoughts.

It was her fault. Somehow she'd alienated the entire church against the Mattson family. Maybe she should leave. But where would she go? Her brothers' obvious relief when she'd said goodbye in Norfolk last fall made it clear they had no use for her, no matter how many clothes she made for their children or meals she cooked for their families. Her sisters didn't care to have another woman in their households. Viola suspected one or two of their husbands had a wandering eye, if some of their flirtations toward her were any indication.

Was there a boarding school back in Charleston where she could teach? A family up north that required a governess? How could she find such employment? Too many questions with no answers. And the most painful one of all—how could she leave her beloved Lavinia and Robbie, both of whom looked to her as they would a mother? Even her sweetest nieces and nephews had not shown her such devotion.

Unable to sleep, she washed her face and went downstairs to be sure the leftovers would suffice for supper. She'd been reared to believe one should perform only necessary tasks on Sundays, so she left the Singer covered rather than start a new sewing project. Perhaps a walk would clear her thinking and improve her mood.

The bright April sun bore down on her uncovered head. Should she have worn a bonnet? Brought her parasol? Again, only questions, no answers. Perhaps she should go back inside in case Lavinia awoke and came looking for her. Instead, she wandered over to the little schoolhouse.

"Nice day."

Viola started at Robert's sudden appearance around the corner of the building. "I didn't see you." She turned to leave.

"You don't have to go." He took off his hat and wiped his forehead with a blue and white handkerchief. "I was just checking the soundness of the walls. This past winter was pretty harsh. Wouldn't want them to cave in on your class." He offered a little grin.

"Huh." Not a ladylike sound at all, but certainly one that expressed her feelings. "My class? Of course." Could one call it a class if only one student came?

"Now, Miss Viola." He drawled out her name as though preparing to dole out some cowboy wisdom to her, as she'd heard his father do with the children. "Don't let those old biddies get you down." Was that sympathy in his voice? In his eyes?

Viola stiffened, refusing to be pitied. "I am not *down*, Robert."

His face hardened. "No. Of course not." He started to walk away but turned back. "All right, let's try something different. With all your experience with little girls, do you think Lavinia is old enough to have her own pony?"

That certainly was a different subject. "Why...why, yes. I had my first pony at four years old. You would of course be certain it has a gentle temperament. Some ponies are quite disagreeable."

He rolled his eyes. "Yes, I know that, and of course I'd be sure. I do know a little bit about horses." He looked her up and down, not rudely, but as though he were assessing her abilities. "So, you ride?"

"Yes. And I would be able and happy to teach her. That is, unless you prefer to. I have pleasant memories of my father teaching me to ride." To her horror, she choked on those last words.

He didn't seem to notice. "Fine. Let's keep it a secret." Once again he turned to leave, then changed his mind. "You want to go for a ride? I have some fencing I need to check. You haven't seen much of the ranch, have you? I mean, being cooped up in the house every day and all."

"I should probably be there for Lavinia when she wakes up." *No. No. I would love to go riding.*

"Suit yourself."

As he walked away, she thought her heart would burst. Oh, to ride once again!

"Wait." The word popped out of her mouth without her permission. "I'll join you for a ride."

Rob knew he must test Miss Viola's riding ability before entrusting his daughter to her. With the wrong teacher, a child could learn some bad habits when it came to handling horses. By the time he'd dusted off Maybelle's sidesaddle and put it on Robbie's little bay gelding, she'd fetched her bonnet and put Pop in charge of entertaining Lavinia after her nap. Rob led the gelding and his own horse, Diamond, and met her by the fence outside the kitchen garden.

"This is Corky." Rob held out a hand to help her step up on the mounting block he'd set up long ago for Robbie.

Instead of taking his hand, she moved to Corky's head and produced a carrot from her pocket. "How do you do, Corky? You're a fine fellow, and I know I'll enjoy riding you." Petting the horse's head with her gloved hand, she spoke to him as though he were human, not in a silly singsong way as some women did with horses. Corky accepted the carrot and nudged her as if to say thank you. Miss Viola laughed. "Oh, yes. We shall be friends."

Somehow managing her billowy skirt, she accepted Rob's help getting settled in the saddle, and they were soon on their way.

"I thought we could ride down to the river." This being spring, he needed to check how fast the Rio Grande was rising and try to determine if they'd have a big flood this year. But he sure wouldn't say that to Miss Viola. Then another thought presented itself. If he did mention possible flooding, that might scare her off. If she made the decision to leave, it would be an easy way to get life back to normal here on the ranch.

Somehow that thought failed to please him. It would be Mother and Maybelle all over again, and Robbie would be the one to suffer the most. She'd only been here a few weeks, and already his son was attached to her. As was Lavinia. And Pop. And Drew. And Will, even though he wasn't here at the moment. And even Rob had to admit he'd miss her cooking.

"It is so beautiful."

Deep in thought, Rob had almost forgotten she rode beside him. "That it is." He pointed to the distant mountains. "Those are the Sangre de Cristos. That's where Will and the cowhands are grazing the herd."

"Beautiful," she repeated, a wistful look lighting her face. "But the mountains appear to be covered with snow. How can they graze?"

"We always send somebody up to check the meadows before we drive the herd up there. Sometimes we have to wait until June or later. This year, the lower meadows had thawed and were greening up just fine, so it was time."

"Ah. I see." She nodded, understanding filling her green eyes. Then she smiled at him.

Rob felt a dangerous thump somewhere in his chest. Time to go on the offensive. "This time of year, all that melting snow fills the river to overflowing. We've had a couple of bad floods in recent years." Like the year Maybelle left. Stunned by the thought, he pulled Diamond to a stop. Why had he never realized that had been her breaking point, when the flood came near to washing away everything they'd built? Easy answer. Because he'd been too busy helping Pop and his brothers save the ranch animals, the outbuildings and the lower barn full of hay.

"I see." She skillfully reined Corky to a stop beside Rob, not in the least bothered by his revelation of possible flooding. "It certainly makes good sense that you built your house on that hill."

"Yep." Coming from a city gal, that was a sharp insight. Maybelle had thought they'd built the house on the hill because it looked more imposing for their neighbors to see, an important factor to her.

Rob nudged Diamond forward, and Miss Viola easily followed. So far, her horsemanship was commendable. "You don't seem troubled by the threat of a possible flood."

She shrugged in her ladylike way. "I grew up in Virginia's Tidewater region. I am accustomed to the whims of various waterways, including the ocean. No need to be troubled by nature if people do all they can to prepare, then trust in the Lord for the outcome."

He reined Diamond to a stop again. He knew this lady had faith, but it was deeper than he'd realized. At least her words suggested it. Would it work out in the middle of a true crisis? As if nature had heard his silent challenge, the unmistakable rattle of a diamondback sounded not ten feet in front of Corky. The gelding fidgeted, then reared up on his hind legs, a scream starting to build in his throat.

"Shh. It is all right." Her voice soft and low, Miss

Viola kept her seat and touched his neck. "Shh. Step back, Corky." She tugged on the reins, and he minded her verbal and silent commands.

Rob pulled his Colt .45 from his holster and aimed at the snake.

"You don't have to kill it." Miss Viola's usually placid expression had turned to fiery determination, yet her posture appeared relaxed. So as not to frighten her mount? "That is, unless your western rattlesnakes are more aggressive than our eastern ones and this one intends to chase us. I have read that cobras in India do chase people. But snakes keep down the rodent population."

Rob had never seen a cowhand who'd faced a rattler with such composure. Land sakes, this woman was something else. He returned his pistol to his holster. "Miss Viola, if you can teach Lavinia to face danger like that, you have my blessing to teach her to ride."

Viola thought she might fall off of Corky right on the spot. How she hid her trembling from both Robert and her horse, she had no idea. And why had she babbled on about cobras in India? Not trusting herself to speak again, she shrugged. She really must stop shrugging. It was not in the least a ladylike gesture and...oh, what silly thoughts! Manners held little importance when she or Corky might have been bitten, might have died. *Thank You, Lord, for Your mercy.*

Once they had ridden many yards away from the snake and Robert had checked the fencing, as he'd intended, she could finally speak without a wavering voice. "I suppose we should get back to the house. I am certain Lavinia must be awake by now."

Robert shook his head and clicked his tongue. "Miss Viola, I'm still pondering how you just shook off that encounter with a deadly snake. Weren't you even the slightest bit scared?"

Yes! Terrified. "Why, Robert, I didn't notice you acting frightened. Were you?"

He snorted out a laugh. "Yes, ma'am. I was scared spitless...for Robbie's horse. And you, of course."

"Humph. Well, then, to set your mind at ease, shall we implement a plan to ensure my safety and that of my charges, both children and animals?"

"You got any ideas?"

"Why, yes." She gave him her sweetest smile.

For some odd reason, he returned a defensive frown. "And that is?"

"You can provide me with a gun." She gestured toward his pistol. "And you can teach me how to shoot."

"Ha!" Chuckling, he scratched behind his ear. "That's probably a good idea. We might find just the right gun in Pop's collection."

His positive response to her request surprised her... and gladdened her heart. Not because she was eager to fire a gun but because of his improved attitude toward her.

That pleasant attitude continued at supper as Robert regaled his family with an outlandish exaggeration of their encounter with the snake. In his telling of it, the beast was within inches of Corky's hooves, and it was eight feet long—though how one measured a coiled snake, she couldn't guess. Further, its rattles sounded louder than firecrackers. According to him, she'd told the snake to "shoo, silly creature"—he said that last in a high, girlish tone—and had calmed her bucking horse with a whisper. Oh, if only that were true. Poor Corky had continued to shudder most of the way back to the barn.

Mr. Mattson and Andrew appeared both duly impressed and deeply concerned. The children listened, wide-eyed. When he finished, they all turned to her with questions and looks of admiration.

Quieting the others, Mr. Mattson gazed at her fondly, as her father used to do. She tucked away the warm feelings his gentle tone gave her for later contemplation. "What have you got to say for yourself, Miss Viola?"

Now, at last composed after her ordeal, she felt heat rising to her cheeks at all this attention. "God is merciful, is He not?" At their agreement, she added, "And, Mr. Robert Mattson, I had no idea you were such a fine storyteller. And such fantastical embellishments! You should write one of those dime novels so popular with people back East."

The responding explosion of laughter from this family, even Robert, demonstrated an acceptance she had not felt since she was sixteen and before her parents had died, which more than made up for the way the wider community had rejected her a mere four years later. If only she could bottle this happy, healing feeling and sip it like a doctor's tonic when disappointments came her way.

Chapter Eight

On Monday morning, Rosa and Agnes arrived to tend the laundry. Having established a comfortable rapport with them during spring cleaning, Viola welcomed them as old friends before heading to the schoolroom with Lavinia. There Elena waited for them by the door.

"Good morning, Elena. You may go in."

"*Buenos días*, Señorita Brinson." Her dark eyes sparked with a challenge and perhaps a little doubt.

"*Buenos días.*" Taking her place at the front of the room, Viola pasted on her teacher smile, accepting the challenge but maintaining her authority. "Lavinia, do you remember I said Elena will be teaching us how to speak Spanish? Do you know what she said?"

"Yes, ma'am." Lavinia nodded. "*Buenos días*, Elena."

"*Muy bien, gracias, pequeña.*" Elena continued talking to Lavinia in her native language as though the child understood.

"Very good, Elena. You may be seated." Viola reminded herself she'd asked for this, but she must maintain some semblance of order. "We will begin—"

Suzette burst through the door, her face flushed. "Guess who's here."

Viola looked out the window to see Señor Martinez helping a pretty Mexican girl step down from a handsome black and red phaeton. What could this outlaw want? "Stay here, girls."

Heart hammering against her ribs, she went out to greet them. "Good morning, Señor Martinez. Or should I say *buenos días*?"

"Ah, you see, *querida*? She speaks our language." Taking the girl's hand, he led her to the porch, pausing at the steps to remove his wide-brimmed hat and give Viola a little bow. Spotless and elegant, his tan leather suit fit his well-built frame perfectly. "Señorita Brinson, we have not been introduced, so I hope you will forgive my *impertinencia*. It is my understanding that you are beginning a school for young ladies, *sí*?"

A bit dazzled by his charming manners and exceptional good looks, Viola swallowed hard. "*Sí*. I mean, yes."

A smile lit his handsome face. *"Bien."* He looked beyond her at Elena. "Ah, I see my next question is unnecessary. You are accepting all girls, yes?"

"Yes, any young lady who wishes to learn etiquette." Viola turned to the girl, who stared at the ground. "How do you do, Miss...?"

"This is my sister, Isabella Martinez. Bella, you must say good morning to Miss Brinson."

She gave Viola a quick glance, then looked down again. "Good morning, Señorita..."

Her brother nudged her. *"Miss* Brinson."

Her light brown complexion turned a little pink. "Miss Brinson."

"I am so pleased to meet you, Isabella. Please come in." Viola waved a hand toward the door.

Looking up at last, Isabella saw Elena, and her eyes brightened. The two girls began to chatter in Spanish.

"Bella." Señor Martinez's gentle, chiding tone was more a caution than a scolding.

She blushed again. "*Sí*, yes, Alejandro."

"*Bien.*" The gentleman stepped up on the porch and took Viola's hand, setting a kiss on her fingertips. "My sister has no mother to guide her, and her older sister has married and gone away to Santa Fe. If you can impart some—*¿qué es?*—etiquette to her, I shall be grateful."

"What's going on here?" Robert's sudden appearance startled Viola more than Señor Martinez's had. Somehow she managed not to jump. Although it was only nine o'clock, he was already covered in dust and sweat. As usual, he wore his gun.

"*Buenos días*, Señor Mattson." His tone restrained, the Mexican gentleman stepped from the porch and faced Robert, his posture guarded, his hands held slightly away from his sides, where a pair of guns sat just below his waist. "I—"

"Oh, look, Robert. I have another student. Isabella wants to join Suzette and Elena." Viola knew her voice sounded high and giddy, but she must intervene before serious trouble began and all their lives turned upside down. "It appears that I shall have a *class*, after all." She gave him a knowing smile, hoping he would remember their conversation the day before when her disappointment had been so obvious.

Robert eyed the other man, then Isabella, then stood there as if considering the situation. Finally, he posted his fists at his waist. "Huh. Well, Martinez, we'd better let these ladies get down to business." He tilted his head toward the phaeton.

Not to be outdone, the other gentleman stepped back on the porch and took Viola's hand for another mannerly kiss. "Miss Brinson, I am entrusting a great treasure to your care. I know you will not disappoint me."

Beyond him, she could see Robert rolling his eyes. Humph! He'd never kissed her hand. In fact, he had barely shown her any manners at all.

"I am honored, señor." She withdrew her hand.

His dark eyes flashed with admiration. "I shall return in two hours? Three?"

"Yes, three."

Robert didn't move until Señor Martinez had boarded the phaeton and driven away. Once the other man passed beyond the front gate, he gave Viola a long look, then walked away without a word.

Rob didn't like having the outlaw show up, but he couldn't object to the man's sister joining Miss Viola's class. At least Martinez treated her with respect. He wouldn't have stood for it if he hadn't. But satisfied Martinez wouldn't return until the ladies finished their class, he went back to work beside Drew and their other hands. He'd even put Robbie to work as they moved wagonloads of dirt into place between the river and the lower outbuildings. They'd started the levee after the flood four years ago and managed to add a little each spring and fall, as time permitted. The project took a long while because the soil needed to settle and pack down into solid earth that wouldn't wash away when the waters rose.

"I think we'll need more help to get this thing finished, Rob." Drew wiped sweat from his brow. "How about I go into town and hire some men?"

"We can't really afford..." Or could they? The money he was no longer sending back East would be well spent if they could get this levee built sooner. "Now that I think about it, maybe we can. Yeah, you head into town and hire five or six men, if you can find them."

"Yes, boss." His brother grinned. "Say, what happened over at Miss Viola's schoolhouse?"

"Martinez showed up with his sister and asked if she could be in the class."

"Well, I'll be switched." Drew's eyes lit up. "That's a good sign. Maybe the fella did change his ways."

Rob shook his head. "I doubt it. He probably has some plan up his sleeve."

"Whatever you say." Drew dusted off his shirt. "I'll saddle up and go to town. Anything else you need?"

"Nope. Just more strong backs to move this project along."

Drew walked a few yards away, then turned back. "You know, Rob, people can change, especially when God gets ahold of 'em. I still think we should give Martinez a chance to prove himself."

"Go to town, Drew." Rob picked up his shovel and started moving dirt into place.

His middle brother was all about reconciliation. Had even tried to persuade Maybelle not to leave. Last Christmas, he'd helped organize *Las Posadas*, the traditional Mexican procession to commemorate the travels of the Holy Family, an event that had united the Americano and Mexican communities in Riverton as nothing else had done. Maybe Drew should be a diplomat.

On Tuesday, Viola sat at the Singer stitching Robbie's new Sunday shirt. The white muslin was easy to work with, so the shirt would be finished in a day or two, if nothing interrupted her.

At the low table beside her, Lavinia practiced her letters on a slate. Although not quite five years old, she was beginning to read and write. Too bad Robbie couldn't spend his days working on his letters and calculations. But Robert said he needed his son's help building the levee. Not one of Viola's nephews could work a long, hard day like this nine-year-old. Still, the child needed his education, too.

On Monday, when she'd realized Robert wouldn't be able to take her to town, she'd asked Suzette to send out the material for Robbie's shirt. The young lady had made the perfect choice. In any event, Viola didn't wish to go to town so soon after Sunday's embarrassing situation. What would she say to any of the church ladies, should she meet them by chance and they deigned to speak to her?

"Miss Viola?" Andrew stood in the parlor doorway, dusty and sweaty from his work. "I won't come in, but Rob sent me to ask if you could make sandwiches to send out to the men."

"Yes, of course." She finished the seam, then set the shirt aside. "Come, Lavinia. We must feed those men. Andrew, will you wait?"

"Yes, ma'am." He joined them in the kitchen and sat

at the table making faces at Lavinia, who giggled in her adorable way. Every time she giggled, Andrew laughed.

"You enjoy the children, do you not?" Viola gave him a sisterly smile. Slicing yesterday's bread, she laid it out and began to spread butter on it.

"Yes, ma'am." He grunted. "We all do. Especially Rob. I haven't seen him so happy since…for a long time."

"Well, I must say I was shocked Sunday evening when he made up that ridiculous story about the snake. Yes, it was a frightening situation, but his exaggerations…" She chuckled at the memory. "I wouldn't have thought him such a storyteller, and I have rarely heard him laugh."

"Oh, he used to laugh all the time. And tease? Mercy, how he teased us younger brothers." He shook his head. "Then Maybelle…" He looked at Lavinia, who stared at him wide-eyed. "Sweetheart, your mama was a beautiful lady." He winked at her.

"Yessir, she is." Lavinia's expression relaxed. "I love her."

In spite of the child's speaking of Maybelle in the present tense, Viola's heart warmed. At four years old, could the girl truly remember her mother seven months after her death? Surely that was a good thing. Those memories would fade soon enough as she grew older.

Sighing to herself, Viola placed several thin layers of leftover roast beef slices on the bread. She packed the sandwiches in a cloth-lined box along with plates, forks and some of the potato salad she'd made earlier. "If this isn't enough, I'll make more for tomorrow." Robert certainly should have warned her about needing meals sent out to his work site so she could plan for it.

"Thank you, ma'am." Andrew gathered the food and left.

As she returned to her sewing, Viola considered Andrew's revelation about Robert. So he used to laugh and tease. Here she'd assumed his disagreeable disposition had caused Maybelle to leave him. Instead, perhaps Maybelle's leaving him had caused his disagreeable disposition. Of course, any estrangement must have two sides, and she doubted she would ever understand what had broken Robert's marriage. It was her business only as far as it affected the children he had placed in her charge.

And at least he had the children. His love for them was more than apparent in every word and action. Further, he never spoke a word against their mother, at least not in their hearing. She could only admire him for that.

A thread of concern wove through her thoughts. Lavinia had spoken of her mother as if she were still living. Would that fade along with the memories? Should Viola address the issue? If only she had an older, more experienced woman to ask. But none had offered friendship, so she must do as she always did—read her Bible, seek God's wisdom and pray.

And perhaps she should give Robert the benefit of her doubts. Perhaps offer friendship and a listening ear. She would begin this very evening after the children were tucked into bed and the adults had gathered in the parlor to while away the hours until their own bedtimes.

But that evening, as they were thus gathering, Robert stormed into the room, anger clouding his face.

"Just as I suspected." He leveled an accusing look at Viola. "Something was stolen from my room, and I know exactly who stole it."

* * *

Miss Viola shrank back in her chair... *Mother's* chair...with such shock and horror that Rob could see she was either innocent or a talented actress. Or perhaps, just as he'd feared, Agnes had stolen the silver picture frame during spring cleaning and had given it to Patrick. He'd seen the exchange himself out by the clothesline. Agnes must have discovered the false floor of his wardrobe and found the one thing of monetary value he'd hidden there. Unhappily for him, it also held great sentimental value. And now it was gone.

"Now, hold on, son." Pop moved up to the edge of his chair. "Before you go accusing anybody of anything, explain yourself."

"Yeah, big brother. Just what are you saying?" Drew wore an uncharacteristic scowl.

Rob ran a hand through his hair, dislodging a shower of dust, and huffed out a long breath. He stared at Miss Viola. Her cheeks had turned bright pink, and her green eyes flashed with anger. To hold on to any bit of his pride, all he could do was bluster his way through this.

"I don't mean you." Though that wasn't exactly true, he kept his eyes on Miss Viola. "One of those women you had out here to do that spring cleaning you insisted on went into my room..." Heat crept up his neck. The house *had* needed cleaning. With years of dust and dirt removed, Lavinia *had* stopped sneezing so much. The whole place just felt better being clean.

Staring down at the white shirt she was making for *his* son, she didn't answer him. He could tell that the delicate hand stitching of the buttonholes took a lot of skill and patience, both of which she excelled at.

"Miss Viola," Pop said. "Would you be so kind as to read to us from the Holy Bible." He waved a hand toward the large family Bible on the bookshelf. "I believe we need a little touch from the Almighty." He looked up at Rob. "Sit down, boy."

Knowing he deserved the put-down, Rob did as he was told. But he was shocked that Pop wanted the Bible read. They hadn't had family Bible time since Mother left. The only time it had been opened since then was when he'd recorded Lavinia's birth. He'd heard his two youngest brothers say the Sharps had Bible reading every evening. Maybe Pop had heard it too and decided it was a good idea.

"I would be pleased to read to you." Miss Viola set aside her sewing, covered the Singer and fetched the large Bible. The heavy book more than covered her lap, and its thick covers rested on the chair arms. From the reverent way she turned the pages, Rob could see she knew her way around the scriptures.

"Mr. Mattson, do you have some particular verses you would like for me to read?"

Pop scratched his chin. "Nope. You choose."

"Very well. I'll open to a random spot." She closed her eyes, turned the large pages, pointed, then opened her eyes. "Here we are. Ephesians, chapter four. 'I, therefore, the prisoner of the Lord, beseech you that ye walk worthy of the vocation wherewith ye are called.'"

She read in that warm, soothing voice she used with the children. Exhausted from the day, Rob couldn't keep from drifting off, until…

"Stop there!" Pop burst out, startling Rob awake. "Read that verse again, Miss Viola."

"'Be ye angry, and sin not; let not the sun go down upon your wrath.'" She looked at Pop, her light brown eyebrows raised in a questioning manner.

"Go on." Pop glanced at Rob. He'd caught him sleeping and probably wanted to make sure he heard the charge on how to deal with anger. As if Pop didn't carry his own load of anger. But Rob wouldn't think of reminding his father of that.

Miss Viola gave Pop a weary smile and continued with the chapter. Several verses later, she read, "'Be ye kind, one to another, tenderhearted, forgiving one another, even as God for Christ's sake hath forgiven you.'"

"All right, that's enough." Pop yawned and stood. "Maybe we'll read some more tomorrow night." He moved toward the door. "Good night, all."

Rob watched Pop leave the room. Had he been convicted about the need to forgive and didn't want to hear any more? Rob's conscience sure had pricked him. God said to forgive, but he'd never forgiven Maybelle. He was too tired to sort it out now, but one thing he did learn this evening—if he ever had trouble going to sleep, Miss Viola's reading of the scriptures would soothe away the tensions of the day, and he would fall asleep as soundly as the children did when she read to them from their Mother Goose book.

Viola wished Robert had told them what had been stolen. How could she help him recover his valuable property if she didn't know what it was? When he'd burst into the parlor with his accusation, she'd been shocked and deeply hurt…and relieved when he said he was not accusing her. That was progress from his earlier veiled claims about the money he'd sent to Maybelle. Now, however, she felt guilty for not defending her friends.

Although she'd not been acquainted with Agnes for very long, she couldn't believe either she or Rosa had taken the item. Or Elena, for that matter. Like Viola, their employment and their reputation in the community depended upon their honesty and integrity. Stealing from a prominent rancher would destroy both of those.

So much for her decision to reach out to Robert in kindness. She would never become accustomed to his temper and yelling, so they could never be friends. No one in her family had ever lashed out at another family member that way, had they? Hmm. No, but they did turn a cold shoulder and refuse to speak to the supposed offender, sometimes for days, causing hurt and isolation. Was one approach better or worse than the other? Neither resolved differences or fostered good feelings among those sharing a household. Only forgiveness could do that, as the scriptures said. So she would forgive Robert for all his faults.

She reminded herself of that the next morning as she swept up his pile of dust from the parlor carpet. And here she thought she'd trained all the Mattson men to clean up before entering that special room. When he shook the dust from his hair last evening, it seemed to be a deliberate defiance of her request.

Forgiveness. Not always easy.

Yet she found it easier while making sandwiches for the men. Doing for others always made her feel better, as did keeping busy in general. Box in hand and Lavinia beside her, she descended the hill upon which the house was built. Andrew saw her coming and started her way, but Robert stopped him and strode across the land toward her.

"Here. Let me take that." He relieved her of the box, but instead of walking away, he gazed down at her. My, his blue eyes were bright today, set as they were in his deeply tanned, well-formed face. As often happened, his height and manliness sent a foolish thrill through her. She swallowed hard, hoping he didn't notice her sudden shyness.

"Smells good."

"Good."

"I helped." Lavinia beamed up at her father.

"You did?" He smiled at her in that tender way that always touched Viola's heart. He truly loved his daughter. Had no doubt loved her mother. His gaze returned to Viola. "Thank you."

"You're welcome." She should return to the house. Why would her feet not move?

"Hey, boss, we're hungry over here!" Agnes's son, Patrick, called out.

The other men laughed.

Robert scowled. "I'm coming." Without another word to her, he turned and strode back toward them, and they eagerly gathered around, all of them taking the sandwiches with unwashed hands, even Robbie.

Viola watched for a moment. As dismayed as she was by their untidy habits, she was more annoyed with her response to Robert's presence. She must stop feeling that way. How could she accept her status as an old maid when she was constantly betrayed by her feminine reactions to that man—a man who was very attractive even when sweaty, smelly and dirty?

* * *

"Hey, boss." Juan Garcia grinned at Rob around a bite of sandwich. "You got a real pretty housekeeper there."

"Yeah, boss." Patrick Ahern snickered. "Seems like I saw some sparks flying between you two just now."

"Maybe the both of you should make a trip to the preacher," Ranse Cable added.

Rob felt his temper rising with each comment. How could he shut these men up for good without alienating them? Joshing was a part of ranch life because it eased the monotony of the work, but he'd lost the ability to take teasing in stride, especially when it was aimed at him and regarded Miss Viola.

"Aw, now." Drew must have noticed Rob's anger, because he went into his peacemaker mode. "Admit the truth. Every one of you would smile at that pretty lady if you thought she'd smile back. Rob's just being polite. And thankful for this fine meal."

"Yeah, right."

Rob didn't look to see who said that. If it was Ahern, he'd have a hard time not confronting him about the theft. But the Irishman was a hard worker, and Rob couldn't afford to lose him in the middle of this work project. He'd take up the matter of the missing picture frame later.

Sandwich in hand, he strode away to check the work they'd done that morning. Drew had been right about hiring the extra men. The work was going faster than he'd expected. In two and a half days so far this week, they had added ten yards to the levee's first layer. The river had already risen a few inches, but the real test would come in late May or early June, the usual flood season. If they could get the levee laid another fifty yards before then, pack it down, then add another layer, it could save the lower barn and corrals in the event of another serious flood.

He bit into his sandwich and was surprised by the spicy taste of mayonnaise. When it came to food, Miss Viola never ceased to amaze him. She must have whipped up the mayonnaise this morning just so they could have tastier sandwiches. He would have to compliment her over supper to make up for his outburst last evening.

He stared up the hill toward the house. She had Lavinia by the hand, and they were laughing. No matter what he thought of her, she was good for his daughter.

When she'd first appeared up there, box in hand, he felt a little kick under his ribs that had nothing to do with hunger. Even in her plain brown everyday dress, which billowed around her in the breeze, she was a sight for sore eyes. All right. He admitted it. She was beautiful. But he'd never admit it to anyone else, especially this bunch of flea-bitten cowboys. And he sure wouldn't admit that her being beautiful and good for his children and a good cook and a soothing reader meant anything at all to him.

No, sir. Not him.

Chapter Nine

Viola finished ironing Robbie's new shirt, folded it carefully and took it upstairs to his room. Like the other five bedrooms, this chamber contained a bed, a chest of drawers and a wardrobe. After placing the shirt in a drawer, she peeked into the wardrobe to see what other clothing needs Robbie might have. Hand-me-down clothes still too large for him hung from pegs. Shoes and boots in varying sizes covered the floor.

A door slammed downstairs, and she jolted. Oh dear, if anyone found her digging in the corners of Robbie's room, what would they think? Robert had come close to accusing her of theft, so he would no doubt think she was snooping for valuables to take.

Downstairs she found Mr. Mattson in the kitchen, his face beaming.

"Miss Viola, I just finished those cradles for Cal's and Jared's babies. How about you and Lavinia and I take them over to the Sharps' place?"

"That sounds delightful." Viola's heart skipped at the thought of visiting the other ranch, where she knew she would be welcomed. Then a sobering thought took over. "However, I fear I am not able to prepare the surrey."

"Huh." He scowled playfully. "Young lady, I'm not so old and feeble that I can't still manage to hitch up a couple of horses."

"No, of course not." At least, she hoped not.

"Well, then, you get Lavinia ready, and I'll meet you by the back door."

"Yes, sir." Doubt lingering, she prepared Lavinia, who danced with excitement over the coming adventure. This would be their first visit to the Mattsons' relatives.

Twenty minutes later, Mr. Mattson drove the surrey to the back door and loaded the two polished, hand-carved cradles, then covered them with an old quilt. "Climb aboard, ladies."

His jolly mood didn't reassure Viola. Short of examining the harnesses, which would surely insult him, she had no choice but to do as he said, and soon they were headed toward the main road. Mr. Mattson's weathered hands shook slightly, but his blue eyes were bright.

Seated with him on the front bench, with Lavinia squeezed between them, Viola stared down the hill toward the river. How she wished Robert or one of the other men would look their way, but it was not to be. Soon they had traveled beyond the bend in the road and out of sight of anyone on the Mattson ranch.

The dry reddish-brown dirt on the road swirled around the wagon wheels, sending a small dust storm over the surrey. Lavinia coughed, and Viola waved her fan in front of both of them. So far, Mr. Mattson seemed impervious to the dust. He acted so pleased with himself, Viola couldn't complain. Unable to perform the harder work on the ranch he'd built from this same soil, he'd found a purpose that would bless his family for generations.

Before they reached Riverton, they came to a fork in the road and took the one leading away from town. Along the way, Mr. Mattson began to chat about his friendship with Mr. Sharp.

"You know, lots of folks back in the South are still fightin' the war. Sharp and I were on opposing sides, but we saw fit to accept the results and put it in the past. Only way to do that was to start a new life in a new land. We brought our families out West, him from New York and me from South Carolina. I taught my sons that hating Yankees would only bring grief. Thankfully, my oldest, Robert, was nine when the war ended, so he was a mite young to form hard opinions." He gave her a sidelong look. "You got anything against Yankees?"

"No, sir." Even though they lived in Virginia, Viola's family had not fought in the war. Not that they had been pacifists, but her father had been a supplier, and even her eldest brother had been too young to fight. She was not exactly certain how their fortune had been rebuilt so quickly after the war. All she knew was that it had run out by the time she needed her share of it.

"Ah, there it is." Mr. Mattson waved a hand toward an arched gateway that led to a large property where countless sheep grazed on a hill.

"Sheep? My, my. I thought this was cattle country."

"Huh." Mr. Mattson sounded a bit peeved. "It was. But now that we've got barbed wire and the land is marked off, the sheep don't ruin the grazing for our cattle like they used to."

"Thank the Lord." She'd read in the *Riverton Journal* that the nearby Colfax County War had ended two years ago, but some of the legal matters had yet to be settled. Comments she'd heard among the Mattson men indicated no one had a claim on their land, which gave her great relief.

"I suppose." His hands still shaking, Mr. Mattson reined the horses to a stop and started to climb down.

Viola set a hand on his arm. "I can do it." She clambered down, unhooked the latch and opened the gate. "Drive through, and I'll close it."

The road took them to a one-story white clapboard house, where it appeared a second story was being added. While not as grand as the Mattson ranch house, it had a homey, welcoming appearance. A Robert lookalike stood on the roof and waved.

"Hey, Pop." Jared climbed down a nearby ladder and trotted to the surrey. "How do, Miss Viola? Lavinia? Everybody will be glad to see you." He tied the lead to the hitching rail and ushered them into the house.

The two sisters, Emma and Julia, and their mother, Mrs. Sharp, welcomed Viola like a long-lost sister. Their kindness brought tears to Viola's eyes, which she didn't have to hide because they had turned their attention to Lavinia, proclaiming their niece the prettiest little girl they had ever seen. Then they fussed over the exquisitely carved cradles that Jared had carried in from the surrey, causing Mr. Mattson to beam with pride.

Coffee and cake were served in the parlor, a room lacking the elegance of the Mattsons' but entirely homey.

"My husband and Cal are out in the pasture," Mrs. Sharp said. "I know they'll be sorry they missed you."

Due to Lavinia's presence, the conversation remained on pleasant surface topics. Still, Viola read sincerity in every word and look. As they prepared to leave, Emma took her aside and whispered her regrets over the church dinner. "We just don't get out other than Sundays, and we assumed you would have heard the news."

Before Viola could respond, Mr. Mattson broke in. "Now, you all must come to dinner on Sunday. The whole family, right, Miss Viola?"

"Yes, indeed." Her heart skipped at the thought of hosting these kind people, although she wouldn't be a hostess in the true sense of the word. Still, it would be second best to having her own home where she could entertain as Mama used to do, and as her sisters and sisters-in-law often did now.

"What can we bring?" Mrs. Sharp asked.

The ladies quickly planned a menu, and soon Viola and Lavinia were back on the road with Mr. Mattson.

"You can see not everybody in this community is stuck up." He clicked his tongue at the horses. "I raised my sons to welcome strangers and help their neighbors."

"That is commendable." Viola could see his hands were still shaking, although not as much as before. Perhaps she should have said something to Jared about it. As it was, Mr. Mattson seemed eager to get home, for he slapped the reins on the horses' haunches and urged them to a canter.

"Yep." He chuckled. "In fact, it was helping the Sharps rebuild their barn last December that took Jared and Cal over there for several weeks. Cal was already engaged to Julia, but Jared fell hard for Emma. They had a double wedding two days after Christmas."

The surrey dipped hard into a hole in the road, almost bouncing Viola out. Lavinia gave out a loud, high-pitched squeal, and the horses bolted.

"Whoa!" Mr. Mattson tugged on the reins, to no avail, at last losing his grip.

Viola grabbed for them, but they slipped out of reach under the surrey.

The galloping horses seemed to know no one held them, and they increased their speed.

"Whoa! Whoa!" Mr. Mattson's plaintive cry reinforced Viola's own fears. His eyes wide, he hung onto the armrest beside him.

Ahead, she spotted the fork in the road. Would the animals know to turn, or would they charge over the embankment on the right and overturn the surrey?

"Surely they will slow down." She couldn't keep fear from her voice. *Lord, help us!*

Lavinia wailed as Viola had never heard her do before.

The horses seemed to know the way home, for they raced around the curve at the fork. An echo of their pounding hooves followed the surrey.

"Whoa!" Robert appeared as if from nowhere and leaned dangerously from his horse to grab the bridle on one runaway's head. "Whoa!" His firm hold and commanding tone had the desired effect, for the beasts gradually slowed to a stop.

For several moments, everyone sat speechless, huffing out hard breaths and sighs. Were the others pondering their mortality, as she was?

"I didn't like that." Lavinia buried her face in Viola's shoulder. "I want to walk home."

At the moment, Viola agreed. She looked at Mr. Mattson, whose pale face and horror-filled eyes gave him the appearance of a much older man. As for Robert, his expression was a mixture of terror and anger, and he seemed unable to speak.

She must redeem the situation. "Well." She used her brightest tone but nonetheless could hear a tremor. "That was exciting. Lavinia, you must thank your father for stopping the horses. But he has them in hand now, so we need not walk home."

Lavinia raised her head. "Thank you, Daddy."

His eyes reddened, and he looked away, then dismounted and retrieved the surrey reins and lifted them toward Mr. Mattson. "Must have been something in their feed, don't you think, Pop? Or the change in the weather. These two probably need some pasture time to get rid of their extra energy."

"Maybe so." Mr. Mattson hesitated to take the reins.

"Go on. We gotta get home so Miss Viola can start supper." Robert gave her a meaningful look. "Right?"

"Yes, indeed." This time her words came out stronger. "And Lavinia must help me."

Mr. Mattson blew out a long, weary sigh and accepted the reins. "Giddup." He slapped them against the horses' haunches and the surrey moved forward.

To Viola's relief, Robert rode by the head of the left-side horse all the way home.

Rob had never been so frightened in his life, not even when the rattlesnake threatened Miss Viola. And once again, she dismissed the near tragedy as if it were nothing. He didn't know what to make of that. Her words had calmed Lavinia right away. On the other hand, how could she have gone off with Pop that way without telling him?

If Rob hadn't gone up to the house to fetch some ointment for Robbie's blisters, he wouldn't have discovered they weren't there. A quick check of the barn revealed the surrey and horses were gone, too. That meant Pop had hitched up the rig, something he'd agreed not to do without help from Rob or Drew. After alerting his brother, Rob had saddled up and ridden toward town. He wasn't far beyond the fork in the road and headed toward town when he saw the surrey being dragged along the other fork at breakneck speed by the usually reliable geldings. But any horse could be startled, so they weren't to blame.

No, it was Miss Viola. At first he thought she just wanted to get out of the house and go to town, so she'd asked Pop to take her. But if they were on the road to the Sharps' ranch, that meant she probably wanted to visit Emma and Julia. Maybelle was always wanting to go off like that, expecting Rob to stop his necessary chores to take her. Miss Viola's selfishness had nearly cost Pop and Lavinia their lives, not to mention her own.

Back at the house, he helped Pop and Lavinia down from the surrey. He didn't dare help Miss Viola for fear he'd start in on her, scolding her like she was a greenhorn trying to be a cowboy. He saw the hurt in her eyes as she climbed down and took charge of seeing his father and daughter safely into the house. Obviously, she had no idea what she'd done wrong. He would take it up with her later this evening and explain why she must not put them all in danger again with her whims. If she argued with him, he might just have to ask her to leave.

At supper, Pop offered his usual prayer of "thanks for the food," but he didn't say "amen." Just sat there, head bowed, for several minutes. Was he having a bad spell?

Rob shared a worried look with Drew, who shrugged and shook his head.

Then Pop let out a long sigh. "Lord, sometimes your mercy overwhelms me, particularly when I deserve it least. Thank you for putting Rob on the right road just when we needed him." He chuckled softly. "And thank you that Emma and Julia liked their new cradles. Amen."

Rob thought he might fall out of his chair. Shame started as a cramp in his belly and climbed clear up to his scalp until he felt like his head was on fire. Pop was so proud of those cradles he'd made, the one important job he could still do for the family. He would have wanted to deliver them as soon as possible, so surely the outing had been his idea all along. To think Rob planned to scold Miss Viola, maybe even fire her. Lavinia and even Robbie would have lost the only mother figure they had in this world. And he would have lost... he didn't know what.

Just as Pop had said in prayer, sometimes the Lord's mercy was overwhelming.

Viola had long ago decided not to let Robert's taciturn ways hurt her feelings, but when he refused to help her down from the surrey, she couldn't deny the pain it caused. She'd still been shaking from the ordeal of the runaway horses and would have appreciated the support of a strong hand, but he had deliberately turned away from her. All the thrill she'd felt when he came to their rescue like a gallant knight of old disappeared, replaced by a promise to herself never to expect any kindness from this man. She was, after all, a redundant woman and therefore not worthy of notice or even the slightest courtesy.

So why did he now stare at her across the dining room table, a hint of kindness in his eyes? Was it his favorite biscuits she'd made, only because it was her job? No, that was not true. She'd made them to prove herself above his petty rudeness. But if that were so, why did his half smile aimed her way cause her eyes to sting with treacherous tears? Oh, she truly must stop feeling…feeling *anything for this man*, for it would only lead to disappointment.

Later, after tucking Lavinia into bed and reading several Mother Goose rhymes to her, Viola couldn't bring herself to return to the parlor for another agonizing evening in Robert's company. Besides, after his ordeal, Mr. Mattson had announced he would go to bed early, and, her mending done, it would be unseemly for her to sit with Andrew and Robert until their own bedtimes. The best thing she could do would be to read her Bible in the privacy of this little bedroom.

Perhaps tomorrow she would write to her sister Virginia and ask her to find any kind of employment for her. Of course, it couldn't be in the Norfolk area because it would bring shame to her well-to-do siblings to have a servant for a sister. But perhaps one of their connections knew of a suitable situation in another city. She would accept any decent employment that would take her far away from the unfriendly people of Riverton—and especially Mr. Robert Mattson.

Except it would also take her far away from Lavinia and Robbie and dear old Mr. Mattson, who surely required help in his old age. In truth, after visiting the Sharps' ranch, she could add Emma, Julia and Mrs. Sharp to her list of reasons to stay. So if she must be a servant, let it be in this house. After all, the Lord Jesus Christ came as a humble servant to all. She must not think of herself as better than her Savior.

Now, if she could just remember that tomorrow when she had to face Robert again.

Chapter Ten

Rob had too much work to do to take time asking Miss Viola what was bothering her. She hadn't so much as looked his way this morning. But she'd fixed a fine breakfast and promised sandwiches at midday, so whatever her problem was, it wasn't keeping her from doing her job. Had she been so scared by yesterday's runaway horses that she would consider leaving? For the first time since she arrived, he knew he didn't want her to go. Beyond taking care of his children's basic food and clothing needs and teaching them their lessons, she imparted to them a calming influence in the face of scary situations. He'd rarely met a lady who could manage that. Maybelle certainly couldn't.

He knew it wasn't fair to compare Maybelle to Miss Viola, but he couldn't stop the thought that his late wife should have been stronger. Like him, she'd grown up enduring the privations of the war. But then, to be fair, when her father had been killed at Vicksburg, her mother had pined away for years before her own death. With no better example to follow, maybe Maybelle learned from her mother to face life's challenges with passivity. In fact, it was her sweet dependency on him that had first attracted him to her. He shouldn't fault her for not rising above the hardships of pioneering in New Mexico Territory.

He thought of the Bible verse Miss Viola had read the other night about forgiveness. He'd put off forgiving Maybelle and all that would mean, maybe like he'd be justifying her abandoning him and Robbie. But could he forgive her for the sake of the children? Pastor Daniel had said forgiveness was an act of will, something a man must choose to do. So, yes, for the children, right now he would choose to forgive his late wife. The peace that filled his chest proved right away that it was for his sake, too. But now, with a levee to build and a ranch to protect from flooding, he couldn't go any deeper with those thoughts. The good Lord would have to work it out in His time.

All morning, the wind blew into the workers' faces, and everyone's eyes stung. Bandanas tied over noses and mouths failed to keep the dust from their lungs. The spring day grew warmer, increasing the sweat pouring down their faces and backs. Rob's arms ached from hours of shoveling dirt into the wagon and moving it from up on the hill to down by the river, and his brain became numb. But as the sun reached its zenith and his stomach started growling, he automatically glanced toward the house, hoping to see Miss Viola appear with her box of sandwiches. In truth, he just wanted to see her and make sure she was all right, maybe share another moment of mutual appreciation as they had yesterday, when he hadn't been able to take his eyes off of her.

"Boss, we got a problem." Juan Garcia pointed upstream, where a floating pine tree had lodged in the levee. With the strong current pushing against its branches, it began to dig away the packed dirt.

"Ahern, Garcia, let's go." Rob and the other two men raced toward the breach, shovels in hand.

After freeing the tree and pulling it over the levee, they refilled the broken embankment and packed it down, then returned to where the others should still be working. Instead, they found them seated around the wooden lunch box, chowing down on sandwiches, cookies and lemonade.

"Have a seat and dig in, fellas." Drew waved a hand toward the box. "Miss Viola has outdone herself today—as usual."

Rob glanced up the hill toward the house just in time to see Miss Viola and Lavinia enter the back door. Unreasonable disappointment stabbed his chest and dashed his appetite. But he needed to keep his strength up for the task at hand, so he forced himself to bite into a sandwich. The explosion of mouthwatering flavor almost set him back on his heels. What had she put in this chicken salad to make it the most delicious he'd ever eaten?

"Hey, Rob, don't you think this is the best chicken salad you ever tasted?" Drew gave him a teasing grin. "Remember what Old Fuzzy said that first day Miss Viola arrived and cooked for us? Said one of us oughta marry her so she won't leave."

While the other men laughed, Robbie stared wide-eyed at Rob.

Instead of smacking his brother, as he wanted to, Rob took another bite and shrugged. He couldn't beat up Drew for joshing, at least not in front of his son. Time to try another tack. "Be my guest."

Again, the men laughed heartily. Their conversation then turned to the cooking successes and failures of wives and sweethearts and other family members.

"Juanita, *mi hermanita*, her *sopapillas* are light as a cloud," said Mendez. "At last she has returned from visiting our uncle in Sonora, for which we are all grateful, for *mi hermana* Angelita does not cook so well." His comical expression of distaste brought more laughter from the other men.

Something nagged at the back of Rob's mind. Last January, the *Riverton Journal* reported that Governor Torres of Sonora, Mexico, had been stricken with smallpox and there had been a deadly epidemic of the disease in the city of Hermosillo. Did the governor survive? And had the disease spread to other areas? Not that Rob was worried for himself. During the war, the Confederate Army had required all soldiers to be vaccinated, and when Pop returned after Appomattox, he made sure the whole family was, too. But what about Lavinia? Had Maybelle taken care of that important safeguard for their daughter's health, as he had for Robbie?

With a levee to build and more work to be done on the barn, he would have to ask Miss Viola to see to the matter—another reason she must stay.

"Yer ladies may be fine cooks," Ahern said in his thickest Irish brogue. "But me mither outshines them all."

Rob stiffened. He planned to fire them both after the levee was finished. Their blatant theft of his silver picture frame couldn't be ignored or forgiven.

"Why, just the other day in the midst of helping clean the big house—" he tilted his head toward the hill "— she brings me her delightful, delectable muffins like she learned to make back in England when she worked in the great lord's house, the ones I was kind enough to share with ye, if you'll recall, Ben and Pete. Now weren't they the tastiest you've ever eaten?"

While the two cowhands voiced their agreement, Rob's heart dropped. Agnes hadn't stolen the silver. She'd been handing her son muffins wrapped in a towel. To think he might have accused them, might have ruined their reputations. Of course, Ahern still might be the one who used the bad branding iron. At the end of summer, if Will reported no lost calves due to rebranding, that would mean Ahern was the culprit, so Rob would see him put in jail.

Could he do the same to Rosa or Miss Viola if one of them had stolen the silver picture frame?

Viola spent all day Saturday trying to think of reasons not to attend church on Sunday. Yet even her need to prepare for entertaining the younger Mattson brothers and their wives and in-laws didn't justify such truancy. In all things, she must exhibit proper behavior for Lavinia's and Robbie's sakes, no matter what it cost her pride. With two roasts and a dozen potatoes in the oven, bread made, breakfast eaten, dishes washed, and the children and her dressed in their Sunday best, she climbed into the surrey behind Robert and Mr. Mattson for the ride to town.

"That's a fine-looking new shirt, Robbie." A teasing

light in his eyes, Mr. Mattson looked over his shoulder at his grandson. "Where'd you get it?"

"Granddaaad." Robbie giggled. "You know Miss Viola made it for me."

"Well, I suppose I do know that. And a fine job she did, too. Did you thank her?"

"Yessir, I did."

Robert's back stiffened, and he glanced at Viola. What had she done now? But instead of criticizing her, he smiled, and his blue eyes brightened like his father's.

"We're mighty grateful to you, Miss Viola. Robbie hasn't had many new clothes in his short life, and he looks mighty fine in what you made. He's never looked so dressed up *or* so grown up."

At his gentle tone, Viola's eyes began to sting with bothersome tears. She stared away at the passing scenery. She simply couldn't keep up with this man's moods or his rare and unexpected words of kindness. "I do believe it is the tie you put on him that gives him such a fine appearance. Now we must complete the picture. With your permission, I should like to make him a dress jacket. I can ask Suzette to bring out the material tomorrow when she comes for her class."

Oh, dear. She was babbling like a child. Such behavior had always brought censure from her oldest sister, Augusta. But no dark look or scolding words came from Robert. Instead, he again glanced over his shoulder with a smile.

"I'd like that. Wouldn't you, Robbie? And while you're at it, you can order something for Lavinia." He winked at his daughter.

How quickly he had learned to forestall rivalry between the two. Viola could only admire him for it.

"And something for yourself," Robert added.

"Thank you, but I have all I need." She couldn't imagine why he kept offering to buy something for her. It was almost unseemly. Her wages from Mr. Mattson were sufficient for her needs. She thanked the Lord every day for His provision in giving her this position at the Mattson ranch.

Now she must turn her thoughts to worship…and another cause for thankfulness. Today, no one gossiped about them, at least not within their hearing. Viola supposed they had tired of her as a topic and had moved on to someone or something else. She enjoyed Pastor Daniel's sermon on loving one's neighbor, echoing the message from Ephesians four, which she'd read the other evening. Of particular note was his emphasis on being kind to one's enemies. She couldn't call the ladies of this church her enemies, but they certainly were not her friends. All she could do was continue to exhibit proper social behavior and hope they learned from her example, even at a distance.

After the service ended, Viola found Suzette and gave her the material order. Then Robert helped Viola and his father into the surrey.

"I'll go fetch the young'uns." He'd permitted them to play with other children for a few minutes.

While Viola knew it was good for Lavinia to meet other little girls, who would no doubt welcome her because she was the daughter of a successful rancher, she hoped the child's beautiful blue dress wouldn't get soiled. She had enough trouble cleaning dust and dirt from the pink shoes. Taffeta ruined all too easily, so the material she'd ordered for Lavinia's next Sunday dress would be made of muslin, as were those the other girls wore. She'd also ordered yarn. It was time to begin knitting blankets for those new babies at the other ranch.

What was keeping Robert? She must get home and take the roast from the oven before it overcooked or dried out or the fire went out or one of a dozen other problems arose. She searched for him among the dwindling crowd. He was tipping his hat to Suzette and shaking her father's hand, perhaps thanking them for letting Suzette attend her school.

He brought the children to the surrey, and soon they were on the road home. Or to the Mattson ranch. She truly must not think of it as home.

Yet as the dinner proceeded with everyone gathered around the table, and later, as she, Lavinia and the other ladies strolled around the property, she couldn't help wishing for a home of her own with loving relatives like this family, who would welcome her warmly and not consider her redundant.

Rob teamed up with Pop, Drew with Cal, and Jared with Robbie and Mr. Sharp for an afternoon of horseshoes. They set up the playing field on the barren area beside one of the corrals. By tacit agreement with his brothers, they drove the iron stakes into the ground an easy twenty-five feet apart to accommodate Robbie… and Pop, though they would never embarrass their father by telling him what they'd done. After much boasting and joshing, the game got underway.

Between his turns at tossing the horseshoes, Rob

gazed around the property, as always, looking for anything that might need to be done in the coming week. In the distance, he saw the ladies and Lavinia walking toward Miss Viola's schoolhouse. He had to admit she sure was putting it to good use after it was no longer needed for its original purpose.

They'd built it for Cal and Julie's wedding present before Cal decided to move to the Sharps' ranch. With no sons and growing older, Mr. Sharp had needed another man to help raise his sheep. Then Jared fell hard for Emma and wanted to move there too after their double wedding.

Used to running the Double Bar M with his father, four brothers and a small son, Rob missed Jared and Cal, as pesky as they'd been as youngsters. He missed Will while he was up at the mountain pasture for the summer. These family gatherings—especially seeing how happy Jared and Cal were—sure did make him wish for…what? He had a big sturdy house that had withstood the harshest New Mexico Territory winters, two fine, healthy children, a growing ranch and healthy cattle, and they all lived in a somewhat peaceful community.

When he and Pop had decided back in '79 to move the family from Charleston, this had been their dream. Of course, they hadn't planned on being abandoned by their wives. But they couldn't go back to South Carolina. By the time Mother had left—returning to the house she'd forbidden Pop to sell—they'd already poured all their money into the ranch. Money they'd worked hard for after losing so much during the war. Then Maybelle left…

The clang of iron on iron shook him from his thoughts. Giggling with excitement, Robbie jumped up and down to the hoots and hollers of Rob's brothers, Mr. Sharp and Pop.

"Dad, did you see that? I got a leaner!"

Shaking off his foolish ruminations, Rob looked down the field to where a horseshoe leaned against the stake. It was the farthest and most accurately his son had ever thrown a shoe. No doubt the shoveling he'd done the past week had grown his muscles, but the accuracy was outstanding.

"Good job, son." He should be watching the game, but his eyes kept wandering back toward the ladies.

Unlike him, his brothers had made good choices in their wives. The Sharp women were the sort a man could count on not to run away at the first sign of trouble. Mrs. Sharp had buried several babies, yet she hadn't let her grief overwhelm her. She'd stayed and helped her husband establish their ranch. That set a good example for her daughters. And they had all befriended Miss Viola, which gave them more high marks in Rob's book. Pop might be a bit shaky these days, but his mind was good. His idea of having these other ladies over would surely encourage Miss Viola to stay. Rob had been wrong. Women did need the company of other women as surely as he needed his brothers working side by side with him.

With Lavinia skipping ahead, the ladies wandered from the schoolhouse in the direction of the barn where he and the other menfolk were.

"Watch out!" Pop pulled Rob back barely in time to keep a horseshoe from hitting his shin. "What's the matter with you, son? You're generally more into the game than this."

"He's watching the ladies." Drew smirked. "One in particular." He was too far away for Rob to smack.

"Do tell." Cal snickered.

"I saw that coming," Jared said. "Brothers, it won't be long before this big brother of ours falls like a sapling in a windstorm."

A grin on his lips, Robbie's eyes followed the speaker of each remark. "Dad...?"

"I'm just watching out for your sister, son." He threw his horseshoe within inches of Jared's boot, exactly where he'd aimed. Jared jumped but chuckled. "You're not to repeat any of their nonsense, you hear?"

Still grinning, Robbie nodded. "Yessir."

"And that goes for the rest of you." Rob glared at each brother in turn. "You hear me?"

His three brothers laughed out loud now. Even Mr. Sharp chuckled under his breath.

"Boys, you mind your big brother." Pop scowled at them. "You cause any trouble, you'll have me to answer to." His affection for Miss Viola ran deep, something Rob needed to guard for his father's sake.

"And don't you forget it." Rob shook a finger at them all.

"Oh, we wouldn't dare forget it, would we?" Drew nudged Cal.

"No, sir." Cal shuddered comically.

"No, sir." Jared snickered. "We wouldn't dare. We've minded Big Boss Rob since we were knee-high to a—"

"How's the game going?" Emma sidled up next to Jared. "Who's winning?"

"Well, Robbie sure has given our team the advantage." Mr. Sharp's praise brought a wide grin to Robbie's face.

Julia tucked herself under Cal's arm and gave him the adoring look that had won his heart, a look he returned. Rob's youngest brother suddenly looked all grown up and the strong protector of the woman he loved.

Rob wouldn't mind having someone special look at him that way, the way Maybelle used to when they first married. What was he thinking? Maybelle had died only last October. Yet long before that, she'd stopped viewing him as her protector, a role he'd failed at miserably. Had her love died long before she did, or had he killed it? No way would he make the mistake of hurting another woman. He was not husband material. Besides, he had a ranch to run, as even Pop had indicated by putting him in charge of all the work.

"You men ready for dessert?" Mrs. Sharp claimed her husband's arm. "'Scuse me, Viola. I should have asked you. Shall we go inside and set out the desserts?"

Drew snickered and gave Rob a knowing look. Rob returned a scowl. Yes, it was obvious. Even the other ladies saw Miss Viola not as a housekeeper but as the lady of the house.

Still basking in the warmth of Sunday's visit with the Mattson relatives, Viola hummed as she and Lavinia made their way to the schoolhouse on Monday. Suzette's horse was tied up at the hitching rail, and she'd already swept the schoolroom floor without being asked. A package wrapped in brown paper lay on the larger table, to Viola's delight.

"Thank you so much for sweeping and for the delivery."

"Yes, ma'am." A mischievous twinkle lit the girl's eyes.

Viola had no time to inquire about the cause of her amusement because Isabella entered the house with Elena and another girl.

"Señorita, Miss Brinson, this is my friend, Juanita Mendez. Her brother works for Señor Mattson. May she come to class, too?"

Viola's heart skipped. "Why, yes, of course. Welcome, Juanita. I am pleased to meet you."

"And I am pleased to meet you, Miss Brinson." Juanita spoke with the same musical Mexican accent as Isabella, but she seemed to have a stronger grasp of English.

"Shall we begin?" Viola waved to the chairs around the table. "Lavinia, you have your assignment, so you may proceed with that."

The older girls practiced walking with shoulders back and a book on their heads, took turns reading from Hosmer's *The Young Lady's Book* and listened to Viola's Bible reading, and in turn, corrected Viola's and Lavinia's Spanish vocabulary and pronunciations. Suzette already had a passable knowledge of the language, having served many Mexican customers at her father's dry goods store.

The morning passed quickly. Viola could hardly believe it when she checked her pin watch and saw both hands on twelve.

"We have had a productive morning, ladies. Now, remember to practice your posture as you sit, rise and walk. Next week, we will discuss the proper way to set a table and where to seat your guests." She gave them a brief outline of the coming lessons, then dismissed them.

Isabella, Elena and Juanita had driven out in the phaeton, so Viola was pleased to watch Suzette ride alongside them as they made their way toward the main road. If these girls from different cultures could be friends, it was a good sign for the community. Perhaps she would eventually be accepted here, too. If she stayed.

She needed both hands to carry the package Suzette had delivered. Material for Robbie's jacket and Lavinia's dress shouldn't make up such a cumbersome load. However, with sandwiches to make for the men and the laundry ladies, she had no time to open it. Work in the kitchen garden and supper preparations took most of the afternoon.

As had become their custom, everyone gathered in the parlor for the evening to say good-night to the children before Viola put them to bed.

"Miss Viola." Lavinia blinked her brown eyes and pointed at the small table beside the Singer where the package sat. "Aren't you gonna open it?"

All eyes immediately turned in that direction.

"Ah. I had forgotten." Just as curious as the others, Viola took scissors from the Singer cabinet drawer and used the point to untie the twine that bound the purchase. She peeled back the brown paper and held up a folded cutting of black fustian. "For Robbie's dress jacket. And this—" she lifted out pale green fabric "—for your new dress, Lavinia. Yarn for blankets for the new babies. Oh! That is a secret. Please do not mention it to Emma or Julia."

The gentlemen all voiced their approval and agreed that Suzette had made very fine choices.

Uncertain about what else was in the package, Viola folded the paper over the top. "Now, off to bed, children."

"Isn't there something else in there?" Mr. Mattson leaned forward in his chair and peered at the package.

A nervous flutter of anticipation filled Viola's chest. She'd planned to look at it later in private. "Very well." She removed the paper and took out more folded fabric, this time an adult size cutting of beautiful white muslin sprigged with tiny blue flowers.

"It's for you." The older gentleman wore a hopeful expression. "Do you like it?"

"W-why, yes. It is lovely." Nothing she could recall from Hosmer's *The Young Lady's Book* informed her of how to react at this unexpected and inappropriate gift. At least it had not come from Robert. "Thank you."

"Suzette made a good choice, didn't she, Rob?" Mr. Mattson didn't turn his eyes away from Viola. As for Robert, he was studiously examining his fingernails.

So this was what he'd been talking with Suzette about yesterday morning after church. Perhaps it had come from him, after all, against all of Viola's insistence that she required nothing from him. Did these gentlemen not understand how that might look to the community? It was not Christmas, the only appropriate occasion for male employers to bestow such gifts on female servants. But then, the community had not seen her entire wardrobe, so perhaps they wouldn't realize the particulars of this one.

"You be sure to get that made up before summer, young lady." Mr. Mattson sat back, clearly pleased with himself.

"Yes, I shall." No matter how inappropriate the gift, she wouldn't embarrass him. Or Robert, whose ducked head didn't entirely hide his frown.

Something wasn't right about the material. Rob could tell by Miss Viola's hesitation and the blush that climbed up her neck to her cheeks. It was Maybelle all over again. Nothing he did was right in her eyes. An ache started to grow in his chest.

"It is exactly what I would have chosen."

Her words, spoken to Pop in that calming voice of hers, soothed away Rob's belly pain as quickly as it had started. From the look in her eyes, he knew she meant it. She'd refused every offer he'd made to buy her something, but coming from Pop, it must be all right. Though he couldn't understand why, he could live with that. Beyond the salary Pop paid her, they all needed to show her their appreciation for all she did for them, from the cooking to the housekeeping to the kitchen garden to…just being here.

Before she came, he'd run the place as best he could while Pop seemed to decline a little more each year after Mother left. Household chores had always been the last thing on Rob's mind. His brothers did their share, of course, but the ranch had lacked a center, a heart. Not so much the *doing* but the *being*. So it was with Miss Viola. Not so much what she did but who she was. And despite Pop's lapse with the runaway horses, since her arrival, he seemed to be gradually regaining his old strength and enthusiasm for life.

Lying awake even after his long, hard day, Rob remembered Old Fuzzy's words the day she arrived. Maybe the old cook was right. Maybe one of them should marry her. Not him, of course. Not Pop, who was still married to Mother. Maybe Drew or Will…

Except that Rob still couldn't find the silver picture frame, and Miss Viola seemed the most likely one to have taken it. But he couldn't confront her about it because Pop would surely defend her, maybe even go back into a decline.

Rob couldn't risk that. He'd just have to pray the frame tuned up. And keep on looking for it.

Chapter Eleven

After church the next Sunday, Mrs. Sharp, flanked by her daughters, made her way across the small sanctuary to claim Viola's company. "It's time you met some of the other ladies."

Before Viola could respond, she saw the distaste in several women's faces and the deliberate turning away of their shoulders. Mrs. Sharp must have noticed as well. "I'm not going to stand for that." She tugged on Viola's arm.

Viola planted her feet on the wooden floor, desperately trying to think of a gracious response to this kind lady. "I—I… May we not put it off for another time? Mr. Mattson seems eager to get home."

In truth, her employer did stand by the door, his blue eyes blazing as he watched the scene. Behind him, Robert wore the same expression.

"There. You see." Viola swallowed her mortification, straightened her posture and lifted her chin. "They are waiting for me."

Sadness filling her eyes, Mrs. Sharp released Vio-

la's arm. "You go on, then. But I'm not done with this."
She walked away.

"Oh, please…"

"Don't try to stop her." Emma stepped over and
hugged Viola. "She's pretty determined."

"You can always count on us." Julia squeezed her hand.

Viola couldn't answer without crying, so she nodded and gave them a weak smile. By the time she'd
walked past Robert and Mr. Mattson, she'd subdued
her emotions sufficiently to speak to the minister without weeping.

"Your sermon was lovely, Pastor Daniel. And so in-
structive. I never considered that when our Lord Jesus
Christ spoke with the disciples on the road to Emmaus,
He was conducting the first ever post-resurrection Bible
study. What an interesting way to express it."

His eyebrows arched as though he was surprised.
"Are you a student of the scriptures, Miss Brinson?"

"W-why, yes." Why should that surprise him? Did
this man of God also think the worst of her, whatever
that might be? Her heart seemed to drop to her stomach, and she could barely force out the words, "Have a
pleasant day, Pastor."

She was already seated in the surrey when Mr. Mattson arrived and wordlessly climbed up. Robert gathered the children from their play, and soon they were
on the road to the Double Bar M. Andrew and two of
their cowhands followed along on horseback. No one
spoke all the way home.

After dinner, while Lavinia took her nap, Viola
strolled around the property. The warm sunshine began

to beat down on her bare head, but she'd walked too far down the hill to go back to the house. The river seemed to call to her, so she found a hard-packed spot on the levee and sat. A cottonwood tree grew several yards away, but she didn't seek its shade. She'd been taught to avoid the sun so as not to develop freckles, but somehow that no longer mattered to her. Her flawless ivory complexion certainly had not brought her the husband Mama had promised.

The river seemed swifter now than it had last week. Branches, wood and even a small animal carcass floated past her. Was she to be like that poor creature, lifelessly swept along by circumstances not of her own making?

"Penny for your thoughts."

Robert's sudden appearance jolted Viola from her self-pity. He settled on the levee upwind of her, and the woody fragrance of his shaving lotion wafted in her direction. After cleaning up for church, he always smelled better on Sundays.

"Oh, I always charge a quarter for my thoughts." Where had such a ridiculous response come from?

Robert laughed, a true, hearty laugh. "And I'm sure they're worth every penny."

My, he was handsome when he laughed…or smiled.

"Indeed they are." Why, it was nothing short of teasing. How unexpectedly pleasant. And what should she say to continue this banter?

His smile vanished. "Miss Viola, I've been meaning to tell you that Juanita Mendez recently returned from Mexico. From Hermosillo, a town in Sonora."

Disappointed at the sudden turn of conversation,

Viola nodded. "Yes. Last Monday she attended class and told us about her lovely visit with her uncle."

"Hmm." For a moment he seemed lost in thought. "Did she happen to mention the smallpox epidemic they had down there earlier this year?"

"No." Uneasiness crept into her. "Have you and your family been vaccinated?"

His eyebrows arched, much as the pastor's had this morning, as though he was surprised by her question. "Yes. That is, all that I know of. I don't suppose you know about Lavinia. I would be grateful if you would check her arms."

"Yes, of course. If she has not been, I would suggest taking her to the doctor in town right away. That is, if Riverton has a resident doctor."

"We do. Doctor Warren."

The matter appeared to be settled for him, yet he remained beside her staring at the river as she had done. What did he see there? Water for life on his ranch or a threat of flooding that could destroy it all? Suddenly she wanted to know more about this man, this strong, sometimes taciturn, sometimes angry rancher who worked so hard to build his family's legacy. She would try to bring him out with his own ploy.

"A penny for your thoughts."

"About this morning at church."

They spoke at the same time. Both stopped. Both laughed softly. Viola felt warmth in her cheeks that had nothing to do with the sun. She didn't wish to discuss her mortifying rejection by the other women, at least not with him.

"Well," he drawled. "I'm not sure my thoughts are

worth a penny, and definitely not a quarter. I just want you to know my family and the Sharps are well regarded in this community. You can't let a few jealous old biddies, or young biddies for that matter, hurt your feelings."

"Jealous? What on earth are you talking about?"

"Dad!"

"Daddy!"

Hand in hand, Robbie and Lavinia raced toward them across the narrow field, giggling as they ran.

Viola usually loved having the children interrupt whatever she was doing. But Robert seemed about to tell her something important that would help her understand why she'd been rejected by the other women. Seeing his joy in greeting his children, she knew the moment had been lost.

"Miss Viola, is it time for pie?" Robbie looked down at her, blue eyes sparkling.

"Time for pie." Lavinia hopped around in a circle.

Robert stood and reached out to help Viola up. "You heard them, Miss Viola. It's time for pie."

Once she was standing, he held her hand a little longer than necessary before dropping it suddenly and grasping his children's hands. "Last one to the house washes the dishes."

The three of them dashed off, with Robert keeping his pace slow enough for Lavinia's short legs to match.

For the briefest moment, Viola was struck with a childhood memory of running with her brothers across a field. Her eldest sister, Augusta, had scolded her, saying ladies did not run. And so she'd never done it again.

Until today.

Throwing such ridiculous ideas to the wind, she lifted her skirts above her high-top boots and dashed up the hill after Robert and the children.

Rob didn't quite know what to make of it when Miss Viola arrived at the house flushed and breathless. He'd been enjoying his run with the children and hadn't noticed her running right behind them. And she was laughing, something he'd rarely seen. Her cheerful mood remained as she served rhubarb pie topped with whipped cream and sat with everyone at the dining room table. Maybe she hadn't been all that hurt by the ladies at church.

No, that wasn't true. She'd been close to tears as she spoke to Pastor Daniel, yet she had commented on the sermon and wished him a good day. After she walked away, the minister asked Pop what was troubling her. While Rob was mad enough to tell him about the other ladies' behavior, Pop had brushed it off as not their place to say. Rob couldn't very well contradict his father, but he'd sure been tempted. He'd also been tempted to tell off those ladies. But Daniel might be a better person to confront them, if only he knew about their unkind behavior.

Like Drew, Daniel was a peacemaker, as he'd shown last Christmas when he and Brother Miguel from the mission across the road had arranged the *Las Posadas* celebration. The nine-day event had brought the Americanos and Mexicans together as a community as nothing else had. Then, on the last night, the girl representing Mary, the mother of Jesus, surprised everyone by giving birth to a baby boy in the Sharps' newly built barn.

As Martinez said weeks ago, María and José had lost their first baby, so everyone considered the early birth of a healthy baby a remarkable Christmas Eve gift. Maybe Martinez did change because of it. Once the levee was finished, Rob would have to visit some of the other ranchers and ask for their opinions of the Mexican landowner. Or not. He didn't trust himself to encounter the ranchers' wives, who'd not extended the courtesy of welcoming Miss Viola to Riverton. Guilt made Rob admit to himself he'd been less than welcoming himself, but—

"And Cal says they'll have a litter of pups this week," Drew said to Pop.

"Puppies?" Robbie looked at Rob, his eyes pleading. "Dad, can I have one?"

"Daddy, can I have one?" Lavinia echoed.

"Lavinia, Robbie, it's *may* I have one," Miss Viola corrected.

"Does that mean we need to get three?" Robbie gave her a cheeky grin while Pop and Drew laughed.

She gave him a mock-stern look. "No, my dear. I do not need a puppy. And you know what I meant."

While the children giggled, Rob scrambled to catch up with the conversation. He hadn't been paying enough attention. Having a puppy or two would be good, especially coming from the Sharps' purebred sheepdogs. They could protect the children when they played outside. Rob's old dog had died several years ago, and they hadn't replaced her. If his quick calculations were right, the pups might be weaned by Robbie's birthday. "We'll have to see about that."

"Da-ad." Scowling, Robbie looked across the table at Lavinia. "Most of the time that means no."

Rob let his son whine without scolding him.

Lavinia didn't appear as disappointed as her brother. She swiped a finger across her whipped cream and gave it to the kitten sitting in her lap. Maybe she didn't need a dog, too. He'd ask Miss Viola for her advice on the matter. He'd begun to see she had a good head on her shoulders, so maybe he should ask her about other things. He just hoped she didn't have him repeat what he'd said about the other women being jealous of her, though he did believe that was the case. She didn't seem to know how pretty she was or how her regal posture and perfect diction and manners set her apart from the far less formal folks around here. None of that bothered the Sharp ladies, but then, that whole family were some of the kindest people he'd ever met.

Later that evening, Miss Viola reported that Lavinia did not have the telltale scar that indicated a smallpox vaccination. As much as Rob hated having to go to town instead of working on the levee with Drew, he'd have to saddle up on Monday morning and head out to visit the doctor. Even if Juanita hadn't been exposed to the disease, Lavinia still needed protection.

Yesterday when he'd mentioned the epidemic in Sonora, Miss Viola's first thought had been to ask if Rob's family was vaccinated. Always thinking of others first. And then she'd run up the hill with him and the children. She was turning out to be far more important to his family than he'd ever thought possible. More important to *him than he'd thought possible*. But every time he had such thoughts, he remembered the silver picture frame. It sure would settle his mind to know the truth of who'd dug into his wardrobe and taken it. He couldn't imagine Rosa would do such a thing. She'd been going in and out of the house on laundry day for years and had never stolen anything.

No, it had to be Miss Viola. And for some downright foolish reason he couldn't figure out, that just about broke his heart.

On Monday morning, Viola left Lavinia in Mr. Mattson's care and made her way to the schoolhouse. As before, Suzette had come early and swept out the week's worth of dirt blown in by the blustery daily winds. They waited until nine fifteen before starting the lessons.

Bringing Elena with her, Isabella showed up at ten o'clock. "Miss Brinson, I am so sorry for being *más que tarde*…so very late. When I stop at Juanita's *casa*, house, I saw she is *muy enfermo*…very sick."

Viola's heart dropped, but she managed not to gasp. Was it smallpox? That meant Lavinia had been exposed last week. "I am sorry to hear that. Is there anything we can do for her family?"

"Hmm. I do not know, Señorita… Miss Brinson. I will have our cook take a bowl of *sopa*, but I think her sister Angelita will care for her."

Heart in her throat, Viola managed to continue the lessons. Then she learned a few Spanish words from Isabella and Elena before dismissing the girls early. "I hope to see you again next Monday. Please remember to discuss smallpox vaccinations with your families."

She returned to the house to find Robert, Mr. Mattson, a gentleman dressed in black and a distraught four-year-old in the parlor.

Lavinia flung herself into Viola's arms. "Don't let him cut my arm off!" Tears flowing, eyes wide with terror, she stared back at the three men.

Viola ignored Robert's harried expression and gently led Lavinia to the couch. With the trembling child on her lap, she brushed her damp hair back from her face. "What makes you think they want to cut off your arm?"

Thumb in her mouth, Lavinia shrugged.

"Miss Viola, would you please—" Robert started to sit beside her, but Lavinia wailed again. He quickly stood and ran a hand through his hair. "Please tell her the vaccination won't hurt."

Viola chided him with a raised eyebrow. "It is always better to tell a child the truth. Otherwise, you will lose her trust." She'd seen it happen with her nieces and nephews more times than she could count. Holding Lavinia close, she asked, "Have you been introduced to the doctor?"

Lavinia shook her head.

"Well, then, that is a good place to begin." Viola nodded to Robert.

He cleared his throat. "Lavinia, this is Doctor Warren."

The graying middle-aged man wore a kindly expression, and his brown eyes exuded patience. No doubt he'd seen many such distraught patients. "Miss Lavinia, I am pleased to meet you." He bowed to her and then to Viola. "And Miss Brinson, at last I am privileged to meet you. Suzette Pursers speaks very highly of you."

For some reason, his remark caused Viola's eyes to

sting. At least one Riverton lady, although still a girl, spoke well of her. "Thank you, Doctor Warren. I am pleased to meet you as well. Forgive me for bypassing further pleasantries, but I am sure you need to get on with your day. Perhaps you're aware that one of my students, Juanita Mendez, may have been exposed to smallpox."

"Yes, Robert told me."

"She didn't attend my class today because she is ill, though we do not know the nature of her illness."

Robert and Mr. Mattson groaned, and their foreheads furrowed.

Remaining calm, as any competent doctor would, Doctor Warren said, "I'll stop by her house on my way back to town."

"Thank you." Viola glanced down at Lavinia, who had relaxed somewhat and now followed the conversation. "Whatever her illness turns out to be, we have all been exposed to it. If it is smallpox, those of us who have been vaccinated can be thankful we will not succumb to it."

"Yes, indeed." The doctor seemed to understand her tactic. "Smallpox is a terrible sickness. Lavinia, have you been vaccinated?"

She raised questioning eyes to Viola. Viola shook her head. Lavinia looked back at the doctor and copied the gesture.

"Oh, dear." The doctor scratched his chin. "What shall we do about that? We certainly don't want you to get sick."

Lavinia pressed closer to Viola.

Viola squeezed her shoulders. "It will be all right,

my darling. Doctor, perhaps you could explain your procedure to Lavinia."

"I can do that." He sat on the other end of the couch. "A little over a hundred years ago, some very clever people found that if they scratched the arm of a healthy person with the, shall we say, *seeds* of the sickness, it kept those people from getting the disease, the sickness. Do you understand?"

Lavinia shook her head, then nodded. "Uh-huh."

Robert knelt in front of her. "Sweetheart, you don't want to get sick, do you?"

The fear in his eyes caused Viola's eyes to sting again. He truly loved his daughter.

"No. I don't like being sick." Lavinia stuck her thumb in her mouth.

Robert chuckled. "I don't either." He glanced at Viola.

"Go on," she whispered. This could be a good bonding time for them, so she prayed he would have the right words.

"Doctor Warren needs to vaccinate you—"

Lavinia stiffened and moved to get off of Viola's lap. "No!"

"Sh." Viola tugged her close. "It will be all right. What would you think if I let the doctor vaccinate me first?"

"Or me?" Robert challenged Viola with a look.

"Or me?" Mr. Mattson spoke from across the room.

Lavinia stared wide-eyed at each of them. A tiny grin appeared, and she pointed at Robert. "You, Daddy."

"Ha." As if he'd won a contest, he grinned as he rolled up one sleeve. "I'm ready, Doc."

"Very well." A bit bemused, the doctor proceeded

to prick his arm several times, applied tiny bits of matter to the cuts, then wrapped the arm with a bandage.

While the doctor worked on him, Robert winced dramatically, clearly not in serious pain.

Lavinia giggled. "My turn." She permitted the doctor to repeat the procedure on her own arm. Although she did squirm at the first prick, she endured the remainder with a smile, probably because Robert continued his histrionics.

Once she was bandaged, Robert held his arm next to hers. "Now we have matching wounds."

"And you were both very brave." Viola sighed quietly to herself, thankful it had gone so well. "Thank you, Doctor. Will you stay for dinner? I plan to make sandwiches for everyone."

Rob ignored his itching arm as he carried the box of sandwiches down the hill to his hungry men and Robbie. Doctor Warren had told him a second vaccination was advisable after seven years, and it had been twice that since his first one. He would have to make sure everyone on the ranch got another one as soon as the doctor replenished his supply.

Once again, Miss Viola had calmed the storm—a storm of Rob's making. He'd been so anxious about protecting Lavinia from disease that he'd barged into the house like a rampaging grizzly bear. She'd been frightened even before he'd blurted out that she needed the vaccination. When she asked what it was, he'd ignored Doctor Warren's warnings and said they needed to cut her arm. He didn't even get to the part about applying the smallpox crusts. She'd begun screaming for Miss Viola and tried to run out of the room.

So far, he'd had no real problems rearing Robbie, but would he ever be the father his sweet little daughter needed? Without doubt, Lavinia needed the influence of a woman. If he were truthful with himself, he'd admit his little girl needed Viola, the one woman he wasn't sure he could truly trust.

Chapter Twelve

"Drew, I need you to take supplies up to the pasture so none of the men will have to come down." Rob hadn't slept much the night before due to worrying about protecting everyone on the ranch from smallpox, not to mention his concern over cattle rustlers rebranding the Double Bar M calves and the constant threat of a flood. Doc said Will and Drew would be safe from the disease until they could get a second vaccination, but the other men might not be protected. That meant they shouldn't come down until the end of summer.

"You can get supplies this afternoon and go up tomorrow. And see if Ranse Cable's been vaccinated and is willing to go with you in case any outlaws decide to help themselves to the supplies on your way there." Ranse, a former gunman and a survivor of the Colfax County War, had turned his life around and become a dependable ranch hand.

Mouth full of pancakes, Drew washed it all down with coffee. "What about the levee?"

Rob huffed out a long breath. "I'll try to hire more men."

"You know," Pop said, "I'm not so feeble that I can't dig a little dirt. If you recall, I did clear this land and build this house only nine years ago. And I've worked shoulder to shoulder with you and your brothers since then."

Rob cringed inside. "Sir, I think your energies are better spent keeping the books." He ducked his head and scooped up a mouthful of eggs, ignoring the annoyance on his father's face.

"Ha." Pop slapped the table. "Shows what you know. Miss Viola's been keeping the books for me for two weeks."

Rob nearly choked on his eggs but managed to swallow the bite. "Do tell." He glared at her across the kitchen table. "When did you volunteer to do that?"

Miss Viola lifted her chin and narrowed her eyes in that snooty way of hers Rob hadn't seen in a couple of weeks. "Mr. Mattson requested that I assist him with the task. If you're concerned about my competence with numbers, remember I am teaching arithmetic to your children at *your* request."

"No, ma'am. I'm not worried about your ability with numbers." *Worried about your honesty, yes, but not your ability.* Rob took a final slug of coffee. "Just surprised. Drew, you ready? Ma'am, will you send Robbie out after he gets up and has his breakfast?"

He said the same thing every morning so he didn't wait for her reply. Though he did think he heard her ladylike "Humph" as he walked out the door. She could get as uppity as she wanted to, but he still hadn't found the silver frame. And why had Pop trusted her with the ranch's finances? The last thing Rob needed was another problem to deal with when they still hadn't heard from Pop's friend regarding the money he'd been sending to Maybelle even after her death.

At Mr. Mattson's cross look, Viola forced a conciliatory smile. "He certainly has a great deal on his shoulders."

"That don't give him any reason to dismiss my offer."

Thank you, Lord. He must have missed Robert's accusing look. Did the man think she was unable to manage a few columns of figures? Or was it worse? Did he still think she'd taken his keepsake, whatever it was— had somehow absconded with Maybelle's money, and therefore couldn't be trusted with the ranch accounts? If she'd taken the money, would she even be here? Of course not.

"No, sir." Viola began to clear the table while Mr. Mattson finished his coffee. "But I do think you might suffer from the heat if you exert yourself out there. I know it would be hard for me. I'm surprised at how hot it gets by midday, and it is only mid-May. I cannot imagine how hot it will be in July or August." She searched her mind for some productive activity to occupy this older gentleman so he wouldn't insist upon working on the levee when it was clear Robert didn't want to take a chance on his father's health. Would his shaking hands even hold a shovel? The disaster with the runaway horses hinted they might not. "Perhaps we could spend our time working on Robbie's and Lavinia's birthday presents."

Before he could reply, the children came running down the stairs, giggling as they always did when they were together. How Viola missed the days when she and her closest sister had enjoyed playing together that way.

Their arrival successfully diverted Mr. Mattson from the idea of going outside to work. After breakfast, when Robbie went out to work with his father, Lavinia wanted only to play with her kitten on the parlor floor. After her vaccination, the doctor had warned she should keep to quiet activities.

When Viola carried the box of sandwiches to the men working on the levee, Robert met her at the bottom of the hill. As usual, he was covered with dirt and sweat and smelled like a hardworking man, but nonetheless, his handsome face and towering stature sent that bothersome tickle threading through her chest. How foolish she was! The man was rude and bossy, and worse, had impugned her integrity.

He took the box. "Doc sent word out with Mendez that his sister's beginning to break out, so it's definitely smallpox."

"Thank you for the information." Viola sighed. "I should let you know that Lavinia didn't have much energy this morning."

Robert looked beyond her toward the house, his forehead creased. "Is she—?"

"She is playing quietly with Puff, so I do not think we need to worry." She started to turn away. "Oh, and I should tell you your father has occupied himself with organizing his library."

Robert chuckled. "Your idea?"

Her cheeks warmed, and she laughed softly. "Yes. I

told him I was interested in finding more books to use in my teaching. Which, of course, is true."

He gazed down at her with that kind, gentle look she had yet to discern. So strange, as though he hadn't treated her as rudely as he had at breakfast. "Thank you, Miss Viola. I do believe you're good for him."

"Hmm. Even when I help him by keeping the books?"

All too quickly, his expression turned hostile. "Thank you for lunch." He spun on his heel and strode away.

Stunned by his abrupt change toward her—again—Viola wanted to call him back, but her pride forbade it. She would wait to tell him she'd discovered some errors in the bookkeeping, which she'd corrected, and had paid an overdue feed bill. Mr. Mattson didn't seem aware of what she'd done, but at least he trusted her. What would convince Robert to do the same? Perhaps when word came back from Mr. Mattson's friend in Charleston, she would be vindicated in his eyes.

For now, she had another dilemma to deal with. The pantry was running low on numerous items. Perhaps she could go to town with Andrew when he purchased the supplies for the men at the summer pasture.

Mr. Mattson agreed to the plan and promised to keep an eye on Lavinia. "I've found some books my wife used to read to our boys when they were small. I think Lavinia will like the stories."

With her young charge safely settled, Viola hurried outside in time to catch Andrew as he drove a wagon past the house. Soon they rumbled up the road toward Riverton. Viola held her beige parasol with one hand and hung onto the side of the driver's bench with the other. As hot as the day was, the stiff breeze made it bearable and also swept pleasant scents of green hay her way.

"Miss Viola, we sure do appreciate the way you look out for Pop." Andrew grinned at her in his sweet brotherly way, then sobered. "I hope Rob didn't hurt your feelings this morning at breakfast."

"He has a great deal on his mind." She wouldn't burden Andrew with her difficulties or cause a breach between the brothers, should he decide to take her side. "We must all do our part to help him." She forced a little laugh. "Besides, you and your brothers have all mentioned he has always been a bit overbearing."

Andrew snorted. "That's putting it mildly." He gave her a sideways glance. "Were your brothers or sisters bossy like him?"

"Yes, indeed. My eldest brother and sister thought they were second parents to us younger ones." And had tried to control their lives.

He chuckled. "I suppose you were the spoiled baby?"

She thought for a moment, recalling how her siblings had always said with some resentment that their parents coddled her. "Yes, I suppose so."

"Yep, that's Cal. Spoiled rotten until…"

He didn't need to finish. His mother's abandonment must have shaken them all.

At Pursers' Dry Goods Store, Suzette met them with an uncharacteristic frown. "We're all worried about the smallpox. Doc Warren vaccinated Pa and me because we meet the public every day, but some other folks are already showing symptoms."

"Oh, dear. Maybe I can help." Viola handed her list to Suzette. "Who is ill?"

"Iris and Mrs. Blake." Suzette took Andrew's list and set both papers on the counter. "Juanita works for them, so Doc thinks they got it from her."

"One would think a banker's family would have the good sense to get vaccinated." Viola bit her lower lip, regretting her words instantly. Just because the two ladies had snubbed her and gossiped about her didn't give her the right to criticize them to other people.

"You'd think," Andrew echoed.

"Humph." Suzette rolled her eyes and shook her head. "Mrs. Blake is concerned about appearances. She said she didn't want the scar the vaccination makes and didn't want Iris to have it either."

"Huh." Andrew snorted. "If it hits 'em hard, they'll have more than a little scar on their arms."

"Do you suppose I can do anything to help them?" Several years ago, Viola had tended some neighbors with the illness. Such a nasty but necessary task.

Suzette shrugged. "I can't imagine why you'd want to help them. Let me get your supplies." She disappeared into the back room.

"Andrew, while you load the wagon, I am going over to the bank to see if Mr. Blake requires help."

"Oh, Miss Viola, I don't think you should do that, considering…"

She patted his arm. "Do not worry. The children will be fine."

He scowled. "That's not what I'm thinking."

"It can do no harm to ask." Viola left before he could say more.

At the bank, she found the teller counting change behind the cage. He set aside the task and greeted her with a smile. "Good morning, ma'am. How may I help you?"

"Would you please tell Mr. Blake that Miss Brinson would like to speak with him?"

The banker soon emerged from a room beside the teller's cage. Worry creased his forehead, but he managed a businesslike smile. "Good afternoon, Miss Brinson. How may I help you?"

"Good afternoon, Mr. Blake. Forgive me for bypassing pleasantries, but I understand your wife and daughter are ill. Is there anything I can do to help?"

He stared at her for several long moments. "Why, I don't know what to say. In truth, I'm at a loss. Everyone is worried about contracting the illness, so no one is willing to nurse them. I'm planning to close the bank so I can take care of them."

"You need not do that. People should have access to their accounts. Give me this afternoon to make arrangements, and I'll come tomorrow morning. Can you manage until then?"

His eyes reddened. "That would be most kind, ma'am, considering—"

"Then I'll come to your house tomorrow morning." Her own eyes burning, she turned and left.

Andrew had finished loading the wagon and helped her up on the bench. "Rob's not going to like it."

She sniffed. "Robert did not hire me, and your dear father trusts my judgment. Now, shall we go? I want to stop by Agnes Ahern's house."

Huffing out his disapproval, Andrew did as she instructed. They found Agnes taking in her laundry. After

Viola explained the situation, the Irishwoman agreed to help.

"Ya know, Miss Viola, I could just go help the Blakes meself. I've had the pox vaccination, an' I've nursed plenty o' sick folk back in the earl's great house in Hampshire."

Viola thought for a moment. Perhaps that was a better plan. But no. This was her opportunity to show the women of Riverton she was not a standoffish snob. "Thank you, Agnes, but I believe your talents will best be used at the Double Bar M. And you will be able to see Patrick every day."

Agnes smiled. "You're very persuasive, miss."

To her surprise, Mr. Mattson agreed to the plan when she presented it to him that evening. "That'll show them what you're made of." Although he'd never spoken of it, his anger over the ladies rejecting Viola was apparent every Sunday at church.

"I don't like it." Robert stood in the doorway, arms crossed and still wearing his dusty clothes after a day's work. "We need you here to take care of Lavinia."

"I am certain you will find Agnes more than competent. She is good with the children, and Lavinia adores her."

Andrew snickered. "Hey, Rob, you sure you're not worried about having to cook your own supper?"

Robert scowled at him. "You ready to leave tomorrow?"

"Yep. Ranse said he'll go, too."

"Then why don't you go to bed and get a good rest before your trip."

Andrew snorted, then winked at Viola before saluting his brother. "Yessir, boss man."

Viola could hardly contain a giggle. Younger brothers and sisters might have to suffer their elder siblings' overbearing ways, but they could also enjoy moments of camaraderie in their misery. While at the Blakes' house, she would miss Andrew, as she did William. She would also miss Lavinia, Robbie and Mr. Mattson. And, despite his disagreeable ways, Robert as well. It seemed she had no control over her feelings toward him. Which was so very unwise of her and sure to lead to a broken heart. Perhaps getting away from him would help her tame her unruly emotions, at least for however long she was needed at the Blake home.

Rob had never endured a longer week in his life. Agnes was the gabbiest woman he'd ever met. From the moment he came downstairs for breakfast until he headed out to the river, she went on and on about one thing or another. When she brought lunch to the men, she stayed and gabbed with her son, who gabbed right back, their Irish accents affecting Rob's own pronunciation of the English language. Every evening, she parked herself in Miss Viola's chair—when had he begun to call Mother's chair Miss Viola's?—and gabbed some more to Rob and Pop.

More than once, she bragged about the time she saw Queen Victoria. But Agnes's favorite topic was Lord Bennington's grand Hampshire estate, where she'd gone into service as a fourteen-year-old. Everything in merry old England was grander, of course. Sometimes Rob wanted to ask why she'd come to America if her em-

ployment there had been so magnificent, but she'd probably launch into another lengthy tale.

By the following Monday, he'd had enough. He left
the men to their digging and saddled up for an afternoon ride through the countryside to clear his head and
to stop the old pain that had returned in his chest. Instead, he found himself headed to town. To the Blakes'
redbrick house. Up the impressive front steps to the columned porch. Taking off his hat. Knocking on the door.

What was he doing? He donned his hat and turned
to leave before anyone answered.

"Robert." Miss Viola's calm, melodious voice
brought him to a stop at the top of the steps. "Is everything all right?"

He turned to see the most beautiful woman he'd ever
known. Not a single blond hair was out of place, and
her apron-covered brown work dress rivaled any lady's
party dress for the way it complemented her ivory complexion and slender frame. The pain in his chest burst
into an ache such as he'd never experienced. Only it
felt more like a desperate longing for something just
out of his reach.

"Is something wrong with Lavinia? With Robbie?"
She stepped toward him and reached out a hand. Instead of sickroom stink, the scent of rosewater came
with her. "Robert?"

He removed his hat again. "No. No. Everything's
fine at the ranch." He couldn't stop staring at those
pretty green eyes. "Just wanted to make sure you're
doing all right."

She smiled, and that wonderful ache in his chest exploded again. "Thank you. We are well…or at least improving. I would invite you in, but the ladies…"

"No. Yes. Of course." A noisy wagon rattled past on the dusty street, bringing Rob to his senses. "Just wondered if you need anything." His words came out rough, cross.

If she noticed, her face didn't betray her. Instead, her gentle smile conveyed compassion. Could this woman actually be a thief? Everything within him shouted no. But he'd been wrong about a beautiful woman before, had given her his heart and had it broken.

"Well, if you don't need anything…" He was repeating himself.

"No. Oh, you could convey my…my love to the children. I miss them." She focused on his eyes as though looking for something. "And your father. And Andrew."

A laugh escaped him. "And me?"

She laughed, too. "Why, no, not at all." Her sparkling emerald eyes contradicted her words.

Somehow her good humor relaxed him. "I can believe that."

"Viola." A weak voice called from within the house. "Who is it?"

"Sounds like you're needed." Rob nodded toward the door. "I should go."

"Yes. I need to…" She reached out to him again. "Thank you for stopping by."

Rob took her hand, noticing for the first time how chapped and red it was. Maybelle's lily-white hands had been such a source of pride to her that she'd refused to do the simplest household tasks. That's why they'd hired

Agnes and Rosa to do the laundry and ate Old Fuzzy's questionable cooking. "You're working hard."

"No harder than you work every day." She tugged her hand away. "Good day, Robert."

She turned back and stepped inside, leaving him bereft.

"Good day," he whispered to the closed door.

She hadn't asked for anything. Never did. But he rode over to the dry goods store anyway and ordered some of that fancy French hand cream Maybelle used to like. "Send it over to Miss Viola."

Suzette gave him a sassy grin. "I'll do that, Rob. Any message with it?"

"Message? No." The hand cream would be message enough. She was part of his ranch, his household. He had a responsibility to take care of her. "Just make sure it's for Miss Viola's use, not the Blake ladies."

All the way back to the ranch, he tried to understand his crazy reactions to Miss Viola. He reminded himself of his doubts about her honesty. And his doubts about his doubts. All he knew for certain was that just seeing her for those few minutes, looking into those kind eyes, touching that chapped hand, had pushed him past a barrier he couldn't even define. As with the flooding Rio Grande, he didn't seem able to build a levee high enough to hold back the flood of emotions that swept over him in her presence.

Viola's knees wobbled so much she needed to lean against the door before trying to walk across the foyer. When she'd opened it to find Robert on the other side, she came close to falling into his arms. How good it had been to see him for those few precious moments, especially since he seemed glad to see her as well. Somehow her finishing school lessons on restraint had kept her from reacting outwardly, but had he noticed her trembling?

And what of her heart? How could she have been so moved by his sudden appearance? Had she not persuaded herself just last night that returning to Virginia would be best for her? Yet his visit, however brief, had revealed a weakness, a fatal flaw she could not expunge from her character. She longed for his good opinion. His admiration. His trust. Perhaps even his love.

Nonsense. This was simply her weariness speaking. She'd slept very little for the past week and didn't expect to for many nights to come.

"Viola." Mrs. Blake's voice sounded louder this time and more demanding. The woman had yet to comprehend that Viola was not her servant but a volunteer who had come out of the goodness of her heart to nurse her and her daughter.

Lord, forgive me. Such self-righteousness had no place in the heart of a Christian. As she often reminded herself, she *was* a servant following the example of her Lord Jesus Christ, and she must not expect more than her Savior received from those He had served. When she considered how He was despised and rejected, she could not justify her own complaints.

"Yes, Mrs. Blake?" She entered the parlor, where the two ladies lay on beds brought from their upstairs bedrooms. "Did you need something?"

"Who was at the door?" Her sharp tone proved her

illness was not as severe as her daughter's, and reminded Viola of her eldest sister, Augusta.

"Robert Mattson. He came to ask if we needed anything."

"You see, Iris." Mrs. Blake managed a triumphant
smile. "He came to see how you are. Now that his wife
is dead, I have no doubt he will court you as soon as
you are well."

"Oh, don't let him in here!" Iris wailed as she pulled
her covers over her head. And no wonder, with her face
covered with blisters.

Viola prayed they wouldn't leave pitted scars on the
pretty girl. These ladies might be snobs and more than
a little foolish, but they didn't deserve the ravages this
disease often left.

"No need to worry, Iris." Viola tucked the covers
back in place. "He has already left."

"Freshen my water." Without so much as a please or
thank you, Mrs. Blake waved a hand toward the pitcher
beside her bed.

Viola sighed inwardly. Yes, the woman was very
much like Augusta, whom Viola could never please,
no matter how hard she tried.

As she made her way to the kitchen, a knock sounded
on the front door. Her heart skipped. Had Robert returned? She opened it to find Suzette grinning so
sweetly she couldn't be disappointed.

"You are a welcome sight, Suzette, but I do not think
it wise for you to come inside."

"Oh, no, ma'am. I don't mean to come in. I just
brought you this." She thrust a small glass jar into Viola's hand. "This is from Rob. It's some of that French

hand cream we carry over at the store. He said it's for you and not to let that Mrs. Blake take it away from you." She blinked her eyes, as though realizing how rude her words must sound. "I mean—"

Viola laughed softly. "I understand." She took Robert's unexpected gift in hand and opened the jar. The pleasant fragrance of lavender and lemon wafted around her. His thoughtfulness brought equally unexpected tears to her eyes. "Thank you for bringing this."

"You're welcome." Suzette giggled. "Those Mattson men. You just never know what they'll do next." She skipped down the front steps, waving over her shoulder as she went.

Viola couldn't argue with Suzette's comment, especially concerning Robert. That man! He never paid attention to her insistence that she required nothing from him. Yet, when Suzette had said he sent the hand cream only for her, her thoughts turned to foolish dreaming. But no, he would no more court her than he would Iris Blake. Still, as she rubbed a small bead of the cream into the back of her chapped hand and felt its soothing properties take effect right away, her heart felt soothed as well and swelled with happiness…and hope.

And despite his orders, she did apply some to her patients' faces. It appeared to heal some of the smaller blisters.

On Thursday, Doctor Warren came for his usual daily visit to his patients, bringing with him a middle-aged woman who bore a slight resemblance to him. "Miss Brinson, may I present my sister, Cassandra Warren? Cassandra trained with Miss Clara Barton and has many years' experience dealing with a variety of diseases. I wired her at the beginning of this epidemic, and she has come to relieve you of your duties."

He spoke in his kindly but authoritative manner, leaving no room for objections. Not that Viola would object. The testing of her Christian charity had grown worse since the Blake ladies had begun to improve.

She exchanged pleasantries with Miss Warren, then gathered her belongings and waited for Doctor Warren, who offered to take her back to the Double Bar M after completing his examination of the patients. When she took her leave of the ladies, Mrs. Blake waved her off as if she were a pesky fly.

Her feelings still stinging from the ungrateful woman's dismissal, Viola almost came to tears as the doctor drove under the archway guarding the drive to the ranch. How glad she was to be home.

Only it wasn't home, was it? But it was no doubt the closest place to a home she would ever have.

Chapter Thirteen

Rob brushed most of the day's dirt from his hair and clothes, then splashed water from the mudroom basin over his face. He didn't bother shaving a second time today. In spite of his fast-growing beard, he'd gone back to shaving only in the morning. As much as he resisted the thought, he had to admit he'd become more fastidious since Miss Viola came to the ranch, probably to avoid her censure. Yep, that was it. He preferred her approving smile to her disapproving frowns. But why?

Before he could examine his thoughts, a buggy rolled into the backyard beyond the kitchen garden. Peering through the window, he saw Doc helping Miss Viola climb down. His heart bounced up to his throat. Without thinking, he grabbed his shaving cup and brush and began to work up a lather. He'd no sooner applied it to one jaw than she walked in.

"Oh. Excuse me." Her face flushed, she hurried past him and into the house. Maybe she'd never watched a man shave before or thought seeing it was somehow improper, like so many other little odd things that didn't pass muster for her.

His chest bursting, he grinned. She was back. Life could go back to normal, whatever that was.

"Hello, Rob." Doc Warren entered the mudroom. "How is everyone?"

"I think we dodged the bullet, Doc." Rob scraped at his beard.

"Thank the Lord. Would you like for me to take a look at the children just to be sure?"

"I'd be grateful if you would."

After Doc went inside, Rob hurried through his shave, then went up the back stairs to put on clean clothes. Once dressed, he headed for his bedroom door but turned back and splashed on some of the cologne that matched his shaving balm. Why? Well, he didn't care to ponder why.

He found Miss Viola and Agnes laughing together in the kitchen. "What's so funny?"

Miss Viola dabbed at her eyes with a handkerchief. "Lavinia and Robbie have decided to become Irish." She nodded toward the dining room, where the children were playing a board game on a card table.

"Leastways from the way they talk," Agnes said.

Rob chuckled. "I admit to hearing a bit of your brogue in my own speech."

"'Tis as fine a compliment as you can give." Agnes moved to the stove to stir the Irish stew she'd served every other day. While tasty, it did get tiresome after a while.

"Well, I'll be goin' home as soon as the muffins

are done, so you can go back to your English ways. Patrick'll drive me."

"I am so grateful to you, Agnes." Miss Viola donned an apron as she glanced at Robert. "Did you need something?"

He crossed his arms and leaned against the doorjamb. "No. Just enjoying…" *Watching you.* "The aroma of Agnes's fine stew."

Agnes gave him a skeptical look, then winked at him. "Sure you are, me boy. An' I'm Queen Victoria."

Before she could begin one of her lengthy stories, he excused himself to join Doc and the children in the parlor.

"No sign of illness, Rob." Doc tucked his stethoscope into his black leather bag. "As you said, you folks dodged a bullet. Not every family did."

Rob walked the doctor to the back door. "Thanks for coming out."

"Glad to." Doc waved goodbye over his shoulder.

Rob watched him drive away. To his surprise, Miss Viola joined him at the back stoop.

"Robert, I wanted to thank you for sending Suzette to the Blakes' with the hand cream." She held up a hand. "You didn't have to do that, but it certainly did make a difference."

Without thinking, he took that hand. Sure enough, her skin was soft to the touch and no longer looked as red and chapped as before. "Nice." *Brilliant observation, Mattson.*

She gazed up at him and smiled. "Yes. Nice." She turned back toward the kitchen.

Again without thinking, he touched her shoulder.

She stopped. "Yes?"

His throat tried to close, but he managed to croak out, "Welcome back."

She smiled again, and they stood staring at each other for he didn't know how long. Finally, she ducked away and went back to the kitchen. Rob had a strong feeling he'd missed an opportunity to…he didn't know what.

Viola didn't know what to think of the way Robert had looked at her. Or why she'd wanted to stand there looking back at him. With supper to get on the table, she would have to examine her feelings later.

What she did know was that she had never enjoyed cooking for the Mattsons as much as she now did. While the Blake kitchen boasted a grand stove and numerous clever gadgets, the patients had not been able to eat more than a little tea or broth or milk toast, and they had not welcomed any of it. At every meal she prepared here at the ranch, Mr. Mattson praised each dish, and the children showed their appreciation by cleaning their plates without being told. Even Robert complimented her cooking skills, and from the kind way he looked at her, she knew he meant it. Perhaps she had truly found a home where she belonged, if only as the housekeeper.

As much as she dreaded going back to church, she dressed Lavinia in her blue dress and wore her own Sunday best for the trip to town. When Robert drove into the churchyard, several women came to meet them.

"What do they want?" he mumbled under his breath.

"Miss Brinson." Suzette led the group. "These ladies would like to meet you."

Aware of the example she must set for the children, Viola forced a smile. "How lovely." She accepted Robert's help from the surrey, then turned to face them.

"Miss Brinson." One middle-aged woman stepped in front of Suzette. "I'm Olive Gentry. We all heard what you did for Gertrude and Iris Blake, and we think that was mighty fine."

"You didn't have to do it," a dark-haired girl of perhaps seventeen years said. "'Specially after the way they bad-mouthed you."

"Hush, Dolores," another woman said. "That's not kindly."

"Well, they did." Dolores added a pout to her cross expression.

"Anyway!" Suzette, a mere eighteen years herself, pushed back to the front. "Mrs. Blake fancies herself the social leader here in town just because her husband owns the bank. But after what you did for them, well—"

"*Wel*come to Riverton." Olive Gentry scolded Suzette with a look.

Viola swallowed the tears trying to clog her throat. How well she understood snobbish women from her own youthful experiences. Except that her mother had been the social leader of her upper-class circle, and no one had dared to snub her or her daughters while she was alive. "I thank you, ladies, for your welcome—"

"Long overdue," Suzette muttered.

"Ladies." Mr. Mattson offered his arm to Viola. "It's not seemly to stand out here in the sun gossiping. I suggest we forget all of this and go inside for worship."

His cheerful tone encouraged Viola almost as much

as Robert's broad smile. She saw him whisper something to Suzette.

She gave him a triumphant smile. "You're welcome."

Viola could only surmise he'd thanked her for the change in the other women. One thing was sure. In this small town, the banker's wife might hold the social reins, but no one was going to snub the family that sold most of life's necessities in their dry goods store.

Rob hadn't enjoyed church this much since he didn't know when. The music lifted his heart to worship, and Pastor Daniel's message on serving others seemed to be a direct reference to Miss Viola's selfless care of the Blake family. She certainly had set a good example for everyone. Not that they wouldn't have done the same, but many had feared their own families might fall ill. A man couldn't fault them for that. Still, she was turning out to be a blessing for the whole community, not just the Double Bar M.

Today she looked mighty pretty in her green Sunday dress and perky little matching hat. His gaze drifted down to a gold brooch with an emerald in the center pinned to her lace collar. He'd never seen that pin before. To his shame, he couldn't stop the thought that she might have taken it from one of the Blake ladies. If only he could find the silver frame, he could put these suspicions to rest. But it was nowhere to be found.

After church, Miss Viola chatted with some ladies who now seemed eager to be her friends, and Robbie and Lavinia played tag with the other children. Even Pop stood apart with some of the older men, while Rob sat alone in the surrey and stewed over his dilemma.

"There's Will!" Suzette ran toward the road, waving at a trio of riders coming their way. "Hey, Will. Hey, Drew."

Many of the other churchgoers moved toward them with greetings.

Right away, Rob sized up the situation. Between his brothers, cowhand Jeb Sizemore rode with his hands tied to the pommel of his saddle. So this was the would-be rustler. Who were his partners? And why had both of his brothers left the herd without trustworthy leadership?

Pop hurried to the front of the group, Sheriff Reilly close behind him. Rob jumped down from the surrey and joined them.

"What've you got there, Will?" Pop looked like he might pop his buttons. "Caught him red-handed, eh?"

"Yessir. And here's one of the running brands he was using." Will untied the iron rod from his saddle and handed it to the sheriff. "You'll be wanting this for evidence."

"*One* of the brands?" Rob moved up next to Pop.

"Yep." Will gave Sizemore a smug look. "He didn't know I'd teamed up with Martinez's trail boss to keep an eye out for rebranding. He had that one for Regalo Del Rey ranch, too." He nodded to Andrew, who handed the sheriff a second rod.

"Martinez's man?" Rob scowled at Will. "And you trusted him?"

Will winced before stiffening his spine. "If you can trust me with our herd of cattle, you can trust me to make decisions like that."

"Now, boys." Pop's voice boomed out. "We'll sort

this out when we get home. Sheriff, we'll leave this scalawag in your capable hands. Will, you and your brother get on home and clean up so you can enjoy some of Miss Viola's fine cooking."

"Come on, Sizemore." The sheriff gripped the bridle of the man's horse. "If that's your real name. I have a feeling you've seen the inside of more than one jail cell."

Rob stared at Sizemore. He'd always considered himself a good judge of a person's character, yet he'd failed when he hired this one. Turning back to the surrey, he saw Miss Viola chatting with the children, keeping their attention as she always did. He'd yet to figure her out. Was she the wise mother figure his children needed to teach them honesty and morality? Or was she a thief? How would he ever learn the truth?

"Bye, Will." Suzette gave Rob's brother a sweet smile.

Dirty from head to foot, Will touched the brim of his hat and gave her a crooked grin. "Miss Suzette."

Rob shook his head. So now it was *Miss* Suzette. If Will addressed her with that formality, he was recognizing that she was all grown up. Next he'd be hogtied and dragged to the altar. Rob couldn't help feeling a little bit jealous. At least Will had fallen for a lady Rob knew to be honest.

As he drove the surrey onto the property, he saw Patrick Ahern coming out of the barn lugging a bale of hay. He tossed it over the fence into the corral where some of the horses were waiting for their dinner. There was another man Rob had misjudged, only in the wrong direction. Ahern had never cottoned to Sizemore, so it was unlikely he was in cahoots with him about the brands.

At least Rob hadn't accused Ahern to his face, so he wouldn't have to apologize to the Irishman.

As for Will trusting Martinez, a known outlaw, Rob would have to take his brother to task about that. If the Lord was merciful, they wouldn't lose their entire herd to the Mexican and his henchmen before Rob had a chance to ride up and take care of the matter himself.

On Monday, seven young ladies attended class, led by Suzette. Viola came close to tears as they sat around the table and gazed at her expectantly. After settling Lavinia at the small side table, she stood before them and made a list of their names.

"Juanita Mendez and Isabella Martinez will join us as soon as their health is restored." She looked for any reaction that might suggest opposition to having the Mexican girls in the class. Instead, she saw only accepting smiles. In fact, several had chatted with Elena before class began.

With Hosmer's *The Young Lady's Book* in hand, she gave the new girls an overview of the lessons.

"It is up to us, the ladies, to bring civilization to our community, first of all through our inner integrity and poise but also through our outward manners. While we know our community is populated by good-hearted people, we also want to be sure our manners reflect what is best."

With her students asking questions and showing eagerness to learn proper etiquette, Viola's morning passed quickly. She dismissed the girls and sent them on their way with the charge to practice their posture and voice modulation.

As she walked back toward the house, the thunder of horses galloping down the drive startled her. She pulled Lavinia to the side as Señor Martinez and three of his vaqueros stopped beside her in a cloud of dust.

"Señorita Brinson, can you please direct me to Señor Mattson?" The anxiety on his handsome face caused her heart to race.

"I believe he's down by the river. They have been working—"

He didn't wait for the rest of her answer. *"Vamos, hombres."* They rode off.

"What's the matter?" Lavinia stared up at Viola.

Viola managed a smile. "Shall we go find out?" Despite her concerns, she didn't run, for that would display alarm and frighten Lavinia.

At the house, she found Mr. Mattson loading his rifle. "Miss Viola, you stay here in the house with Lavinia." He started toward the back door.

"Lavinia, go find Puff and see if she wants some milk." Viola followed Mr. Mattson outside and caught his arm. "You must tell me what is happening."

"That Mexican and his henchmen came here to attack—"

"No, no. They are not here to cause trouble." She'd seen their faces, and they were not the faces of men intent upon evil.

He pulled away. "You leave it to us men, little lady. Now get back in the house." He scurried away.

Eyes wide with fear, Lavinia came outside carrying Puff. "Are they going to shoot us?"

Viola knelt down to her level. "Why would you think that?"

"Yesterday Robbie said they're cattle thieves."

"No, my darling, I am sure they are not. You have nothing to fear." But if she truly believed that, why was her heart hammering against her ribs?

At the sound of rapidly approaching horses, Rob lifted his head, and his blood ran cold. "Martinez!" He yelled to the other men as he raced up the riverbank, dropped his shovel and released the restraining strap on his holster. He'd been too busy to practice his quick draw, but Will was pretty fast. With his brothers and the four other men, maybe they could drive off the Mexicans. But what about Robbie? At nine years old, his son didn't need to be in the middle of a gunfight.

"Señor Mattson, I have news." Martinez reined his horse to a stop some fifteen feet away. "*El diluvio*, he is coming." He waved a yellow paper. "My cousin in Alamosa sent the telegram."

"Who's coming?" Rob's nerves settled as confusion took over. Apparently, Martinez hadn't come to start a range war.

"Señor Mattson." Mendez stepped up beside him. "It is the flood you expected. It is coming."

"You must move your herd up from your lower pasture." Martinez waved toward the south. "I and my vaqueros will help, *sí*?"

"*Sí*. Gracias!" Will shouted as he thumped Rob's arm. "Rob, we need to saddle up and get our bull up from the pasture."

"Right." Rob shook off his momentary stupor and ran up the hill. In that pasture they had thirty head of breeding stock and their expensive bull, all too valuable to risk in the mountains. If they were swept away in the flood, the Double Bar M would be ruined. "Robbie, go up to the house and take care of your sister and Miss Viola."

Robbie dashed away while Rob's brothers and the other men ran for their horses.

Rob approached Martinez. "I'm mighty grateful for the warning."

"*Sí*. But we have no time to talk. What would you have me to do?"

"Head down to the pasture and start rounding up the herd. If you can manage the bull, get him first and bring him up, then the rest." Charlemagne was mighty cantankerous, but maybe they could wrangle him. If not, the bull favored Drew, so he might have to go after him.

"We can do this." Martinez waved to his men. "*Vamos.*"

Would wonders never cease? Despite Rob's distrust of the man and the way he'd rebuffed him, Martinez had come to the rescue. Shaking his head, Rob headed for the barn to fetch his horse.

Carrying his rifle, Pop ran toward him with the gait of a much younger man. "What's happening? Where's Martinez?"

Rob paused long enough to explain. "Why don't you go back to the house and make sure the young'uns are all right?" He strode toward the barn again.

Pop kept pace beside him. "I know it's not the young'uns you're worried about, son, but I'll be all right. It's time I got back to running my own ranch instead of leaving it all on your shoulders."

"Yessir." This was not the time to argue.

Drew had already saddled Rob's horse as well as his own. Leaving Pop to saddle his mount, they rode out ahead of the others and met up with Martinez and his men. About half of the cattle had been rounded up, and the vaqueros now drove them up the hill far out of the broader riverbed.

As expected, Charlemagne wouldn't budge, not even to follow his cows. He pawed the ground with one front hoof and snorted, threatening to gore anybody who came close. Drew dismounted several yards away from the bull and spoke in his peacemaking voice.

Rob held his hand up to keep the other men from approaching. With a wave, he directed them to skirt the scene and go after the rest of the herd. He stayed close in case Drew needed his help. If need be, he'd shoot the bull rather than lose his brother, but it would be a terrible loss.

"Come on, old man," Drew said. "Let's get out of this sun and go up to the barn." He held a lariat behind his back and pulled a carrot from his pocket. "I know you want this, so just mosey on over here and you can have it."

Charlemagne snorted and stamped again, then slowly lumbered toward Drew. Pleased to be munching on the carrot, he didn't seem to mind the rope going around his neck.

"There's more where that came from." Drew scratched the bull's head. "Let's go now."

Huffing out a sigh of relief, Rob followed his brother in case Charlemagne changed his mind about cooperating. He didn't and was soon in the special pen they'd made for him when he'd broken out of the last one.

Within two hours, Will and the other men brought the rest of the herd into the front pasture by the road. They'd even saved the new salt licks Rob had foolishly put out last week before the river gradually began to overflow its banks.

After Rob saw everything settled, he rode to the back of the house. To his surprise, Miss Viola, the laundry ladies and the children had set up a table and were serving sandwiches, cookies and coffee to the men. Martinez stood a little too close to the lady for Rob's liking, but when she deliberately stepped away from the man, Rob ceased his worrying.

"Martinez." He held out his hand. "I don't know how to thank you. I also don't know why you would help us."

Martinez gripped his hand and shook. "Do not the Holy Scriptures tell us to help our neighbors? Your brothers discover the bandido who would steal our cattle and save both our herds. We work together, *si*?"

Rob grunted. *"Sí."* He couldn't entirely release his concerns about this man until he talked to Will, but it sure would be good if they could put all animosity behind them. The Colfax County War, fought over land grants and settlers' rights, had seen too many men killed, so a petty range war between two ranchers would make no sense.

Martinez sipped from his cup. "Ah, señorita, your coffee is *excelente*. And these cookies are *delicioso*. You must give *mi hermanita* the recipe, no?"

"Why, thank you, señor." The flush on Miss Viola's face from the heat of the day made her even prettier than usual. She smiled at Martinez, whose fancy duds didn't appear any worse for wear from his dusty afternoon of herding cattle. "I'll give Isabella the recipe next Monday when she comes for class."

"Got any more coffee?" Rob eyed Miss Viola.

"Yes, of course." She filled a cup and gave it to him, along with the smile that always caused that stirring in his chest.

"Amigo." Martinez nudged Rob's arm. *"Un momento."*

"Sure." Rob followed the man several yards away from the table. "What can I do for you?"

"The señorita, she is not, eh, *prometida*, promised, is she?"

"Uh, no. Why do you ask?"

Glancing at Miss Viola, Martinez smiled respectfully. "Then may I have your permission to call upon her?"

Rob wanted to laugh but thought better of it. Miss Viola hadn't shown the slightest interest in the Mexican. "Well… I don't know. She's—"

A distant rumble interrupted him. A dozen or so wild rabbits dashed up the hill and across the pasture, followed by two coyotes that seemed not to notice their usual prey. Instead, they and various other wildlife all ran for their lives. The rumble grew to a roar.

"Here she comes!" Pop yelled.

"Will, Drew, you and the men go down to the barn and hitch up the wagons and the surrey. Bring them up by the house." Rob scanned the property, searching for other potential problems. Except for the bad flood four years ago, the yearly deluges rarely reached the upper barn, but they never knew how high the water would rise.

Miss Viola touched Rob's arm. "Shall I pack a bag

for the children in case we need to leave?" Her voice sounded calm, as always. The trust in her eyes, trust in *him*, gave him the answer he needed for Martinez. No, she wasn't promised, but she also wasn't available for courting.

If anyone was going to court Miss Viola Brinson, he would be the one.

Her heart racing, Viola gazed up into Robert's brilliant blue eyes as he stared down at her. Despite the more imminent danger of the flood, she knew her heart was also in danger. Any moment now, the intense protectiveness she saw in his expression could turn to mistrust and hostility. She could never understand what she'd done to cause the change.

"No. Packing might just scare them." He took off his hat and ran a dusty sleeve over his equally dusty forehead. "The flood may reach the barn, but it won't reach us here on the bluff." He gave her that little grin that made her heart jump.

"Very well." She turned her attention to the river. Living in Norfolk, she'd experienced many hurricanes, which had brought violent winds, rain and rising water upon the land. Here, although the ground beneath her feet had begun to shudder like an earthquake from the coming deluge, the day was clear, and the wind no stronger than usual. To her surprise and relief, no great wall of water moved along the riverbed like a mighty ocean wave breaking onshore. Instead, the flow widened rapidly and increased in speed, and the level rose, bringing with it branches, trees and dead animals.

Lavinia moved closer to her and took her hand. Even Robbie seemed agitated.

"Children," she said, "shall we watch the water rise? Isn't it interesting? Did you know the Rio Grande is much like the Nile River in Egypt? It floods every year, bringing nutrients needed to help the vegetation grow."

Robert gave her a sidelong look, then winked. "Always the teacher."

She hid a grin. He really shouldn't wink at her, but to her shame, she'd come to love it when he did. "Nature is the teacher. We simply must pay attention to it. Children, look." She pointed to several snakes slithering up the hill. "They are fleeing the flood. I see a red racer and a garter snake. Those are harmless. What do you see?"

Lavinia hid her face in Viola's skirt.

"I see a rattler!" Robbie cried. "Dad, can I shoot it?"

Robert looked at Viola before answering. "No, son. If we give him a wide berth, he won't trouble us. He's just runnin' scared like the others."

Soon the roar of the flood drowned out all conversation. It lapped up close to the top of the levee, pulling away portions of the hard-packed soil Robert and his men had worked so hard to put in place. She saw his shoulders slump but could think of no words to encourage him. The flood would have to play out as it would. *Lord, please have mercy on this family. On all the families in the path of the flood.*

"Señorita, may I speak with you?" Señor Martinez extended a hand toward the front of the house. "I believe we'll be able to hear each other better over there."

Without thinking, Viola looked at Robert. While she

didn't require his permission, she had a strange longing for him to intervene. But he was looking toward the river and didn't seem to notice her conversation with Señor Martinez.

"Come along, Lavinia. It's not so loud in the front yard. Bring Puff."

Señor Martinez winced in his charming way, but he also smiled. He must have hoped they would be alone. When they arrived at their destination, he invited Viola to sit with him on the front porch. They settled in two chairs while Lavinia chased her kitten on the grass.

"This is a beautiful ranch, señorita. I think you are *muy* happy here, *si*?"

"I am content." Oh, dear. She'd chosen too mild a word. His expression changed from resigned to hopeful.

"I would be honored if you would visit my hacienda. And of course Isabella would be delighted to have her teacher visit."

"Well, I—" How could she refuse his invitation without insulting him? How could she accept without giving him the wrong idea? "Perhaps…"

To her relief, she was interrupted when Robert's boots thumped on the wooden porch boards. "Say, Martinez. Why did your family establish Regalo del Rey ranch so far from the river? Was it to avoid these floods?"

Viola gave him a welcoming smile. Señor Martinez, however, looked none too happy at his coming. Remembering Robert's hostility toward him, she hoped they would not argue. Perhaps his friendly question about the man's property indicated a change of mind.

"Ah, that is the tragedy, Robert Mattson." Señor Martinez sighed dramatically. "You know my great-grand-father received from the king of Spain the land grant situated on a bluff like yours. Hence the name Regalo del Rey... Gift of the King. But the river, it changed course one year, moving far from us. This is the way of things." He shrugged. "But you must no longer call it Regalo del Rey. At last *Navidad*, when God so merci-fully spoke to my heart, I give my *rancho* a new name, *Regalo si el Salvador. ¿Entiendes?* You understand?"

Giving the man a warm smile, Robert nodded. "Gift of the Savior. Yes, I understand." Then he shrugged. "And I hope you will understand me, my friend." He glanced at Viola. "My father needs Miss Viola to run his house, and I need her to teach my young'uns."

The gentleman's eyes narrowed briefly. "*Sí, mi amigo.* I understand." He stood and touched the brim of his sombrero. "I do not think the flood will cause you any serious harm, so I and my vaqueros will go now."

"Thanks again, *amigo*. You have been a good neigh-bor. I won't forget your coming here to warn us." The two men shook hands, and Señor Martinez strode away.

"And just what, exactly, was that all about?" Viola fully understood, but for some foolish reason, she wanted Robert to say it.

He shrugged and gave her that charming little grin of his. "Nothing much. I just noticed he wanted to come calling on you." His blue eyes twinkled. "And you didn't appear to cotton to the idea."

"Oh, I see." Viola stepped down from the porch, and he followed her. What a thrill his protectiveness gave her. Now she wouldn't have to insult the gentleman by refusing him herself. More than that, it hinted at Robert's own feelings for her. "And you took the responsibility of answering for me?"

"No, no. Not at all. In fact, you were managing things quite well." He ran a hand down his black-stubbled jaw, and dust showered down onto his shoulder. "But as I said, we need you here." He walked toward the corner of the house.

Foolishly, she swung around in front of him to keep him from leaving. "You need me here?" Her pulse raced. What was she doing?

"Sure. Pop needs you. Lavinia and Robbie need you. Will, Drew..."

"But not you, of course."

For more seconds than she could count, he stared down at her, frowning, as though looking for something. Her heart hammered against her ribs. Did he notice her trembling?

At last, his expression softened. "I—" His voice sounded rough, and he cleared his throat. "It's good that you're here." Like Señor Martinez, he touched the brim of his hat before walking away.

Her face flaming, Viola couldn't move. What had she hoped to accomplish by confronting him? Some grand declaration? From *this* taciturn man? But then, hadn't he backed up her refusal of Señor Martinez's request in the most diplomatic manner? As disappointed and embarrassed as she was, she would have to be satisfied with that.

Chapter Fourteen

The ranch hands took turns watching the water level. If it rose any higher than the top of the levee, Rob planned to empty the lower barn to save the rest of the equipment, maybe even build temporary storage for it up on the bluff.

Some problems were easier to solve than others. While he'd been able to help Miss Viola fend off Martinez's request to court her, he couldn't stir up the gumption to do it himself. But why not? What was courting anyway? Wasn't it just two people spending time together to see if they were compatible? He should try to spend more time with her away from the rest of the family. He needed to be careful though. After one unsuccessful marriage, he couldn't stand the idea of a second failure.

Wait a minute. When had he started thinking of Miss Viola and marriage in the same sentence? After all, he had to consider Lavinia and Robbie. Then there was the missing silver picture frame. If he found out she took it, he'd have to deal with that. As for that gold pin, he'd wait to see if the Blake ladies made a fuss about it. He was a coward for not just having it out with her. But Pop would surely kick up a ruckus if Rob accused her, maybe even begin to decline again. Rob couldn't risk it.

But Miss Viola wasn't a coward. When he'd witnessed her courage about the flood, when he'd looked into those pretty green eyes and had seen how she trusted him, he couldn't believe she was a thief. Besides, he liked being around her. Her calm ways affected everyone for the good, especially his children. So he would try to spend more time with her without calling it courting.

Yep, he was a coward. But it was the only way he could figure out how to solve the problem of being attracted to her while fearing she was a thief.

Will had convinced Rob that Ranse Cable and Old Fuzzy, along with the four other cowhands, could manage the cattle herd in the summer grazing range. Then when Will offered to go for the mail for the third time in a week, Rob's suspicions grew about his next younger brother being sweet on Suzette. Every trip to town gave him a chance to see her, especially since her father was the postmaster. He rarely returned home until midafternoon.

Today, though, he came home before noon and handed Rob a letter. "This is probably what you've been looking for."

"Well, I'll be switched." Rob pulled out his pocketknife and slit the envelope open. "I'd begun to doubt Mr. Lucien Martin was still alive after all these years." He scanned the letter, then reread it slowly. "Of all the..."

His head felt like it was about to explode. Some people made such clever excuses for their sins that they could persuade a saint.

"What's it say?" Will tried to look over Rob's shoulder.

Rob moved away. "I'll tell everybody over dinner."

"I got another one here for Miss Viola." Will held up the envelope. "From one Mr. Endicott Brinson, *Esquire*." He chuckled. "I always knew she came from quality."

"A fancy word at the end of a man's name doesn't always mean quality." Rob had a strong impulse to snatch the letter, but he had no right to read her mail. Just what did this brother of hers want?

Viola ladled out the soup for everyone, then took her place at the dining room table. The letter Will had given her seemed to burn a hole in her pocket, but she would wait to read it. When she was a child, Endicott had rarely spoken to her in a kind way, and he'd been all too pleased to send her away to Charleston to care for Maybelle's orphaned child. She dismissed her unhappy memories and turned her attention to Robert. The letter he held would no doubt settle his mind about the money he had been sending to his late wife.

"Pop, you'll be glad to know Lucien Martin and his family are well and prospering."

"Good to know that." Mr. Mattson waved his hand impatiently. "Now get to the good stuff."

Everyone laughed except Robert. "Turns out Edward Purcell is a decent man and an honest lawyer. He wasn't pleased by the way the minister and his wife treated Lavinia and was real happy when Miss Viola arrived."

Viola's heart ached at the memory of the frightened child she'd encountered last fall. From their first meeting, Lavinia had latched onto her as if she were a lifeline.

"As to your letter not reaching me until shortly before you came here—" He looked at Viola. "He discovered they had withheld it until he demanded they send it." He snorted. "Turns out the so-called minister wasn't a man of God at all. He was a charlatan who preached that Christians should take a vow of poverty, and all the while, he cheated his congregation out of their money. When he found out I'd been sending money to Maybelle, he tried to get the bank to release the funds to them. They're still at it. Says they deserve payback for all they did for Lavinia." Robert's voice took on a hard, angry edge. "And Lucien says Purcell quit advising them because they're still trying to adopt Lavinia to get at it."

Viola saw the terror in Lavinia's tear-filled eyes. Robert should have waited to announce this news until the child was in bed. "Well, imagine that." She used her bright, cheerful tone, and spoke perhaps a little too loudly. "What nonsense."

Robert caught her unspoken message. He gave Lavinia a big grin. "Yes, ma'am. Downright silly, if you ask me. You've got a daddy right here, and nobody's ever going to take you away from me."

While everyone echoed Robert's proclamation, Lavinia jumped down from her chair and ran into his arms. "I love you, Daddy." She sobbed into his shoulder.

Whispering his love in return, he caressed her hair

with such a gentle gesture that Viola could no longer hold back her tears. How different from the way he'd ignored his daughter when they first arrived. Her tears ran down her cheeks, but thankfully, everyone's attention was on the child and her father, so she had time to dab them away with her napkin.

"We all love you, sweet pea." Andrew's eyes had turned red, too. "You're our little prairie rose."

"Now, which is she?" William smirked at his brother. "A sweet pea or a rose?"

"Enough of that." Mr. Mattson banged his hand on the table. "We'll hear the rest after the children are in bed. Let's eat."

That afternoon, Viola decided to work on her new dress. Mr. Mattson had asked about it, and she certainly wanted to finish it before the party she'd planned for her students. After hearing Robert's good news, she'd lost interest in reading her own letter. Endicott had never done anything but scold her, so she was in no hurry to learn about his latest complaint. Instead, she wanted to bask in the knowledge that Robert now knew for certain she'd not been involved in the confusion about the money he'd sent to Maybelle.

After the children went to bed, the adults gathered in the parlor. Viola used the time to darn Lavinia's stockings.

"All right, Rob. Let's hear the rest of that letter," Mr. Mattson said.

"It's not much." Robert unfolded the page. "I asked him about Lavinia's clothes and toys, and he said that so-called minister and his wife wanted to show this 'rich' little girl how other people lived so she wouldn't value belongings. It was all part of their scheme to extort more money from me." He huffed out a laugh. "Rich? Not by a long shot. They sure were barking up the wrong tree. We live from one year to the next raising these cattle."

"Their actions were outrageous." Viola had not been impressed by the couple, but in the six months she had been in Charleston, she hadn't realized the depth of their scheming. What clever crooks they were, pretending to be honest, but, as the old saying went, so cold and calculating that butter wouldn't melt in their mouths. "Right when Lavinia needed to feel secure, they took away the things she was most familiar with."

The Mattson brothers mumbled their similar disgust.

"I'll ask Blake if he can wire for the money." Robert refolded the letter and returned it to the envelope. "He'll know what to do."

"Good plan." Mr. Mattson stood. "With all that settled, I'm going to bed."

"Sleep well." Viola set aside her mending and picked up her shawl. "Robert, if you think it is safe, I would like to go out on the front porch and watch the moon rise. It's a full moon tonight."

His eyebrows arched with surprise. "I'll go with you in case the coyotes are roaming around."

"Oh. Very well." She'd planned to enjoy a few quiet moments to herself, though in truth, she was not disappointed. Maybe now they could get past the last of his doubts about her.

With his family always around, Rob hadn't found a way to get alone with Miss Viola. Why hadn't he thought sooner to invite her out to the front porch in the evening? They settled in two wooden chairs, from where they could see the glow of the moon coming over the distant eastern prairie. The breeze carried her gardenia perfume in his direction, reminding him of Mother's gardenia bushes that grew outside their home in Charleston, where she now lived. The pleasant childhood memory relaxed him. But now that he was here at last with Miss Viola, what should he say?

"Nice night." *Very smart, Mattson. Just the way to charm a lady.* It had been so long since he'd courted, he had no idea how to begin.

"Yes. It is pleasant now that the wind has died down. The moon certainly is beautiful. Back East in Norfolk, and later in Charleston, I always enjoyed watching it rise over the ocean."

Rob wasn't watching the moon. On the shadowed porch, the dim light from the lantern in the window beside her shone on her profile, revealing a relaxed smile. Mercy, she was beautiful. He should tell her that, but somehow the words wouldn't come.

"Mr. Martin's letter must have relieved your mind."

"It did." He should say more. Should apologize for suggesting she had somehow used the money for herself. Again, the words stuck in his throat. "What about your letter? What did your brother have to say for himself?"

"I have no idea."

"You didn't read it?" Stupid question. If she'd read it, she would know what it said.

She laughed softly. "If you knew my eldest brother, you would understand why I am putting it off."

"Tell me about him."

She gazed at him for a moment, then sighed. "Endicott is rather overbearing, as are most eldest brothers of my acquaintance. They think they know everything and can tell their younger siblings what to do."

"Hey, watch what you say." He punctuated his warning with a grin. "I'm the oldest brother in my family."

"I rest my case." She gave him that smile that always turned his insides to mush.

"Oh, now—"

"Just ask your brothers." Her teasing expression turned serious. "I am thankful Endicott gave me permission to care for Lavinia, even though his motivation was not to help our distant cousin."

An odd, protective feeling stirred in Rob's chest. "No? Then what was it?"

She sighed, as though surrendering to end-of-the-day weariness. "The family had not known what to do with me for several years, not since a few years after our parents died." She stared at him for a moment. "Do you know what a redundant woman is?" She stood and faced the darkened front yard. "I shouldn't have said that."

Now Rob saw red. What a passel of miserable miscreants, treating their own kin that way. He stood and turned her to face him. "Viola, you're not a redundant woman in this house. I don't know what we would have done without you these past few months." Had she noticed he didn't say *Miss* Viola? That he wanted to dispense with that formality and get to know her better?

Even in the dim light, he could see her tearing up. His anger vanished, replaced by an unfamiliar tenderness in his chest.

"Thank you, Robert. I am gratified to know that."
She stood still, staring up at him.

Like a magnet, her gaze pulled him closer, urging
him to kiss her. She seemed to move closer to him, too.
Should he complete what they both seemed to want?

A door slammed inside the house. She jumped back.
"Good night, Robert."

Just like that, she was gone, leaving him with more
guilt about his past treatment of her than satisfaction
over his first fumbling attempt to court her. But at least
now he knew a little more about her. And just maybe
he could find a way to make it up to her for the way
her family had treated her. As for the silver frame, even
if she'd taken it, he'd forgive her. If he could forgive
Maybelle for all the grief she'd caused him, and especially Robbie—and he truly had forgiven her—then
he wouldn't hold it against Viola. They'd straighten it
out somehow.

Viola wanted to kick herself. Why had she said to
Robert what she'd never said aloud to anyone else, not
even Virginia? Now he would consider her someone
to be pitied.

Or not, if their almost-kiss was any indication. And
he'd insisted she was not redundant in this house. They
needed her. *They*, not he, despite that same almost-kiss.
But she could be satisfied with that. Perhaps she'd found
a home at last. No, best not to rest too comfortably in the
idea. Oh, why did her thoughts go around in circles that
way? And why oh why had she almost let him kiss her?

Determined to gather her wits, she found a kerosene
lantern and carried it up to the bedroom. Time to read

Endicott's letter. In the lantern's soft light, she slit open the envelope and pulled out the page.

> My dear Viola,
> I trust you are well. Diana and I miss you terribly, as do the children. Now that you have discharged your duty to Maybelle, we insist that you return to us.
>
> I am sure you will be interested to know that Albert and I have entered into a business partnership with Percy Magnuson, who will provide the funding if we agree to his terms. Mind you, this venture will bring us all great success, not to mention wealth.
>
> Poor Percy lost his dear wife last year and requires a mother for his four children. He is eager to see you again. Just think of it, my dear. At last you will have the opportunity to be of use to your family.
>
> Please return to us as soon as possible.
> Your loving brother,
> Endicott

Viola could hardly contain her laughter. If she'd read this letter earlier today, she might have resigned herself to marrying the disgusting middle-aged man who had tried to maul her at one of Endicott's parties four years ago, long before his poor wife died. He'd been the first one who called her redundant after she'd rebuffed him.

But Robert had dismissed such a cruel claim about her. Had said she was needed here. Despite her earlier confusion, she held that thought close to her heart, for being needed was preciously close to being wanted.

She set the letter on the vanity and prepared for bed, but sleep would not come.

How cruel of Endicott to claim she'd been of no use to the family. Had she not cared for his children, without payment, so he and Diana could go off to Europe for a year? Had she not cooked for Albert's family, without payment, when their cook quit? Even her sisters had not defended her against their husbands' unwanted advances. And now they thought she could be summoned back to Norfolk like a servant and sold into marriage so they could ensure the success of their business venture. Her first reaction had been to laugh. Now she could only cry herself to sleep.

And wish that Robert truly had kissed her.

Once Viola went to bed, decency prevented Rob from looking in on Lavinia to be sure she was sleeping well. But when he heard mewling sounds coming through the door of the room they shared, he was tempted to discover the cause. Maybe it was Lavinia's cat, but he doubted it. Viola must have received bad news from her family and was shedding a few tears. Even though it was none of his business, he would ask her about it tomorrow. With his work on the levee stalled until the river subsided later in the summer, he had fewer chores to do around the ranch. That would give him a chance to spend more time with her. She'd opened up to him about the way her family treated her, which still angered him. If he asked just the right way, maybe she would confide in him.

In the morning, however, she wore her usual sunny smile as she served breakfast to the family. How she managed to do that day after day, he had no idea. He couldn't decide whether to ask about the letter and risk her tears or ignore it completely. But then Pop solved his dilemma.

"Miss Viola, I know you received a letter yesterday. We were so caught up in Rob's news that I forgot to ask about yours." Pop helped himself to several pancakes and poured on maple syrup.

If Rob hadn't been watching her, he would have missed her wince. Real fast, she pasted on her pretty smile and shrugged.

"It was nothing important." She seemed to be avoiding eye contact with everyone, especially him. "However, I do want to discuss something truly important before Robbie gets up. I have heard a rumor that his birthday is coming in two weeks. What do you usually do to celebrate?" Now she gazed at Rob expectantly, causing his heart to jump. "Cake? Presents? A party with his friends?"

He didn't miss how she changed the subject, but that letter was anything but "not important." Even so, he let himself be diverted. "Sure. That'd be real nice."

She laughed. "Which?"

"All of them," Drew said. "That boy worked like a man on the levee. He deserves something special for his tenth birthday."

"Yep. He's all grown up now." Will nodded soberly. "Next year he can help us drive the herd up for summer grazing."

For a moment, worry crossed Viola's face. Then she

gave Will a chiding look. "I trust you do not mean that. Therefore I'll forego lecturing you on age-appropriate occupations for children." She waited until the laughter died down. "Do be thinking about what we should do so I can prepare." She glanced toward the inner door, then whispered, "I plan to sew another shirt for him, but is there something else he would like?"

While the others took her hint and whispered their ideas, Rob pressed a hand to his chest. Not because it hurt but because of the overwhelming...what? Gratitude? Affection? Maybe even the love he felt for this good woman. In only a few short months, she'd taken to his children like a natural mother. Being housekeeper and governess was not a job to her. She clearly enjoyed making this house a home for all of them. And, dared he hope, a home for herself where no one would ever think to call her redundant.

Rob looked at her hands. They'd healed well and were no longer reddened and chapped. That French hand cream he'd bought had done its job. And now he wanted to heal the inner woman who'd been so cruelly treated by her family. And maybe complete that interrupted kiss.

To please Mr. Mattson, Viola finished her dress that afternoon before cutting out Robbie's new blue chambray shirt. Sewing relaxed her and gave her a sense of satisfaction. It also gave her a chance to sort out her feelings about Endicott's letter, which she'd set aside until she could frame a respectful response. Recalling Mama's sweet patience and the excuses she made for all of her children's faults, she reminded herself of what she owed her older brothers. If not for that year of tending Endicott and Diana's home and children, she wouldn't have the skills to keep house for the Mattsons. If not for cooking for her brother Albert's family, she wouldn't have learned so many clever tricks in the kitchen, thanks to their former cook's notes in the cookbook she'd left behind.

Every time hurt and anger arose within her, she countered it with memories of her siblings' finer qualities and happier childhood memories. It didn't always work, but she had to try, or she would crumble under the fear that she would have to do as her brothers had asked. To keep herself from such a foolish notion, she wrote Endicott to say she was unable and unwilling to leave her present employment.

After tending the Blake ladies during their illness, Viola had not only gained new students for her classes, but church had become a pure pleasure for her. Of course, Pastor Daniel's sermons and the music always inspired her. In addition, the other women now accepted her, chatted with her after services and even hinted they might drop by the ranch for a visit. When the pastor preached about the blessing of hospitality, Viola decided she must ask Mr. Mattson's permission to hold a tea for the ladies. Inviting the mothers would give her students an opportunity to display the lessons they had learned. And, dearest to her heart, it would prove to them she was a worthy member of their society. Perhaps even Mrs. Blake and Iris would attend. But first she would entertain Robbie's friends for his birthday party.

The morning of the party, Lavinia and Robbie were

all giggles as they bounced around the house like rubber balls. When the five guests arrived midmorning, Robert and his brothers took the boys outside to play baseball.

"Why can't I play, too?" Lavinia gazed longingly out the back door.

"They play too roughly, my darling. When you're a little older, you will be able to keep up with them." Viola took her hand and led her to the kitchen table. "Shall we finish decorating the cake?"

The shouts and thumps coming from the yard convinced her she'd made the right choice for her little charge. Her own nephews had never been permitted to make such noise or to be so rowdy. While she'd always appreciated that before, now she wondered if boys needed to be allowed to expend some of their youthful energy instead of suppressing it.

At dinnertime, the men and boys brought the rowdiness inside. With much jostling and teasing, they gathered around the dining room table for sandwiches and lemonade. While the others ate under the supervision of William and Andrew, Robert brought the wooden ice cream maker to the kitchen, where Viola poured in the creamy mixture she'd concocted. Robert then set about cranking the machine's handle.

After ten minutes or so, he added more ice and rock salt to the tub. "We make a good team, don't you think?" He winked at her.

As always, his winks made her heart skip. She probably should scold him but couldn't bring herself to do so.

"Don't you think?" he repeated, adding a funny little grin.

He was flirting with her! How on earth should she

respond? Recalling the way her sister Virginia used to flirt with her beaux, Viola lifted her chin and sniffed.

"A good team? You and I? Why, Mr. Robert Mattson, whatevah do you mean?"

After several minutes, he finished cranking, laid a tea towel over the ice cream maker and stepped over to her, still grinning impishly. He didn't speak, but merely stood there, gazing into her eyes. As always, his impressive height and strong male presence caused that odd little thrill to course through her. In spite of his active morning of playing ball in the heat, she could still catch the scent of his woody cologne, which added to his allure. Somehow she couldn't summon her inner old maid to dash such a foolish reaction. In fact, she could barely breathe.

"I mean," he murmured in his baritone voice, "you and I work well together." He reached up and brushed a wayward strand of hair from her face. "And I hope we can continue to do so."

As if to confirm his wish, he kissed her cheek right below her ear. A pleasant shiver swept down her side, and her knees threatened to give way. Somehow she managed to grasp the back of a chair. "I believe—" Her voice wobbled. She cleared her throat. "I believe it is time to serve the cake and ice cream." With great difficulty, she brushed past him and took the everyday dessert plates from the cupboard. "We will use these. Such rowdy boys cannot be trusted with your mother's fine china."

Robert leaned down and spoke close to her ear, sending another pleasant shiver down her side. "We'll talk more about this later." He gave her a smug smile as he took the dishes from her, grazing her hands with his big rough fingers in a way that somehow didn't hurt.

That man! He knew how he affected her. And he had kissed her! On the cheek, but still a kiss. And she didn't possess a single weapon to defend herself from falling for him. Perhaps she should write to Endicott again, accept his offer, flee this place and protect herself from inevitable heartbreak.

Rob's hands shook so bad he almost dropped the small plates as he carried them to the dining room. What had gotten into him, teasing Viola that way? And giving in to the temptation to kiss her, even if just on the cheek?

Easy answer. Without even trying, she'd captured his heart, and he wanted to let her know. As she'd poured the ice cream mixture into the tin canister, her rose-scented perfume had mixed with the vanilla flavoring to create a heady fragrance. She looked so pretty, so accomplished, so...*right* in this house. He'd known he had to say something. But instead of talking about their being a good team, which they were, he should have just told her how pretty she looked. How glad everybody was that she'd come to live here. How glad *he* was. Did she understand from the kiss what he felt for her?

She brought in the cake and set it in front of Robbie, whose wide grin and shining eyes showed what a fine time he was having. She even taught the boys a clever little ditty to express their good wishes for health, happiness and many more birthdays to come. Her sweet singing voice, which he'd begun to notice in church and when she sang lullabies to Lavinia, only added to her appeal. Clearly, she loved to entertain, even if it was rascally boys. She'd made a fine hostess when his youngest brothers and the Sharp family had come over that one Sunday. And next week when the ladies came for tea, she would truly shine. This woman had brought much happiness to this house.

No matter what he found out about the silver frame, he wouldn't mention it. After all, if they married, everything of his would be hers as well.

"Isn't it about time for presents?" Will had bought Robbie a new hat and was eager to give it to him.

The boys cheered as they set their gifts on the table—an arrowhead, a jar of honey, a whittled toy soldier and other items, most made at home with varying degrees of skill. Lavinia had embroidered an awkward *RDM* in the corner of a man-sized handkerchief made from an old bedsheet. Rob suspected Viola had secured the stitching. The lady herself presented Robbie with the new chambray shirt she'd made. Pop gave him a new hand-carved board game. Drew gave him a pocketknife. And finally, Rob set a long, brown-paper-wrapped gift in front of his son.

"My rifle!" Robbie tore off the paper and held up the gun, careful not to point it at anyone. "Thanks, Dad."

"We'll start your shooting lessons tomorrow." Rob had received his first gun from Pop at ten, horrifying his mother. But his shooting skill had come in handy as they crossed the continent from South Carolina to their new home in New Mexico Territory, both for protection and provision. Seeing the light in Viola's eyes as she viewed the rifle, he recalled her request to learn how to shoot. He still needed to decide what would be the best gun for her to carry for safety.

After their guests left, Rob surveyed the mess. If he helped Viola clean it up, he'd have another chance to talk with her.

"Miss Viola." Drew picked up some of the last crumbs from the cake plate and popped them in his mouth. "Can I help you clean up?"

"I'll do it." Rob jerked his head toward the door, silently ordering his brother from the room.

Drew smirked. "Sure. I'll just go and, uh, find something else to do." He laughed as he walked out.

Viola appeared to be concentrating especially hard on the dishes she was washing. Rob grabbed a tea towel from the rack Pop had hung on the wall and picked up a wet plate.

Viola gasped softly. "I didn't see you there." Her cheeks turned pink. "You do not have to help me. I'm sure you have other things to do."

"Nope." He stood next to her, his shoulder almost touching hers. She edged away like a skittish filly. He decided not to follow, or he'd ruin everything. Maybe she was afraid he'd kiss her again. "Say, it's been two weeks since you got that letter from your brother, and you still haven't told me what he had to say." He hadn't meant to blurt out the question like that. Now he *had* ruined everything.

"Oh." Her voice sounded thin and high. "Nothing to worry about." Her shoulders slumped just a little, then she straightened. "He has found a—" She pulled in a deep breath. "A position for me in Norfolk and wants me to return as soon as possible."

Rob didn't realize he'd dropped the plate until it crashed onto the floor and shattered into a dozen pieces.

Chapter Fifteen

Muffling a scream, Viola jumped. "Mercy, Robert. Are you all right?"

His dropped jaw and the paleness beneath his tanned complexion said he was anything but all right. "W-what sort of position?"

As she fetched the broom to sweep up the shattered plate, guilt crept in. Why had she given him her news so casually? Because for one wild moment, she'd decided to throw out a veiled challenge to see if he would say he cared, that his kiss on her cheek had truly meant something. If his face was any indication, he did care, but she needed to hear the words.

"Actually, he has a commercial opportunity that my marriage to his business partner will solidify." No, no, no. She should not have said that. Why was she risking her future this way? After all, had she not turned down Endicott's offer?

"Ha!" Rob took the broom from her and attacked the mess with a vengeance, sweeping the shards into the corner and resting the broom against the wall above them. He returned to her and gripped her shoulders. "Viola, if you marry anybody, it's gonna be me." He blinked, as though surprised by his own words.

Her eyes burned, and her knees threatened to buckle. "W-why, Robert, you do not have to rescue me."

He stared into her eyes with such tender intensity that she felt her doubts begin to fade. "Why not? You've rescued this whole family. We want you here. We need you here. And with your say so, I'm going to write that brother of yours and tell him he can find another way to *solidify* his opportunity."

Her heart dropped. Her threatening tears subsided. "I see. Well, it is a decision I'll need to make." And had already made. She pulled away from him. "Now, I must finish these dishes so I can begin supper."

He touched her shoulder, but the contact failed to give her the usual thrill. "What did I say wrong?"

She gave him a quick smile, then concentrated on her work. "Nothing." It had all been quite lovely, but he hadn't made it personal between the two of them. If he couldn't say he loved her, she couldn't bring herself to stay. Was she being foolish? Probably. But she could see no difference between keeping house for a businessman who didn't love her and a rancher who would not confess that he did.

"So you won't marry me?"

"Oh." Foolish anger sent heat flooding her cheeks. "Did you propose?" Now she sounded like her often-cross eldest sister, Augusta.

He huffed out a long sigh. "I thought I did."

"No. You said you were going to marry me. And that—"

Before she could finish, he gripped her arms again,

pulled her close and kissed her right on her lips! Now her knees did buckle. If he hadn't been holding her, she would have fallen to the floor and shattered like the dish he'd dropped.

He moved back a few inches. "I'm not good with words. Can you live with that?"

She moved back a few more inches and grabbed a chair back. "I need to hear the right words. Can you live with that?" Where had she found the strength to challenge him that way?

He turned away, running a hand through his hair. Then he turned back to her wearing that impish grin. "All right, then. Will you marry me?"

She tried not to smile but failed. "Why do you want to marry me?"

"Because I—"

She could see the struggle in his face, but no matter how Maybelle had hurt him, she wouldn't accept anything less than a declaration of his deepest feelings. "Go on."

"I love you." It sounded more like an apology.

"There. That didn't hurt, did it?" *Viola, what are you doing?*

He stepped over and chucked her under the chin. "Your turn."

Now she laughed. "I love you, too, although I cannot imagine why."

He laughed and pulled her back into his strong arms. "Oh, Viola darlin', I can't imagine why either."

She leaned her head against his broad chest and could hear his heart pounding.

"So, will you marry me?" His heartbeat seemed faster.

She'd risked so much to bring him to this point. Now she understood what he was risking. "I would be very pleased to marry you, Robert *darlin'*."

As he kissed her again, this time with such intensity that she felt her own pulse increasing, she heard a soft male chuckle coming from the next room. Had Mr. Mattson been listening all this time? If so, that chuckle said all she needed to hear. Not only did the old gentleman approve of her, he also had probably planned it from the day he asked her to be his housekeeper.

She was wanted. She was loved by the man she loved. And she'd finally found a home.

The back door slammed, meaning someone was coming in. Rob didn't care. He could stand here holding Viola for the rest of his life as the calming comfort of her embrace seeped into his chest and healed more hurts than he could name.

The unmistakable sound of whining and whimpering cut into his thoughts.

"Hey, what's going on here?" Jared's needling voice made it clear he knew the answer to his own question.

Rob kissed Viola lightly before letting her go. "Sometimes I think I have too many brothers."

Laughing, she peered around him. "Oh, how adorable." She broke away and rushed to greet Jared and Cal, but mostly the black-and-white puppies they each held. She took one in her arms, not seeming to mind when it licked her face. "What a sweetie."

"Where's Robbie?" Cal held the second pup. "We thought we'd give him a choice of which one he wants."

Rob had forgotten about their promised gift. "I'll call him."

Pop must have already done so, because Robbie raced into the kitchen with Lavinia not far behind. Both children squealed happily, and each took a puppy.

"Well, I guess that answers that." Rob looked at Viola. "Do you mind two dogs to clean up after?"

She blinked in her adorable way. "It isn't my decision, Robert. You and Mr. Mattson must decide."

He tugged her to his side. "It's a family decision, you included."

"Whooeee!" Jared howled. "Big brother, I wondered when you would get your head on straight."

"Good job, Rob." Cal clapped him on the shoulder, then kissed Viola's cheek. "Welcome to the family, Miss Viola. Julia took one look at you last April and said it wouldn't be long."

"Thank you, Cal." Viola's face turned pink. "Are Julia and Emma well?"

Just like her to turn the attention away from herself. Rob loved her all the more for her concern for his expecting sisters-in-law.

"Hey, Pop." Jared nodded to their father. "What do you think?"

Pop chuckled. "I think I can help train these pups so it won't be so hard on our Miss Viola."

Lavinia's kitten chose that moment to enter the kitchen and head for her water dish. Lavinia set the puppy down, but before she could reach Puff, the pup decided to investigate this new arrival. Her tail suddenly three times its normal size, Puff hissed and arched her back, then scrambled up Rob's leg, digging tiny claws into him on her way to his shoulder.

"Ow." He couldn't help but laugh despite the sting she caused. He tried to grab her, but she was now climbing down his back and out of reach.

The puppies yipped and wiggled, clearly wanting to make friends with this tiny critter. By now, Lavinia was crying for her kitten. Drew and Will chose that moment to come in, their laughter and foolish comments adding to the confusion.

"Now, now." Viola gently tugged Puff from Rob's shirt and cuddled her out of the puppies' reach. "She isn't hurt, Lavinia, merely frightened."

"Don't mind the pups, sweetheart." Jared crouched down to Lavinia's eye level. "They're used to our cats, so they won't hurt her."

Rob rubbed his neck where the kitten had scratched him. "I'm more worried about Puff hurting the puppies."

"All right, now." Viola handed Puff to Lavinia. "Everyone out of the kitchen, or we won't be eating supper until midnight."

While more laughter erupted from the others, Rob could only gaze at his darling lady with admiration. Nothing ruffled her feathers.

"Robert, sit." She pointed to a chair. "I need to clean those scratches so they won't become infected."

"Yes, ma'am."

She dabbed medicinal alcohol on his neck, but he barely felt the sting. Just having her touch him, take care of him, soothed away all pain.

Viola watched as her nine students penned their invitations for next week's tea. If everyone accepted, the schoolhouse would be full to overflowing. Most important to her, if all the ladies came, it would mean they had accepted her into their community. Everything had to be absolutely perfect, from dust-free floors and furniture to the displayed papers the girls had written to the apple tarts Viola planned to make.

Ever since Robert declared his love last week, Viola had felt more at home with each passing day. Even the summer heat didn't bother her as she tended her housekeeping duties. With a home and a purpose and a man who loved her, she had never been so happy, even as her parents' cosseted youngest daughter. How glad she was that she had written Endicott to refuse Mr. Magnuson's offer.

The day before the tea, Viola scurried through the house, dusting and scrubbing while the children worked on their lessons at the dining room table. Maybe it was because Mrs. Blake might come up to the house at some point tomorrow, but Viola kept hearing Augusta's scolding voice in her mind. *You missed several spots, Viola. You are careless and lazy. No sensible man will ever have you.* In Viola's mind, the two women spoke with one voice. She enjoyed being diligent in her work, but she did not care for their nagging.

"Miss Viola, I finished my schoolwork." Robbie held up a slate with his arithmetic problems neatly computed. "May I go help Pop with his carving?"

"Me, too?" Lavinia jumped down from her chair, a hopeful look on her sweet face.

While she preferred to keep Lavinia close, perhaps it would do no harm for her to visit her grandfather. He would see to her safety, and Viola could get her work done.

"Yes, my darlings. Run along."

They scampered out the back door, and Viola stirred the wood in the firebox to be sure tonight's supper chickens would bake evenly. Then she mixed some biscuit dough.

As she rolled it out on the table, a sharp knock sounded on the front door.

Who could that be? Everyone in these parts came to the back door, a custom she'd learned to accept.

Brushing flour from her hands and hair from her forehead, she made her way through the house. Beyond the oval glass window in the door, she saw two gentlemen and a lady, all well-dressed. Her heart seemed to stop beating.

With a trembling hand, she opened the door. "Endicott. Augusta." An unpleasant shiver swept through her. Her earlier ruminations seemed to have summoned her eldest siblings and... "Mr. Magnuson."

"Just as I suspected." Augusta pulled the screen door open and charged through. "You look a fright. Flour all over you, and your hair a mess."

Suddenly an incompetent little girl again, Viola cringed. "Come in, gentlemen." She ushered them all into the parlor, exchanging pleasantries as best she could. "Please sit down. I'll make tea."

"And be sure to fix your hair before you rejoin us." Augusta sauntered around the parlor, swiping her white gloves over the side tables and mantelpiece.

Back in the kitchen, Viola's hands shook as she poured hot water into the teapot and spooned in tea leaves. When Robbie slammed through the back door, she almost dropped the porcelain pot.

"Miss Viola, can we have some cookies?" He grinned in his adorable way. "Pop sent me."

"Yes, of course." While she placed the cookies on a plate, Robbie peered through the inner door. "Who's that?"

"Shh. Just run along." Odd. She hadn't noticed how scruffy Robbie looked earlier. He needed a haircut and…no! She wouldn't let Augusta's presence affect her thoughts toward the children.

In the parlor, she set the tea tray on the coffee table and smiled at her sister. "Would you like to pour?"

"Not at all. We shall see if you have forgotten your social graces." She gave Endicott a smug look.

Tea poured and further pleasantries exchanged, Viola addressed her brother. "To what do I owe the pleasure of this visit?" As if she didn't know.

"Why, to respond to your ridiculous letter and to straighten out your nonsense." He nodded to Mr. Magnuson. "Percy, I leave it to you."

From the lecherous look in Mr. Magnuson's eyes, Viola could see he was still the oily philanderer she remembered. He crossed the room, knelt by her chair and leaned far too close. The smell of cigars on his clothes and breath nearly overwhelmed her. "My dear, I can understand why you didn't respond to my proposal, delivered as it was through your brother. And in a letter! Such a thoughtless misstep. That's why I came to propose in person." He glanced around the room. "Such a shame you should be living, not to mention *working*, in such a disputable place. Why, you should have your own staff of servants to care for your every need."

"But—"

"But we will see to the matter." He lifted her hand and slobbered a kiss on it, then held on when she tried to pull away. "We will sweep you away from all this and take you back to my Virginia mansion. Call your maid and have her pack your things—"

"If you please…" Viola tried again to pull away. "Let me go!"

"Viola!" Augusta suddenly loomed over her, with Endicott beside her. "You are an obstinate, selfish girl. For once in your life, do something for your family. Come away with us this instant and marry this excellent man. You are blessed to have such a worthy man willing to take on the responsibility for such a—"

"There, there, now, Augusta." Mr. Magnuson swayed toward Viola again. "At least she retains a modicum of her youthful beauty with which to grace my home and entertain my business associates." His oily smile turned her stomach.

Rob hadn't felt this lighthearted in years, if ever. Even the most tedious work around the ranch seemed enjoyable. He pounded a final nail into the new corral gate and wiped sweat off his brow, but his mind strayed to his upcoming wedding. Honoring Viola's wishes, he'd agreed to wait until mid-October, which would make it just over one year since Maybelle died. Once roundup was completed, cattle taken to market and proceeds divided with his brothers, he might even have enough money to take Viola on a short honeymoon trip. That was, if she wanted to go.

For Rob's part, he prayed the Lord would show him how he'd failed in his marriage so he wouldn't repeat his mistakes. His poor wife hadn't been made for life in the West any more than Mother had. No wonder they'd both fled back to Charleston.

But Viola wasn't Maybelle or Mother. She took things better, from hardships to dangers to the pranks his brothers had begun to play on her to show her they'd already accepted her into the family. Whether it was a frog in her apron pocket or a garter snake in her sewing basket, she always reacted with her usual calm. He knew they had something planned for the ladies' tea, had even given his permission so long as the prank didn't do any real damage, but he stayed out of it. He was having too much fun being in love to engage in tomfoolery.

"Dad! Dad! Come quick." Robbie raced toward him looking scared. He grabbed Rob's hand. "You gotta come."

Rob allowed himself to be tugged across the barnyard. "What's wrong?"

"Some men came to the house, and Miss Viola's not too happy about it."

"Men?" His son's alarm became his own as he broke into a run. He stormed through the back door and followed the sound of voices to the parlor. Two men and a woman stood over Viola, their posture nothing less than threatening. Cold rage swept through him.

"What's going on here?" Hand itching to draw the gun at his side, he instead strode to her chair and set that hand on her shoulder. "You all right, darlin'?"

"Oh, Robert." Her breathless response and the way she grasped his hand told him all he needed to know.

"What are you people doing here?" He leveled a menacing look at the man who resembled Viola.

"Who do you think you are?" The middle-aged woman lifted her chin in the same stuck-up way Viola used to do. "This is none of your business." She glared at Viola. "Is this filthy, disreputable individual the sort you've been *working* for?" She looked beyond him, and her eyes widened with apparent fear.

Rob heard and felt his brothers and maybe Pop come up behind him. "This most certainly is my business." He'd been raised to be a gentleman toward ladies, but it took all his self-control to answer this woman with manners. "Miss Brinson is my fiancée. We will be married in October. Settle that in your mind as you get out of my house."

As indignant protests burst from all three visitors, Viola stood and nestled under his arm. "Thank you." Her adoring look settled his nerves. His lady, always calm in the face of adversity.

Viola had never seen Endicott anything but self-possessed and aloof. Now her brother's pale skin turned red, and his eyes blazed.

"You are mistaken, sir. My sister is promised to another, far more worthy man." He urged rotund, wide-eyed Mr. Magnuson up beside him. "The dowry has already been paid."

"Dowry?" Robert snorted out a laugh. "What sort of medieval world do you come from?" His brothers laughed with him. "Out here, nobody buys a wife like she's some sort of heifer. And a grown woman makes her own decision about who she'll marry." He released

Viola and stepped close to Endicott. "And trust me, Brinson, it *ain't* your pasty-faced friend here."

"How dare you?" Mr. Magnuson lifted both of his chins and tried to look dignified, as if that were possible for the old lecher.

Viola chided herself. No need to be hateful. With Robert beside her, the man could no longer harm her.

"Let me take him outside, Rob." William took a step toward the intruders.

"No, brother. Allow me." Andrew joined him.

"That's all right, boys." Robert held up his hand. "I think these three scalawags understand us now. Don't you?" He glared at Endicott, who tugged at his starched linen collar.

"It's all over, folks." Mr. Mattson, sounding younger than he had since Viola first met him, moved between the opposing parties. "Now do you folks want to stay for supper, or do you want us to, shall we say, *usher* you back to the train station?"

Endicott straightened. Though not a short man, he still appeared small next to Robert. "Just as I said, Magnuson. These people are heathens. We have wasted a journey. Shall we go? And you—" He glared at Viola with a look that once would have destroyed her. "Our parents always coddled and spoiled you. Now look at the result. You are willful and selfish, and you are no longer a part of our family. Do not expect to come around begging for my help when your marriage to this...this uncouth ruffian fails."

He plopped his hat on his head and strode from the room as if he'd somehow won the day. Mr. Magnuson followed, more like a mongrel with its tail between its legs.

Augusta, however, lingered long enough to lean toward Viola with a sneer. "The very idea! You are a worthless, ungrateful girl. You will be sorry—"

A growl emanating from Robert interrupted her and sent her scurrying after the men.

While the Mattson men guffawed, Viola tried to blink away tears. "If you will excuse me, I must see to supper."

"We'll make sure those scalawags leave." William nudged Andrew, and they left the room.

Viola started toward the kitchen on trembling legs, but Robert pulled her back into his arms and gazed into her eyes.

"You all right?"

She forced a laugh. "Not if my biscuit dough has gone flat."

Mr. Mattson chuckled. "I'm sure it'll be fine."

While the dough was indeed fine, Viola was not. Why had Augusta been able to plunge her back into her youthful self-doubts? Were Robert's love and the support of his family not enough to keep her uncertainties from returning?

She didn't have to search long for an answer. Mrs. Blake, with her constant nitpicking about the way Viola had taken care of her and Iris, had planted the seeds of self-doubt all over again. Now Viola must make certain everything was perfect so the banker's wife could have nothing to criticize.

Despite the hullabaloo of the day before, Viola was her usual efficient self, preparing a fine breakfast to send the menfolk off to work well-fed. Rob watched in amazement as she bustled about the kitchen with her customary smile, making sure everyone was ready to face the day. Oh, how he loved this woman.

"If you do not mind, gentlemen—" she set a bowl of scrambled eggs on the table "—I'll prepare sandwiches for your lunch. After that, Lavinia and I will be making tarts for the tea and will need the kitchen to ourselves."

"Sure thing, Miss Viola," Will and Drew answered together...and a little too fast for Rob's ease of mind.

Will winked at her. "We'll stay out of your way, sis."

An hour later, Rob and his brothers worked in the corral with the two ponies they'd brought over from the Simpson ranch. The one that took to the sidesaddle easiest would be purchased for Lavinia. So far, the little black gelding seemed best, but they needed to be sure he wouldn't buck with the added weight of a rider. Rob kept glancing toward the house to be sure Lavinia didn't come outside and discover her birthday surprise. He could just imagine his daughter and Viola riding side by side around the ranch.

"Ouch!" Will gripped one hand with the other. "Just got a mean splinter from the fence. I'll run up to the house and get it out and be back in two shakes."

Giving Drew a nod, he took off before Rob could express his doubts about the seriousness of the injury. His brother was up to something, but Rob couldn't leave the ponies to stop him. When Will came back, the grin on his face gave him away.

"All right, Will, what did you do?"

"Me?" Will snorted. "I'm as innocent as a lamb."

Rob snorted, too. "Right. I just hope you didn't get in Viola's way."

"Not at all, big brother." His grin got a little too wide. "She just fetched the tweezers from her medicine kit for me. I did the rest."

The pony chose that moment to buck, so Rob let the matter go. After all, he'd given his brothers permission to pull a prank. But now, after her family's visit had upset her, he wasn't sure that was a good idea anymore.

"Can I help now?" Lavinia had been at Viola's elbow all morning, begging to help.

"You *may* watch me." Most of the time, she enjoyed teaching the child how to cook and learn from her childish mistakes. But these tarts were too important to trust to four-year-old hands.

Viola spooned the apple mixture into the tart shells and folded the top over them. She'd tasted the mixture shortly before William came in with his splinter, so she knew it was her best ever. After baking the pastries for twenty minutes, she drizzled a sugar glaze over them. Only when she saw the haphazard glaze design did she realize she was trembling. No matter. The flavor, cinnamon, nutmeg and exact amount of sugar would surely impress even Mrs. Blake, if the lady and her daughter deigned to attend.

As promised, Suzette arrived right after lunch to sweep and dust the schoolroom and place the chairs in a circle. The other ladies began to arrive at two o'clock. Viola greeted them at the door.

"Welcome, Mrs. Gentry. Dolores. Mrs. Arrington. Alice. Mrs.—" Viola swallowed hard. "Mrs. Blake. Iris."

"Humph." The banker's wife pushed past Viola and

scanned the room with narrowed eyes. "Come along, Iris. We shall see exactly what this supposed school is teaching these impressionable girls." She glared at Juanita and Elena. "Well, at least you hired maids to properly serve our tea."

Just like Augusta. Viola bit her lower lip to keep from telling the officious woman what she thought of her. But what a bad example that would be for her students. "Juanita and Elena are two of my students. Furthermore, they are teaching us to speak Spanish so we can better communicate with all our neighbors."

"Indeed." The woman huffed out an indignant sigh as she chose a chair near the refreshment table. "Well, someone should serve us, and the sooner the better. Sit down, Iris."

Poor Iris, whose pretty face still bore reddish small-pox scars, blushed and sent Viola an apologetic smile. Apparently, her illness had changed her on the inside as well, but for the better.

"Soon enough, Mrs. Blake." Viola put on her most professional air. "First, the girls will present a program."

"Humph." The old grouch repeated her favorite word.

Viola silently scolded herself for such thoughts. She hadn't been able to stand up to Augusta, but she must not let this woman intimidate her.

"Oh, hush." Olive Gentry plopped herself down beside Mrs. Blake. "If you're gonna spoil this for our girls, you can leave."

Before the banker's wife could respond, Viola clapped her hands. "Class, if you will take your places, we can begin."

The girls lined up in two rows at one side of the

room to sing in harmony a song Viola had composed. As they began, she had a moment of doubt. Was the song too silly?

"Welcome, all our friends so dear. We hope our tea will bring you cheer. Sit back to see what we have learned. We hope your praises we have earned."

To Viola's relief, everyone smiled and applauded. Except for Mrs. Blake, of course.

"Please be seated beside your guests and present your lessons as we planned."

One by one, beginning with Isabella, the girls demonstrated their ability to walk, sit and rise again with a book on their heads. Then each one read her essay on what etiquette meant to her. They completed their presentation with a display of their drawings. Although their skills couldn't be compared to Viola's classmates at boarding school, these guests were effusive with their praise.

"Now we shall have our refreshments." Viola nodded to Suzette and Dolores. As her best students, they had the privilege of serving the tea.

While Dolores set out small tables, Suzette poured boiling water from the stove into several teapots and added tea leaves.

"This is one of my father's best English imports," she said. "It is called Earl Grey. Don't you just love the fragrance? It's bergamot. It takes only five minutes to brew."

Dolores passed out dessert plates, then took the napkins from the tray of tarts and offered them to the ladies.

As they took their first bites, Viola's heart skipped.

They would surely love the pastries. Her success would be complete.

"Ugh! What in the world?" Mrs. Blake spat out the bite she'd taken and wiped her lips with her napkin. "Are you trying to make us sick?"

Viola gasped as the other ladies also spat into their napkins. "Oh, no." She took a bite and felt the apple filling bite back. "What—?"

She didn't have to finish her question to know the answer. William had ruined her apple mixture while she fetched the tweezers for his splinter. How could he have been so cruel? No, how could *Robert* have been so cruel? He always laughed at their pranks, and she had no doubt he'd given his brother permission to spoil her tarts with some tongue-stinging hot spice. It might even have been his idea. Scrambling to regain her composure, she forced a smile.

"Well, that is certainly a surprise. Suzette, hurry and serve the tea so we can get the taste out of our mouths."

"Not on your life." Mrs. Blake stood. "The very idea! So this is how you teach these girls proper manners?" She pulled Iris to her feet. "Come along, daughter." She glared at the other women. "If you have any sense at all, you will follow me out that door before she poisons all of you." Nose in the air, she marched out, Iris in tow.

As the other women looked around to see who else would leave, Viola's eyes stung, and she couldn't speak. This situation couldn't be redeemed, no matter what she said or did.

"Seems the Mattson brothers aren't happy we didn't invite them to our tea." Suzette giggled.

Dolores joined her. Juanita, Elena and Isabella stared

at them for a moment, then began to laugh, too. Soon the entire room rang with the laughter of all the ladies.

All except Viola.

Watching from the barn door, Rob saw Viola running toward the house, sobbing her heart out. He didn't need to ask why. Whatever Will had done had backfired, and the lady Rob loved suffered for it. He raced across the barnyard after her and reached the kitchen in time to hear an upstairs door slam.

"What's going on, son?" Pop came out of the parlor as Rob made his way upstairs.

"Nothing. I'll handle it." But could he? He'd never even seen her cry before. Should he let her cry herself out? His hand made the decision for him. He knocked on the door. "Viola? Sweetheart?"

"Go away." Her voice sounded thick with tears.

Rob's chest ached for her pain. "Sweetheart, please let me in." No, he couldn't be alone with her in the bedroom. "I mean, please come out here. Let me—"

She yanked open the door and glared up at him. "What do you want?" She brushed her handkerchief across her blotchy tear-streaked cheeks. "Haven't you done enough?"

"Me?" Rob took a step back even as guilt crept in. He should have stopped Will. Should have declared her tea off limits. He'd never seen her lose her composure this way. "Look, I—" He reached for her hand.

"Do not speak to me!" She slammed the door. The lock clicked in place.

Rob could hear rustling and thumps, sure sounds she was packing her belongings.

"Now, Viola, don't do anything you'll regret. I mean—that I'll regret." He brushed a hand down his cheek. "Please, can't we talk?"

"You knew what this tea meant to me. Why did you have to ruin it?"

He could hear the pain in her voice. "Aw, come on, sweetheart—"

"Do not sweetheart me. You let William ruin my tarts. You *let* him!" She reopened the door. "Would you be so kind as to prepare the surrey. I want to go to the train station." She turned away, then back to him. "Or should I ask Suzette to take me?"

"Nobody's going to take you—"

"Mr. Robert Mattson, I am hereby releasing you from our engagement." Her complexion began to fade to its usual ivory. Her expression was colder than steel. "Even after meeting my sister and brother, you still had no idea what that tea meant to me. You may as well have put a rattlesnake in the school room. No wonder Maybelle left you."

Her words stabbed him in the heart just as surely as if she'd plunged in a knife. He returned her cold look. "I'll get the surrey."

The eastbound train wouldn't go out until tomorrow, but he would put her up in the hotel in town. What he would tell the children, especially Lavinia, he had no idea.

Viola thought she might throw up. Never in her life had she been so deliberately cruel to anyone. At the harshness of her words, the depth of Robert's pain was written across his face. But what did she expect after his own cruelty to her? Destroying her tea was an unforgiveable assault on all she held dear. Now who would turn the girls of Riverton into young ladies with proper manners? Well, that was no longer her concern. She would never fit into this untamed, ill-educated land.

She would return to Norfolk and accept Endicott's offer. Despite supposedly casting her out of the family, he would never miss a financial opportunity. And at least Percy Magnuson would never destroy her gatherings. In truth, he wouldn't dare because it would reflect badly upon him and damage his business. But never mind. At least if she married Mr. Magnuson, she would live in a civilized society.

Civilized. But loveless.

The tea was meant to be her crowning achievement. Her victory over Mrs. Blake and her ilk, who were no different from the society women who had stopped including her back in Norfolk when it became clear that she was redundant to her family and could bring them no social advantage. Here in this wild country, her tea would have demonstrated proper behavior while creating a society where she would be respected. Where she could hold her head up as she attended church or walked down the street instead of ducking around a corner when the likes of Mrs. Blake came her way. What a victory that would have been. Instead, now she had to run back to her family in shame and beg them to take her back.

If she hadn't fallen in love with Robert…and she did love him, loved him still…his betrayal wouldn't have hurt so badly. Why had she fallen for a rough, thoughtless rancher with mud on his boots and dirt under his fingernails? Where had her self-respect been when she let her guard down? When her *pride* had been at stake? Everything she'd done since coming to Riverton had been for the purpose of showing her family how wrong they were about her value. Now her life was in ruins, and she had no way to repair it.

She removed the last of her personal items from the bureau drawer and placed them in her trunk. She ran her hand around the floor of the wardrobe to be sure she hadn't missed anything, then straightened Lavinia's bed, which was rumpled from her nap. Everything must be left in perfect condition. As she tucked the quilt under the mattress, her fingers struck a hard object. She pulled out a book wrapped in a red kerchief. No, it was a frame. Was this the object Robert had claimed was stolen? Why on earth was it under Lavinia's mattress? Now he would think she'd stolen it and would have all the more reason to be glad she was gone. A renewed bout of tears overcame her, but she managed not to sob out loud.

A knock sounded on the door. "Miss Viola?"

Suzette! Oh, no. The girl must not see her this way. She brushed away her tears and blew her nose. "One moment, dear."

Goodness, her weepy voice gave her away. Never mind. Suzette was the only person in the world who had accepted her as she was and admired her for it. She opened the door, expecting her friend to fall into her arms and weep with her.

Instead, Suzette stood with one hand on her hip, the other resting on the doorjamb in a very unladylike pose. "Well, good. I'm glad you got over—why, Miss

Viola, are you still crying?" She laughed. *Laughed!*
"Oh, come on, now. You aren't gonna let a little prank
make you cry. Didn't you hear us all laughing? Nobody
was hurt, and not one of us—well, except that stuffy
old Mrs. Blake—minded the chili seasoning. Why, we
use it in our cooking all the time. 'Course, not in our
sweets." She laughed again, then squeezed Viola's hand.
"Pranks like that aren't meant to hurt your feelings.
They're meant to show you're accepted. Didn't you tell
me about the frog the boys put in your pocket? Didn't
you tell me about the snake? Even I would have jumped
out of my skin over the snake, but you laughed when
you told me about it."

"Yes, but—"

"Aw, come on, Miss Viola." Suzette gave her a chiding smile. "We love you. All of us do, but one cowboy
in particular. You gonna let a little misplaced pride ruin
your life?"

Pride? She couldn't argue with that. Her own
thoughts had convicted her before Suzette said a word.
Only now did it sink in. For all her thoughts about wanting to emulate the Lord Jesus Christ in humility, she
had desperately clung to her pride, the sin the scriptures
said He hated most.

"Come on." Suzette grasped her hand. "Let's go
downstairs and—"

Viola pulled back. "I cannot." Not after what she'd
said to Robert about Maybelle. Oh, how could she have
lashed out at him that way? She knew how much he
grieved over his failed marriage. She hadn't been acquainted with her cousin, but from what he said, she'd

been quite fragile. Now how could Viola fix what she'd broken?

"Yes, you can." Suzette huffed out a cross breath. "I won't drag you down there. In fact, I'm going home. But—" She wagged a finger in Viola's face. "When you're ready, you need to tell Rob and Will that you forgive them. You hear me?"

Viola forced a smile at her student's bossiness. "I'll try."

"And I'll see you in church this Sunday, you hear?"

Viola nodded. "I hear."

Despite her agreement, she would still have to deal with the issue of the missing frame. If she'd simply left it behind, Robert would never believe she hadn't taken it. Now, if she gave it to him as a peace offering and explained where she'd found it, perhaps he would forgive her for her harsh words.

Lord, please help him forgive me.

Chapter Sixteen

His heart heavier than it had been since Maybelle abandoned their marriage, Rob harnessed the gelding to the surrey, then led it to the kitchen garden gate. He'd known Maybelle was unhappy out here, but he'd thought Viola had made her peace with the rougher parts of New Mexico Territory. For one little prank to drive her away made no sense for an otherwise sensible woman. If she hadn't made that comment about Maybelle, he might try to talk her into staying. But he refused to live with another sharp-tongued woman. Good thing he'd discovered this about her before they married.

He found the whole family waiting for him in the parlor. His brothers shuffled their feet, guilt written across their faces. Robbie and Lavinia stared at him wide-eyed.

"What's going on, son?" Pop asked. "They tell me Miss Viola is leaving."

Before he could respond, the lady in question came down the stairs and entered the room.

"Miss Viola," Will said. "I never meant to hurt you."

"Me neither." Drew gave her an awkward grin.

"Never mind. I forgive you." She gave them a soft smile. "Robert, as I was packing, I found this." She turned that smile toward him as she handed him the missing silver frame. "What a lovely wedding photograph of you and Maybelle. Of course, the frame is a bit tarnished, but we can clean it."

His knees threatened to buckle. "You *found* it?" He couldn't keep the accusation from his voice.

"Y-yes. It was under Lavinia's mattress." She blinked those green eyes and tilted her head, innocence personified.

"Right where you hid it?" His feelings still raw from her remark about Maybelle, he jerked the frame from her grasp.

"Dad—" Robbie said.

"Hush, son. This is between Miss Brinson and me." He took a step closer to her.

Eyes blazing, she moved back. "No. It is not. There is nothing between you and me." She glanced at the children, and her expression softened. "If you will excuse me." She hurried from the room and ran up the back stairs.

He started to follow her to force her to confess, but Robbie grabbed his arm. "Dad, I'm sorry."

"What are you talking about?"

"I—I found the picture and wanted to show it to Lavinia."

"You *found* it? But it was hidden in my wardrobe."

Robbie stared at his feet. "Awhile back, right after Lavinia came here, I peeked in your room and saw you looking at it. Then I saw you put it away." He offered a little grin. "My wardrobe doesn't have a false floor, but I wish it did, 'cause I would have put it there."

"Don't change the subject. You know it's wrong to dig in other people's belongings."

Robbie shrugged. "I know. I'm sorry. But I wanted to show the picture to Lavinia. She said she forgot what Mama looked like." He shuffled his feet. "Sometimes I forget, too."

"She's so pretty." Lavinia stood up beside her brother, tears filling her brown eyes. "I love her." She reached out and touched the picture.

Rob set it on the table, then sank down in a chair and gathered his children in his arms. "And she loved you both very much." He could barely choke the words out, but it was true. For all her faults and failings, Maybelle had loved these little ones.

And what had he done? Accused a wonderful, beautiful, *innocent* woman of stealing. And probably destroyed any chance he might have of reconciling with her.

"Well, now you've done it, boys." Pop dropped into his chair like he'd been hit. "Driven off that dear lady who's the best thing to happen to this ranch since your mama left."

Truer words were never spoken. In fact, Viola Brinson was the best thing to happen to this ranch *ever*. She'd healed too many problems to count. As for her harsh words about Maybelle, they were also true, but very unlike her to say them. That just revealed how hurt she'd been by the ruined dessert. But why?

He didn't have to think too long to figure it out. From the first, the women of Riverton had been rude to her.

Sure, she'd been a bit snooty, but maybe that was due to shyness. He hadn't exactly welcomed her either. Wasn't it the responsibility of home folks to welcome newcomers, as Suzette had? Instead, Viola had reached out to them, offering to teach their daughters, then taking care of the Blake women, then organizing her little social, which wasn't so little to her.

After the way her family treated her, he should have noticed she'd been nervous as an untried filly about the social. She'd wanted so much for the women to like her. If only she could realize they'd changed their minds about her. They did like her. Now he'd added to her pain by accusing her of stealing and thus destroyed any possibility of making things right with her.

This wasn't the first time he'd mistaken the character of other people. Patrick Ahern turned out to be a loyal employee, not a cattle rustler. No longer an outlaw, Martinez turned out to be a selfless neighbor who saved the Mattson herd from the flood. Why did Rob always think the worst of other people? It all came back to Mother and Maybelle. He might have forgiven them, but the effects of their abandonment still impacted his thinking. He needed to let it all go. *Lord, help me forgive others as You've forgiven me. Help me move on from all offenses, real and imagined.*

Robbie and Lavinia huddled in the corner, whispering. They glanced at him, then took off like a shot, running upstairs before he could stop them. He didn't want to anyway. Maybe they could convince Viola to stay, and he could have another chance to make amends to her. Yes, he was a coward to let his children fix things, but maybe they could at least open the door.

* * *

Viola sat on the bed staring out the window. Robert's cruel accusation was the proverbial last straw. And here she'd wanted to make peace with him after Suzette so sweetly and wisely scolded her. She had no idea why that frame had been under Lavinia's mattress, but she could see why Robert had called it valuable. Not only was sterling silver expensive, but the picture must have reminded him of happier days.

"Miss Viola!" Robbie called through the door.

"Miss Viola!" Lavinia echoed him.

Her heart ached to think of leaving these darling children. "Come in."

Once inside the room, they fell into her arms crying.

"Miss Viola." Robbie wiped at his tears. "We hid the picture of our mama under Lavinia's mattress because we like looking at it. We didn't want to put it back in Dad's room 'cause he'd just hide it away again."

"Ah. I see." That explained everything except Robert's accusation.

"I told Dad." Robbie gazed at her with pleading eyes, as did Lavinia. "Please don't leave us. We love you, and we want you to be our new mama."

"Please don't go." Lavinia renewed her tears. "We love you."

Viola shook herself inwardly. What a baby she'd become, all hurt feelings and thinking only of herself. Another sure sign that she was indeed very proud, as Suzette had suggested. "And I love you both, as did your mother."

"Promise you won't go." Robbie gazed at her with eyes so like his father's.

"I... I won't go." If nothing else, she could still keep house. After all, Mr. Mattson, not Robert, had hired her. And of course she would care for the children.

It took three handkerchiefs to dry all their tears. At last Viola felt herself composed.

"Now, if I am not mistaken, I hear someone's tummy complaining about being hungry. Shall we go fix supper?"

The children giggled. "Yes, ma'am," they chorused.

As they made their way down the back stairs, Viola considered what to serve. She could make a quick stew from the leftovers of last night's roast and some biscuits to go along with it. She might even whip up a quick dessert, a very special one. Her own stomach growled at the idea, a sure sign she was ready to leave her self-pity behind.

Rob wasn't about to take Viola to the Riverton hotel so late in the day, so he unhitched the surrey and put the gelding in the stall. Grabbing clean buckets from their hooks, he milked the two cows. Will and Drew had made themselves scarce, so he had to carry the full buckets to the house himself.

As he neared the back door, the aroma of beef stew met him. Maybe Pop had taken on the chore of fixing supper. With the milk to strain, Rob couldn't check right away, but the smell tantalized him the whole time. After entering the mudroom, he strained the milk through cheesecloth into clean gallon jars, then carried the first one to the icebox in the kitchen. And almost dropped it.

There stood Viola at the kitchen table, kneading biscuit dough like she'd done since that first day in April.

She cast him a glance so brief he almost missed it. How could she look so beautiful in a hot kitchen on a hot July day, and after all she'd been through? His heart seemed to stop beating. He could not let this woman go, but how could he fix the mess he'd made? *Lord, help me. Give me wisdom. Help me win her back.*

"Sure smells good." Not the best thing to say. He wanted her to know he loved her for herself, not because of what she did. Of course, she did everything well. And it sure did show her good character to fix supper for all of them this particular evening.

"Supper will be ready in half an hour." She swiped the back of her floured hand over her forehead, leaving a white trail.

Oh, how he wanted to brush it away just to touch her.

"Robbie told me about the picture." She didn't look at him as she used the tin biscuit cutter to cut rounds of the dough before placing them on a baking sheet. "I assume that takes care of that particular matter."

Rob set the milk in the icebox. Time to visit the icehouse and cut another block. Maybe tomorrow morning. "Yep. I was a numbskull to think you'd taken it."

A tiny smile lifted one corner of her lips. "That you were."

"It would mean a lot to me if you could forgive me for being a mule-headed fool."

"I could do that." She stopped her work and looked up at him, her green eyes glistening. "It would mean a lot to me if you could forgive me for what I said about Maybelle leaving you."

He didn't hesitate. "I could do that." He stepped over to her and brushed the flour from her forehead. "Viola,

I'm so sorry. I do love you with all my heart. Please don't go."

Tears splashed down her ivory cheeks. "Very well. I'll stay…for the children."

"Just the children?"

"Well, maybe for your father and William and Andrew." She puckered her lips as though trying not to smile. "I shall manage to tolerate you."

He chuckled. Or tried to. Emotion made it sound more like a gurgle. "Will you still marry me?"

She paused a little too long for his comfort, then sighed happily. "I will still marry you."

"Oh, my darlin'." He pulled her into his arms and planted a kiss on those inviting lips. For some reason, she didn't seem inclined to let him go but leaned into him and kissed him back with an enthusiasm he'd never seen in her before.

"That's more like it." Pop's voice cut into their private moment. "Now get out of the kitchen, Rob, so your fiancée can finish fixin' supper. The young'uns and I are starving."

As if not to be left out, Robbie and Lavinia poked their heads in the kitchen, giggling.

"See. I told you, sis." Robbie side-hugged his little sister. "Grown-ups can be awful silly sometimes, but they generally work things out." At that moment, the boy sounded surprisingly grown-up himself.

Seated at the kitchen end of the dining room table, Viola felt her heart full to overflowing with joy and love. The stew was not the best she'd served due to an extra ingredient, but the men seemed to like it. She'd made sure to set aside portions for Lavinia and Robbie before adding the hot flavoring.

"These biscuits are the best you've ever made." Robert's praise might have been a bit excessive, but it warmed her heart. "And you did something special to the stew. It's real tasty."

"Yes, I added some of that chili seasoning you all are so fond of." She took a sip of water to cool the burn. She supposed it was a flavor she would need to get used to. And being with this family more than made up for it, for they were so very different from the one she came from.

Yes, family. Soon to be *her* family. A loving husband, precious children, fun-loving brothers and a man who had loved her with paternal affection since she first arrived. And she had friends who loved her, too. In Viola's opinion, one in particular, Suzette Pursers, had proven to be the true social leader for the ladies of the community, despite her mere eighteen years. Even before that, Viola had loved her as a true friend, a sister.

The conversation moved on to other topics, mostly projects to be done around the ranch, the river's lowering, the fall roundup.

"Say, Lavinia." Mr. Mattson gazed lovingly at his granddaughter. "I understand somebody has a birthday coming up. Would you happen to know who that is?"

Lavinia's eyes lit up. "Me. Me!"

She bounced in her chair, but Viola didn't correct her. Maybe she could be more lenient about manners and such. After all, did she not teach her students that the most important manners were being kind to and accepting of others?

"And just what might you want for your birthday?"

Mr. Mattson's blue eyes twinkled. "I'm used to getting presents for boys, but what on earth should I get for a pretty little five-year-old girl?"

"Yeah, sweetheart," Andrew said. "You gotta tell us what you want. A new doll?"

"How about a new dress?" William asked.

Viola glanced at Robert and gave him a little smile. She was as excited about the pony as he was. How fun it would be to teach Lavinia to ride.

"I want a rifle like Robbie's." Lavinia spoke in all innocence.

The men had the grace not to laugh.

"Well, honey, you just make a list," Robert said, "and we'll each get you something special."

"Miss Viola." Mr. Mattson had cleaned his plate and looked at her expectantly. "I'm ready for that dessert, though I can't imagine how you managed such a fine meal *and* dessert after entertaining the town ladies all afternoon."

Robert and his brothers all seemed to groan, as though their father had misspoken and shouldn't have brought up the subject. Time to save the day.

"Why, it is no trouble at all, gentlemen. Lavinia, if you and Robbie will clear the plates, I'll bring out the newly made tarts."

Soon she'd placed filled dessert plates in front of each person. Once she sat down, they began to eat.

"Delicious, as always." Mr. Mattson savored the first bite.

Eagerly following his example, Robbie and Lavinia voiced their agreement.

Robert and his brothers didn't manage to swallow the first one.

"Um, well…" Barely able to speak, Robert took a gulp of coffee. "I've never tasted a savory dessert quite like this one." He set down his fork. "I believe I'll save the rest until later."

"What's savory?" Lavinia blinked her brown eyes at her father.

"Salty, sweetheart. Usually it's a good thing, like popcorn. But most folks usually put sugar in an apple dessert, not salt."

"Mine's not salty." Lavinia ate another bite.

"Mine's not either." Robbie copied his sister.

"And there you have it." Mr. Mattson guffawed. "Looks like you boys got a dose of your own medicine."

While William snickered, Andrew spat out his bite and sent an apologetic grimace in Viola's direction. Soon they were all laughing. And Robert was gazing at her, not as if she'd put an unpleasant taste in his mouth, but as if she were, well, the woman he loved. And she loved him more than she had ever thought possible.

Thanks to Mr. Blake, Maybelle's funds had been transferred to the Riverton bank. With the interest that had accrued, it provided the children with savings that would help them establish their own lives when the time came. Viola persuaded Robert that Lavinia must be taught to manage her own money as she grew older so she wouldn't be ignorant of…or cheated out of…what was rightfully hers. At his agreement, she had all the more reason to love him.

The two months before the wedding passed quickly. Robert purchased a small gun for Viola, a derringer, and taught her how to shoot it. Now she carried it instead of a stick as she and Lavinia walked around the ranch.

Lavinia's birthday was a happy family affair, with her new pony being her favorite gift. Viola set about teaching her to ride each day. Like her father and the rest of the Mattson family, the child seemed to have a gift for relating to animals large and small.

After the birthday party, Robert announced he would ride to the mountains with William for the cattle roundup. As much as Viola loved him, she was happy to have him out of the way so she could complete her wedding dress. Perhaps he'd noticed her quickly hiding the white satin fabric whenever he entered the parlor.

The roundup took the better part of three weeks. By the time Robert, William and their cowhands returned, Viola had finished her gown and made a matching one for Lavinia. All the while, she'd continued her classes with her young ladies. Each one shared her excitement about the coming wedding. Even Iris, whom Mrs. Blake had hoped would marry Robert, joined in her happiness *and* Viola's class. Although her mother had not changed, Iris appreciated the sacrifice Viola had made to become their nurse.

On a Friday morning in late September, as the men drove only a few cattle under the Double Bar M sign, Viola watched with deep concern.

"Oh, dear." She stood beside Mr. Mattson on the front porch. "Does this mean the rest of the cattle were stolen?"

He chuckled in his paternal way. "Nope. They've already loaded the cattle bound for market onto the trains headed to the Kansas City stockyards. These will feed the family through the winter, except a few of those heifers that'll be seed cattle for next year."

"Ah. I see. One more thing for me to learn about cattle ranching." She moved toward the front steps. "I cannot wait to greet Robert. I have missed him so much." *And cannot wait to be in his arms again.*

Mr. Mattson touched her arm. "You don't want to do that, my dear. He'll come to the house soon enough."

"But…"

"After he cleans up a bit." He winked. "Driving cattle isn't a dainty business."

As his meaning sank in, she laughed. "Yes, of course." It would be much more pleasant to greet Robert with a kiss if he didn't smell like, well, a hardworking man.

At their October wedding, he smelled finer than ever wearing the new manly French cologne Suzette had ordered specially for him for the occasion. With her dear friend Suzette as her attendant and Lavinia as her flower girl, she walked down the aisle of the Riverton Community Church on Mr. Mattson's arm. The sanctuary was crowded to overflowing. Agnes, Rosa and several cowhands, along with Señor Martinez and his family, took up a large portion of the room. The town ladies who had ignored Viola the first few times she'd entered this church now gushed over her, saying she was the most beautiful bride they had ever seen.

In the sunlight beaming through the east window, Robert's blue eyes sparkled like sapphires. He'd never looked so handsome. Beside him stood Robbie, his best man. Having four brothers, Robert claimed he hadn't wanted to choose one of them, lest there be some hard feelings. Viola suspected he wanted his son—soon to be *her* son—to be an important part of the ceremony, as his sister was.

Cal and Julia, Jared and Emma, Mr. and Mrs. Sharp sat in the front row, with William and Andrew behind them. Julia held her son, and Emma cradled her daughter, newborn cousins for Robbie and Lavinia and already adored by the entire family. The dearest wish of Viola's heart was that she and Robert would also be adding to the family.

Even the Blakes attended the wedding and following reception. Of course, Mr. Blake had always been friendly to the Mattsons, seeing as they kept their considerable proceeds from the sale of their cattle in his bank. Mrs. Blake remained cool and standoffish, but that only left her by herself as the others crowded around Viola and Robert.

"Señora Mattson." Señor Martinez swept off his ornate sombrero and bowed deeply. "You have my deepest congratulations." He bowed to Robert. "And congratulations to you, *mi amigo*. You have married a beautiful, gracious lady."

"Thank you, Martinez." Robert reached out to him, and the men shared a firm handshake. He leaned toward the Mexican and whispered, "As a wedding gift, can you head off the shivaree for us?"

Señor Martinez threw back his head and laughed. "Not for a moment, *mi amigo*. Not for a moment! Your brothers have already engaged my, shall I say, *services* to add to the celebration. As promised, I shall bring my caballeros and our mariachi band to serenade you this very night."

"What do you think, darlin'?" Robert whispered in her ear. "Shall we slip away before anyone notices and avoid all that foolishness?"

"Oh, no. I think it will be fun." In her previous life, Viola might have been dismayed to think of such shenanigans, as Agnes would call them. But now she welcomed the idea of neighbors who so freely celebrated her happiness with her, no matter how late it kept her up on her wedding night. Like the chili seasoning in the tarts, it was all in fun.

He chuckled. "All right. Just remember, nobody's gonna make you do anything you don't want to do, including me."

"Oh?" She smirked. "Did I not promise to obey you a mere half hour ago?"

"Huh. Yeah, you did. But I have a feeling I'll be obeying you more than the other way around."

"Hmm." She adjusted his tie, though it required no adjusting. "I think I can live with that."

She could also live in this wonderful community that had welcomed her at last. She did not require a position as social leader to find contentment, for she now had many dear friends, all of whom loved, encouraged and supported each other in this wild country. And now she truly was no longer a redundant woman but wanted, needed and loved.

As for the man of whom she had thought, *No, no, Lord, not him* when she first saw him, she could now say, "Yes, yes, Lord, *that* man."

* * * * *

Dear Reader,

Thank you for choosing to read *Finding Her Frontier Family*. This story is set on a fictional ranch beside the Rio Grande near the fictional town of Riverton, New Mexico Territory.

This book is a sequel to my Love Inspired Historical novella, *Yuletide Reunion*, which was published in the 2015 anthology *A Western Christmas*. In that story, the community comes together to rebuild Job Sharp's burned-down barn. During the rebuilding, Job's daughters, Emma and Julia, fall in love with Jared and Cal Mattson, two younger brothers from a nearby ranch, who have come to help. Of course, the two couples marry and live happily ever after. But what about their three older brothers? The oldest is Robert, estranged from his wife and now a widower with two children who need a mother. A deeply wounded man, Rob definitely needs his own love story. While it appears that William has already found his love in Suzette, be looking for Andrew's romance, coming in a future Love Inspired Historical!

So why does this Florida gal write a story set in New Mexico Territory? Well, my sister lived for many years in a beautiful, real-life adobe house beside the Rio Grande. During my many visits to see her, I was inspired by the history of the area. I have long wanted to write stories set on her land, although I've tweaked the descriptions for the sake of these characters. After all, it takes place in 1887, and of course life was harder back then. No phones, no television, no running water. Meals were cooked on woodstoves, and the settlers faced many natural and human dangers every day. Still, our hardy ancestors managed to survive and build strong communities. I love to create characters whose fictional lives mirror the courage of these people so we can learn from them.

I love to hear from my readers, so if you enjoyed *Finding Her Frontier Family*, please write and let me know. Please also visit my website: louisemgougeauthor.blogspot.com, *find me on* Facebook: facebook.com/LouiseMGougeAuthor or follow me on BookBub: bookbub.com/profile/louise-m-gouge.

God bless you.
Louise M. Gouge

LOVE INSPIRED

Stories to uplift and inspire

Fall in love with Love Inspired—inspirational and uplifting stories of faith and hope. Find strength and comfort in the bonds of friendship and community. Revel in the warmth of possibility and the promise of new beginnings.

Sign up for the Love Inspired newsletter at **LoveInspired.com** to be the first to find out about upcoming titles, special promotions and exclusive content.

CONNECT WITH US AT:

Facebook.com/LoveInspiredBooks

Twitter.com/LoveInspiredBks

Get 4 FREE REWARDS!

We'll send you 2 FREE Books plus 2 FREE Mystery Gifts.

FREE Value Over **$20**

Both the **Love Inspired®** and **Love Inspired®** Suspense series feature compelling novels filled with inspirational romance, faith, forgiveness, and hope.

YES! Please send me 2 FREE novels from the Love Inspired or Love Inspired Suspense series and my 2 FREE gifts (gifts are worth about $10 retail). After receiving them, if I don't wish to receive any more books, I can return the shipping statement marked "cancel." If I don't cancel, I will receive 6 brand-new Love Inspired Larger-Print books or Love Inspired Suspense Larger-Print books every month and be billed just $5.99 each in the U.S. or $6.24 each in Canada. That is a savings of at least 17% off the cover price. It's quite a bargain! Shipping and handling is just 50¢ per book in the U.S. and $1.25 per book in Canada.* I understand that accepting the 2 free books and gifts places me under no obligation to buy anything. I can always return a shipment and cancel at any time. The free books and gifts are mine to keep no matter what I decide.

Choose one: ☐ **Love Inspired Larger-Print** (122/322 IDN GNWC)   ☐ **Love Inspired Suspense Larger-Print** (107/307 IDN GNWN)

Name (please print)

Address   Apt. #

City   State/Province   Zip/Postal Code

Email: Please check this box ☐ if you would like to receive newsletters and promotional emails from Harlequin Enterprises ULC and its affiliates. You can unsubscribe anytime.

Mail to the **Harlequin Reader Service:**
IN U.S.A.: P.O. Box 1341, Buffalo, NY 14240-8531
IN CANADA: P.O. Box 603, Fort Erie, Ontario L2A 5X3

Want to try 2 free books from another series? Call 1-800-873-8635 or visit www.ReaderService.com.

LIRLIS22

SPECIAL EXCERPT FROM

LOVE INSPIRED
INSPIRATIONAL ROMANCE

*Cowboy and veteran Yates Trudeau returns home to his
family ranch bruised and battered and carrying a
life-changing secret. When he bumps into
Laurel Maxwell, the girl he left behind, she might just
set him on the path to healing that his body—and his
heart—so desperately needs…*

Keep reading for a sneak peek at
The Cowboy's Journey Home,
part of the Sundown Valley series by
New York Times *bestselling author Linda Goodnight.*

Had he really come to the woods before going to the
ranch house? She had a feeling she was right and that
he had. She wondered why—another habit of journalists.
She needed to know everything, especially motives.

Yates's gaze seemed glued to her face, and she fought
off a blush that would let him know he still affected her
on some unwanted, visceral level. People say you always
remember your first love. Yates had been her first and
only.

She'd spent the better part of a year waiting to hear
from him and another year getting over him.

Now here he was in the flesh, stirring up old memories.
At least for her.

The annoying blush deepened. Laurel turned her
attention toward the children and the dog. With a smiling

Justice in the center, they formed a circle of petting hands and eager chatter.

"Those aren't all your kids, are they?"

A small pain pinched inside her chest. "Sunday school class." To turn the focus away from her, she asked, "Was he really a military dog? Like a bomb or drug sniffer?"

"Explosives."

"Did something happen to him? Why'd he retire?"

Yates's face, already closed, tightened. "Stuff happens. Soldiers retire. Look, I should go. Enjoy your picnic."

With a snappy military about-face, he started to walk away.

"Yates, wait."

He paused, gazing back over his shoulder.

"After you get settled, come by the *Times* office. I'd love to interview you and the dog for the paper." She put her fingers up in air quotes. "'Hometown Hero Returns' would make a great feature."

"No interview. We're civilians now. Nothing heroic about that." Turning away, he gave a soft whistle. "Justice, come."

Before she could say more, Yates and his dog disappeared into the foliage.

Don't miss
The Cowboy's Journey Home *by Linda Goodnight,*
available August 2022
wherever Love Inspired books and ebooks are sold.

LoveInspired.com

When a cold-case serial killer returns, FBI special agent Fiona Kelly has one last chance to stop him before he claims the prize he's always wanted—*her.*

Don't miss this thrilling and uplifting page-turner from bestselling author

JESSICA R. PATCH

"*Her Darkest Secret* by Jessica R. Patch grabbed me in the first scene of this edge-of-your-seat suspense and didn't let go until the end!"
—**Patricia Bradley**, author of the Memphis Cold Case novels

Available now from Love Inspired!

LOVE INSPIRED
LoveInspired.com